A CURIOUS LADY

"I apologize," Matt said.

"Why?"

"Because I was tempted to kiss you and I've no right to do so . . . yet," he added, rather spoiling the innocence of his explanation.

Babs bit her lip. "You need not apologize. I was . . . rather hoping you would."

He turned back. "Why?"

She was silent for a long moment and then, determined to lighten what had become far too serious, smiled a rather mischievous smile. "Curiosity?" she asked, her head tipped to one side.

He chuckled and gestured up the path. "Shall we return before I succumb to temptation and satisfy your curiosity?" he asked.

"If you insist."

His smile broadened. "You are, as I have suspected, something of a minx."

"Yes," she said, glancing at him from the corners of her eyes. "But you are a bit of a rake, so that is all right."

Books by Jeanne Savery

The Widow and the Rake

A Reformed Rake

A Christmas Treasure

A Lady's Deception

Cupid's Challenge

Lady Stephanie

A Timeless Love

A Lady's Lesson

Lord Galveston and the Ghost

A Lady's Proposal

The Widowed Miss Mordaunt

A Love for Lydia

Taming Lord Renwick

Lady Serena's Surrender

The Christmas Gift

The Perfect Husband

A Perfect Match

Smuggler's Heart

Miss Seldon's Suitors

An Independent Lady

Published by Zebra Books

AN
INDEPENDENT
LADY

Jeanne Savery

ZEBRA BOOKS
Kensington Publishing Corp.
http://www.kensingtonbooks.com

With many thanks to our Canterbury friends,
John, Jill, and most of all Alistair, who sent me
the Church of England marriage rite from
an 1839 copy of the Book of Common Prayer.

Prologue

Silence filled the great old church. The groom, surprised, looked down at his bride. The bishop, an elderly relative of the groom, pushed his head forward, turning his good ear slightly nearer. When there was still no sound from the young woman gripping her bouquet, he looked up from his book, his thin brows arched questioningly.

A rustle of clothing from the front row and a hissed, "Sissie!"

The bishop cleared his throat and repeated, "Louisa Maria Susanna Morgan, wilt thou have this man to thy wedded husband, to live together after God's ordinance in the holy estate of Matrimony? Wilt thou obey him, and serve him, love, honor, and keep him in sickness and in health; and, forsaking all other, keep thee only unto him, so long as ye both shall live?"

Louisa Maria glanced up, her skin so white it was nearly translucent, her eyes so wide open they had a painful look about them. "I—"

Another long pause ensued.

"*Sissie.*"

The insistent whisper from the front row of those gathered to witness the wedding could be heard throughout the church, but only those nearest the front heard the bride gulp.

"—cannot."

A new silence filled the nave. Then, an embarrassed giggle from halfway back in the congregation. Louisa's father rushed forward and grasped her arm.

"You fool." Sir George shook her as he growled into her ear, "You say it proper."

"I . . . cannot."

"Say it!"

She stared mutely at nothing at all.

"If you won't say the words, I'll repudiate you. Do you hear me?" He waited. "Speak now or never say another word!"

The girl hung her head.

Sir George stared at her in outrage, a baffled look about him. And then, roaring, flung her from him. "From this moment forth you are none of mine!"

The girl caught her balance. She looked at him, still mute. Mutely she turned to the man she had jilted, a sad bewildered look. Then, dropping her bouquet, her head hanging, she turned and walked slowly up the aisle. A low buzz and murmur increased in volume but the bride did not appear to hear it.

Another rustle and shuffle and an elderly woman moved away from the first row. She turned up the aisle after her granddaughter.

"Mother, if you go after that . . ." Sir George glanced around, seemed to realize where he was, and, speaking in less ranting tones, substituted, "that *traitor,* you will never be welcome in my house again."

She stopped, glared at him over her shoulder, and, head high, setting her cane firmly with each step, walked at a slightly faster pace. Each step took her nearer the high, over-large, doors at the back of the nave.

"You'll never get another pence from me!"

"I've my jointure. It will do," she said, her voice firm and clear.

The mutter from the crowd grew.

Lady Dewsbury-Morgan had nearly reached the back of the nave when there was another shuffle, another rustle, from the front.

Sir George very nearly howled, his overly ruddy complexion fluctuating from that to a sickly yellowish-white and back to the purplish hue.

His wife tipped up her chin and stared at him, her mouth set but a trifle wobbly, just a hint of fear in her eyes. Then she too started up the aisle.

"I repudiate you! You are no wife of mine!"

"I know," she muttered. After a step or two, she added, "But then I never was, really. More a convenience, I think." She raised her voice. "Mother Vivian, wait for me."

A dowager and her daughter, overhearing her ladyship's murmur, looked gleefully shocked and turned to repeat her words to others. "What did she mean by it?" hissed one very young woman to another.

Up near the altar, the groom jerked loose from the shock. He patted his coat here and there until he found and pulled a plump purse from a hidden pocket. He handed it to his cousin and closest friend who, his mouth agape, stood like a post at his side. The groom whispered something. The friend blinked, then shook his head. The groom insisted. The friend shrugged, took the well-stuffed purse, and disappeared into the shadows to one side of the nave, hurrying toward the back.

Matthew Adam Woodward Riverton, by courtesy, Lord Calder, turned to the man who should, at this moment in time, be, by law, his father. "You swore she was willing."

"Of course she was willing!"

"No coercion? You didn't beat her or lock her in her room on bread and water?" asked Calder laconically and saw the truth in Sir George's expression. He turned to the elderly cleric and took him by the arm. "Come along, Uncle."

The man was more a great-uncle, possibly great-great-uncle, and not terribly steady on his feet. "Hmm? What? What's to do, Nevie?"

"There is nothing else to do. Not here."

One

"But where can she have gone?" asked Lady Morgan.

Lady Dewsbury-Morgan's eyes were not so good as they once were, but they were not so bad that she could not see objects as large as her granddaughter. She searched the crowd of idlers waiting to gawp as the wedding party left the church and then looked beyond, her red-rimmed eyes surrounded by deepening wrinkles of concern. "Should have hurried more. Stupid knees." She lifted her cane and poked a lad lolling to one side of the church door. "You. Where did the chit go?"

"Don't know what yer mean."

"She means, you dolt," said a bored male voice, "the girl that came out of the church. Where did she go?"

"'Tweren't no girl," insisted the ragged youth, his gaze sharpening with curiosity.

Lady Dewsbury-Morgan's mouth compressed into a tight line. She took one last look toward the crowd in the street and then, determinedly, stomped back inside. She glanced around, nodded, and headed toward a side door, her daughter by marriage on her heels and the groom's cousin ambling along behind.

The latter was beginning to feel a trifle worried but, as yet, did not allow the emotion to spoil the expression of exquisite boredom that was required of a town buck wishing to follow Brummell's lead.

"Louisa Maria would have taken one look at that crowd

and been unable to move into it," said Lady Dewsbury-Morgan. "She'll have gone out another door. With luck, this one." She pushed open a smaller side door and stepped out, followed by the others.

Quentin Riverton moved down the half dozen stairs and questioned a few people loitering nearby. He returned to where the women waited. "She headed that way," he said, pointing.

"The river," muttered the older of the two women, paling.

That startled the cynical man from his pose of indifference. He glanced down the street and gulped. "Rather that, than marry my cousin? She cannot be such a fool."

"She hasn't a very good impression of marriage," said the elderly lady with more than a touch of acid. "Much as I dislike to admit it, my son is not a good husband." She ignored Lady Morgan's stumbling excuses and explanations and feeble attempts to exonerate her husband.

"There's a hackney," said the young man, waving down the jarvey. "I'll check elsewhere while you go straight to the nearest bridge. I'll buy that horse if I have to and—" He pointed to where a would-be Corinthian bent over his horse's neck, flirting with a maid who was supposed to be polishing a door knocker. "—we'll find her."

He handed the two women into the smelly carriage, gave orders to the driver, and then, remembering his errand, stuffed the groom's purse into the elderly woman's hand before hurrying away.

"My daughter!" Lady Morgan sobbed. Once.

"None of that. We must be strong."

After a long moment's silence, Lady Morgan whispered, "What if she succeeds? What will her father say if we fail to find her?"

"You mean will my son have you back?" Lady Dewsbury-Morgan bit back the words on the tip of her tongue, forced herself to remember how different this cowed creature was before her marriage, before Sir George deliberately and systematically turned that bright-eyed hopeful woman into the mouse she'd become. "If we must, we will live together on my jointure. But we will *not* fail. She is on foot and I doubt she is moving quickly. We will reach her in time."

But the street was congested and the carriage was slowed by it so that it was some time before they stopped at the end of the bridge and got down. Lady Dewsbury-Morgan thrust a few coins at the driver. She didn't see his appreciation of her largesse because her eyes were on the struggle in the middle of the bridge. Two rather young boys were attempting to hold a woman not a great deal older back from clambering onto the edge of the parapet.

"Where did Riverton get to?" asked Lady Dewsbury-Morgan of herself. "Never a man around when you want one. Only when you don't." She hurried as quickly as she could in the trail of her son's wife who had picked up her skirts and run to clasp her daughter in her arms.

"Sissie, Sissie, you mustn't," crooned the mother.

Louisa Maria stood rigid in her mother's embrace, her gaze trained on the river, her eyes huge in her stark white face.

Lady Dewsbury-Morgan arrived a trifle out of breath. She leaned on her cane and eyed her granddaughter. Then, very deliberately, she slapped the girl. Hard.

Louisa collapsed against her mother and, silently, sobbed and sobbed.

Quentin Riverton arrived at Calder's rooms to find Matthew sprawled in his favorite chair, a glass clutched between his two hands. Quentin stared down at his bleary-eyed cousin. "You are castaway," he said accusingly.

"Definitely not. Merely a trifle in my altitudes," said Calder with dignity and the careful enunciation of the inebriated. "Where is she? Is she all right?"

"I don't know. Somehow, I missed them. But the girl didn't jump. I do know that."

"Jump . . ." Calder half rose to his feet, then dropped heavily back into his chair. "The river?"

Quentin nodded. "I found a pair of lads who were full of it. They'd been holding her back from climbing the railing when the ladies arrived. And then the three went off in the hackney and that was that. I couldn't find them."

"But they found her? They have her in charge?" There was an urgency to Matthew's voice that surprised Quentin. "Coz, tell me."

"Oh yes. The two Morgan ladies found her."

Shock had sobered Calder a great deal and his thinking was more rational. "What do you mean the boys *told* you the tale? Why were you not with the ladies?"

"Harrison—you know Freddy Harrison?" Calder nodded, one impatient shake of his head. "Tried to talk him out of his horse so I'd have more freedom, be able to move about faster than in a carriage, you know?" Calder nodded. "The damn fool insisted he needed the sway-backed knock-kneed creature and would not sell him to me!"

Calder, relieved that Miss Morgan was not lost in the stews of London, facing dangers she could never have imagined, laughed at his cousin's irritation. "Harrison never could buy a decent horse. He would deny it, of course, but it is my belief he is not so ignorant as he seems, merely so soft-hearted he cannot bear to think what will happen to such animals if he does *not* buy them."

The two fell silent then. Quentin searched for and found a clean glass. He poured himself wine from the bottle his cousin had very nearly finished. Calder motioned for him to fill his glass as well, and the two sipped and stared into the fire.

"Matt," said Quentin after a time, "what will you do now?"

Calder drew in a deep breath and let it out again. "Well . . . I don't know, do I? I suppose I'll hunt for her, won't I? She's my fiancée." After a moment he added, "I still want to marry her."

"But . . ."

"Yes?"

"Well, isn't it obvious she doesn't wish to marry you?"

"Oh well, now I know there is a problem—" Calder waved it away. "—I can woo her properly, can I not? She may be shy, but she is not stupid. She'll have me in the end," he said with the rather dead voice of a man who knew, and regretted knowing, his value in the marriage market.

Nearly a week later, Lady Dewsbury-Morgan stared around a drab ill-furnished bedroom and grimaced. "The rooms are poky and not clean," said her ladyship with a touch of acid. The three had come to Reading to Louisa's old nanny's little cottage, but it was small and they were very much in the way. They could not stay there but it was difficult to find a suitable place when they could afford so little.

The solicitor's clerk, to whom she spoke, shrugged. "Ain't in much state to complain, are you?" he asked, sneering.

Her ladyship turned a glare on the young pimply-faced man and, although he could not explain why, he felt himself turning bright red. Nervously, he cleared his throat.

Having cowed him nicely, Lady Dewsbury-Morgan

drew in a deep breath. "I do not like your tone, young man, but the sentiment," she said, still more acid in her voice, "is, unfortunately, not far from the truth." More gently, she added, "Anna, what do you think?"

Lady Morgan cast a sad look around. "Does it matter?"

"You, Anna, are nearly as big a clunch as your daughter. Of course it matters," said Lady Dewsbury-Morgan bitingly. She glanced around. "We can rid ourselves of the dirt, but that mattress will have to go," she added, pointing with her cane. "The owner said furnished. He must supply furnishings that may be used."

The clerk pursed his lips, as two contradictory notions fought for his attention. His mentor, Mr. Deaton, had a soft spot for this old lady. On the other hand, the dwelling's owner was a skinflint. The young man was not at all certain how the two would mix. "I'll tell Mr. Deaton," he said. "He'll do what he can."

Lady Dewsbury-Morgan nodded. She looked around once more. "Very well. We'll take it on a quarter's lease with an option to renew. Assuming that mattress is replaced."

The clerk looked impressed. "That's using your noggin," he said, nodding. The rooms were priced too high for the poor, but the nobs were unwilling to live there. The owner's miserly ways had brought it to such a sorry state one must stretch to call the quarters genteel. Still, given how long it had stood empty it was likely that, offered a full quarter's rent, the mattress *would* be replaced.

"We may want to move on if things do not work out," said Lady Dewsbury-Morgan to Anna once all was settled, "but, then again, we may make friends and find a new life for ourselves in which case we will extend the lease. Very well," she repeated. "Let us retrieve our possessions and Sissie."

They had left the girl in the care of her old nurse who had a small cottage just west of Reading, her front gate opening onto the Bath road. The rooms they had just rented were near the center of town and Lady Dewsbury-Morgan did not look forward to the long walk. Unfortunately their finances were such that hiring a hackney was not to be thought of—not until needed for the transport of their pitifully few belongings.

Her son was not one to go back on what he'd said and the women had not asked if he would do so. They knew from the moment they made the decision to follow Sissie up the aisle that they were on their own. At least, Lady Dewsbury-Morgan knew it. She wasn't convinced Anna had realized it, but torn between a husband she feared and a daughter she loved, Lady Morgan had bravely chosen the daughter. They had, as the expression went, made their bed.

"Or, in this case," muttered Lady Dewsbury-Morgan caustically, "*unmade* it!"

They were near the edge of town when a young lady was pushed right into their path from a door a few steps above the pedestrian pavement. She tumbled to the flagstones.

"And don't come back!"

A bundle fell just beyond the sprawled maid, opening and strewing her possessions into the street. The door slammed and the young person pushed herself up, looking into Lady Dewsbury-Morgan's face.

"Well, miss? Can you move?" asked her ladyship not unkindly.

"Oh. Oh, yes. Very sorry."

The tones sounded far more educated than expected and her ladyship's brows arched.

The maid moved, gasped, and reached for her thigh. She pulled away a chunk of glass that was sticking into her skirts. A seepage of blood followed. And, with knowledge, pain registered. Then, although she swallowed a sob and her jaw clenched, she scooted to one side.

Lady Dewsbury-Morgan heaved a sigh. "Anna, pick up the, er, hm, *young person's* possessions while I see how badly she is hurt. And while we do that—" She turned to the young woman. "—you may tell us what *that* was all about." She gestured with her cane toward the closed door and then, bending stiffly, she knelt at the woman's side.

"Oh, m'lady, you mustn't," said the woman. "Re-elly."

The voice was pitched higher than the first honeyed tones and the words given the sound of a quite different class. Her ladyship cast the maid a quick look and then forced the surprising chit's skirts far enough up her leg she could see the cut. It was not deep but was rather long. Her ladyship took up her reticule and opened it. She pulled a small bottle from it.

"Not very good gin, but it will clean the wound," she said and poured about half the contents into it. The stranger gasped and then bit her lip, tears spurting from the corners of her tightly closed eyes. "Yes, it stings," added her ladyship, "but better that than that it goes rotten on us."

"Us?"

"You need a—uhmm—*position*, do you not?" asked Lady Dewsbury-Morgan.

The young woman bit the other side of her lip.

"Well?"

"You don't know why I was let go."

Her ladyship allowed her gaze to rest on the maid's dark red hair, pert nose, and decidedly firm features. "Very likely you lost your temper. Don't lose it with me."

The maid chuckled and then struggled to her feet.

"Actually, I am not offering you a position," said Lady Dewsbury-Morgan, her eyes narrowing.

"Actually, I do not want one," said the young woman in her original voice. "Going out for a maid was a ridiculous notion, I suppose," she added thoughtfully.

"I rather thought you might be willing to give up whatever scheme you've been playing at. Still, you need a roof over your head until you organize yourself, so come along. You can use my cane and I will lean on Anna and you may tell us your story as we walk."

Lady Dewsbury-Morgan grimaced when her hip gave her fits for a moment after she straightened up. One knee added a minor chorus to the singing pain, but, except to regret the gin that might have eased the aches, wasted when she'd poured it into the stranger's wound, she ignored them.

"You tell yours," she repeated and added, "and we'll tell you ours. Come along, Anna. Sissie will be worrying."

"Do you think so?" asked Lady Morgan anxiously. "Will she be—all right when we get home?" she added breathlessly.

"I don't know if she'll ever again be right in the head, but we will pray for her."

"What is wrong with her?" asked the limping maid-who-was-not-a-maid.

"She had a shock," said Lady Dewsbury-Morgan shortly, overriding Lady Morgan who would have explained more fully. "She won't talk. Not a word. But we'll talk about *our* problems later. While we walk you may entertain us with *yours.*"

"It is, I suppose a rather old-fashioned tale," responded the chit, speaking slowly. "I was engaged in my cradle to a man I've never seen. He went off to India, you see. And now . . ." She paused.

"Now he has returned to England, is that it?"

"Yes. My guardian refused to even consider sending him to the devil for me. To the right-about, I should say. He would not listen to me. He would not so much as allow me to finish my arguments!"

"Men are like that," said Lady Morgan earnestly. "It is the way of things."

"Yes, and the result is that we women must go to extremes in order to convince them when we are serious."

"Oh, but . . ."

Lady Dewsbury-Morgan interrupted her daughter-in-law. "Yes, I can see how you might feel that way. Well, we will manage somehow until you decide what to do. No, Anna, do not protest. The girl cannot be allowed to wander the streets. She would find herself in who knows what sort of difficulties. Think of your own daughter and have a little Christian charity. What we do for this woman is, in part, paying for what those lads did when they kept our girl safe until we got to her!"

"Now that sounds like a real story," said the young woman. "I will find it excessively interesting, I am sure!"

The four women settled into their cramped rooms and into a routine that, Babs—more formally known as Miss Barbara Ruthven—knew would soon feel claustrophobic. She looked up from the bread she kneaded to where Louisa sat podding peas.

She'll be all day at it, thought Babs and then chided herself for her lack of sympathy. *Poor dear. Will the child ever again speak?*

The pompous doctor, consulted at Babs' insistence, said not. Babs was unconvinced. She sought for something to say to the silent girl.

"Ah yes. Were you looking out the window this morning, Louisa Maria? Did you see that knife grinder and the lady across the street argue? What a rumpus that was. Do you think he substituted a cheaper blade or did she try to get something better from him than what she'd given him for sharpening? We will never know, of course, but very entertaining, I thought. And the words! I learned six new words." Babs chuckled, a warm golden-honey sort of sound. "You mustn't tell me they are words

I should not add to my vocabulary. My old governess would hand me more than a scold if I were ever to use them where *she* could hear. Still, they are so very colorful. She-dragon, for instance. Have you ever heard anything which better describes that harridan?"

Babs continued talking, rambling on about this and that, until her bread felt properly elastic and ready to rise. She put it in the bowl, turned it to butter all sides, and covered it with a clean cloth. Not for the first time since she came to live with the Morgan women, she blessed her governess, her housekeeper, and her long-time cook. When she'd turned eleven the three women had combined forces, forcing her to learn all sorts of things she'd assumed she'd never need to know. It was quite amazing, really, how much she had retained that she hadn't a notion was in her head. Cookery was only one talent her present circumstances had brought to her attention. In fact, she was rather proud at how deft she was with a stew pot!

After setting the bread to rise where a small fire on the hearth warmed the inglenook, she joined Louisa Maria and picked up a handful of peas while searching her mind for something else about which she could talk. She hadn't a notion why it felt the right thing to do, but talking to Louisa had become a habit. She was certain that, occasionally, she saw a response in the chit, a flickering of the eyelids, for instance, and, another time, a stillness that followed a comment.

"I wonder how I might discover if my uncle has forgiven me," she murmured. "I told you about my uncle, did I not? No, perhaps I have not. He's very nearly old enough to be my grandfather. My father had a different mother, my real grandfather's third wife. But that is unimportant. That Uncle William is elderly, *is*. He was reared in the last century and is, therefore, fustily old-fashioned and cannot see why I object to wedding someone I've never met. A man years and years older than myself who has been out of England so long he has undoubtedly forgotten anything he ever knew about polite society and proper behavior. You understand, do you not? After all, you had no wish to wed the man your father chose for you."

Babs almost allowed an exclamation to escape her. Louisa's skin had paled and her hands had stilled. She *did* hear. Or more to the point, she listened to and understood what was said to her. Babs drew in a deep breath. "So," she continued, doing her best to cover up her surprise, "how can I discover if my uncle has had a change of heart without *his* discovering where I am—in case he has *not*, you see?"

"Ah," said Lady Dewsbury-Morgan. "There you are. Did you finish your books? I mean to go to the library and will return them for you if you wish."

The library was Lady Dewsbury-Morgan's only extravagance. Her jointure would be barely adequate to keep the four of them. She knew she had no business spending the necessary for the privilege of taking out books and reading newspapers and, as their circle of acquaintance grew, having a place in which to pass an hour or so talking to them.

Life would be unbearable if they had no outlet whatsoever other than each other. Besides, the expenditure would not leave them to starve. They might find themselves wearing more layers as the seasons turned to autumn and then winter, when extravagance now meant they would be unable to afford quite as much coal as they'd like—but they'd not starve.

"Books?" asked Babs. "Oh. Yes. Louisa Maria, will you please go to our room and get your grandmother the books you will find on the dressing table?"

Obediently, Louisa Maria rose and left the kitchen.

"She heard you!"

"I think she hears everything. I talk to her. Or at her."

Babs grimaced. "Occasionally she reacts in some way. She just refuses to talk."

Tiny lines around Lady Dewsbury-Morgan's eyes deepened with tension. "Do you think . . . ?"

"Eventually." Babs nodded. "Yes, I believe she will recover, but it will take a lot of patience and a lot of kindness. Poor child."

"She isn't all that many years younger than you yourself," said her ladyship, her voice dry.

"Centuries younger," said Babs. "Centuries."

Lady Dewsbury-Morgan nodded her understanding. Louisa Maria had been kept close. Even her season was carefully monitored. At first she was seen only briefly here and there and, on those occasions she was taken into society, she had been watched every moment. Her father had acted as if she were the most valuable gem in his collection, a fragile gem, one that would crack or perhaps shatter at a touch. Or was she like a flower he thought would bruise if allowed the least little contact with reality?

Whatever the case, Louisa Maria had little knowledge of the world, of men; of anything that might prick the bubble of the dream world in which she was reared. Worse, she was given little opportunity to add to her small store of knowledge.

Her life had been very like that of a fairy-tale princess imprisoned in a tower by a bad fairy. Or by an ogre? It was certainly true that the only pain the chit ever knew came from her father. Sir George was not a gentle soul and had no patience and, living in a household of women as they did, he was her only experience with the male of the species. It was, perhaps, not surprising she'd rejected her affianced husband. The man's eyebrows alone had very likely scared the child out of her wits!

"My son is a fool," said her ladyship, her bitterness obvious in her voice. "I told him how it would be, but he said that fragile innocence was just what a man wanted in a bride. She was his daughter. I couldn't interfere— Could I *not,* you would ask?" she added as if Babs had expressed surprise. "Bah! You have the right of it. It was merely that I *didn't* interfere. I *should* have."

"You couldn't know how frightened she was of anything beyond the tight, closely guarded little world she'd known from childhood," soothed Babs.

"I knew she hated going to parties. Even balls. She is an excellent dancer, but, when she could, she discouraged possible partners, and avoided joining the sets even with men I had thought she liked—or at the least, that she didn't dislike."

"What she undoubtedly did *not* like, was having a partner. Someone who asked questions she didn't know how to answer, who expected her to know how to play the game of love, do you not agree?"

"Ah! You refer to the quick flirtatious look or the light-hearted and meaningless comment." Lady Dewsbury-Morgan sighed. "I wish . . ."

"Shush. My governess always said that wishing something is other than it is is a waste of time. One accepts what is and goes on from there."

Lady Dewsbury-Morgan eyed her. "What would *you* have done if we had not come by at just the moment you were ejected from that house?"

Babs grinned. "I am not a total fool. I wear a linen belt around my waist into which I have sewn several coins. Enough to get me home if I decide to return."

"I think you should."

"Go home?"

"Yes. Your guardian must be worried sick. Or have you sent word that you are safe and well and I unaware of it?"

Babs' lips compressed. "I have tried to think of a way to do that very thing, but I'll not have him know where I am." She drew her lips in, pursed them . . . sighed. "Others will be worried as well."

Lady Dewsbury-Morgan nodded. "I've a friend who can be trusted. She has been an invalid for decades and does not go about society. I will write her and enclose yours within my own. She will forward it for you without giving her address, but it will come from somewhere other than here."

Babs hesitated for only a moment, then nodded. "Thank you."

Louisa Maria had not returned. Babs went to find her and was unsurprised to discover the girl standing perfectly still in the middle of their bedroom staring at nothing at all. Babs touched her, turned her, moved her to the bed, and helped her sit and then lie down. She sighed. Louisa Maria needed exercise but it was difficult here in the city where people stared. She had to be led, encouraged to move along, so that, when they did go out, they became a raree-show for idlers.

Mousy little Lady Morgan had gone with them not long after they all moved in together, and then, standing firm just when she should not, had demanded they not subject the child to rude stares and the occasional cat-call. It was Babs' perhaps cynical belief that the mother cared more for her own sensibilities than for Louisa's.

Babs took the books to Lady Dewsbury-Morgan who handed them to Lady Morgan who put them in her basket. "We won't be too long," said Lady Morgan, with a nervous glance down the hall toward the bedrooms.

"We'll be as long as it takes," contradicted Lady Dewsbury-Morgan. "By this time I'd have thought you'd have learned that Miss Ruthven deals with Sissie far better than either you or I."

"It's probably because I am more her age," said Babs tactfully.

"It is probably because you do not treat her like an imbecile or fear her as if she were mad!"

"I do not treat my daughter as if she were mad!" said

Lady Morgan, hurt that anyone would think such a thing.

But, thought Babs, *you do tend to treat her as if she were stupid.* She didn't say it, however. *And holding my tongue when I feel so strongly about the subject,* she told herself, *is a big improvement over the brash young woman I was before I began this adventure. Then I'd have said my piece and damned the consequences. Oh, I was so sure of myself!* She chuckled at the rueful thought and then, putting it from her mind, set herself to composing the letter to her guardian.

Nearly two weeks later, Lady Dewsbury-Morgan sat at a table in their circulating library reading the most recent London newspaper. The lonely life they were leading was becoming a problem, the hours more and more difficult to fill. They had taken the rooms one by one and cleaned them from top to bottom. They had polished and scrubbed and brushed and done all those things that make an abode as decent as possible. That was finished and, except for the dusting, which took a handful of moments, and the daily sweeping, which took only a few more, there was little to do.

So, as had become her custom in order to waste a bit of burdensome time, she had taken up the paper, would begin with the society news, turn to the political and war news, and, when all else failed, actually read the advertisements.

She had commented on one or two items to Lady Morgan who sat beside her deep into the first volume of a lurid Gothic novel, but had given up when she got no response. The war news was encouraging in one sense, but not in the more personal. As usual, she skimmed the lists of those who died—this time in northern Spain on the Plain of Zadora near a place called Vitoria—hoping she would not see a name she recognized. It was a futile hope.

Her ladyship reminded herself to write notes of condolence to two women who had once been friends. That she had not spoken to either in decades was not relevant. The marriage she had made to save her father from the poorhouse had accomplished that goal, but it had also separated her from the milieu into which she'd been born. She was invited to the larger, less select, society do's—but mostly by the type of hostesses who invited everyone they ever knew in the hopes of filling their rooms in the manner of a proper "squeeze."

Her ladyship sighed. If only she had kept up a more personal relationship with one or two of her bosom bows, then, when worse came to worse, she might have had recourse to more pleasant surroundings than they found themselves in now. Her one sincere friend from the old days was the invalid she'd mentioned to Babs. The lady lived in restricted circumstances and could not be asked to deal with the three of them—which was, perhaps, the reason they'd remained in touch? That they could not be expected to visit each other?

She called herself a nincompoop for, even for a moment, allowing herself to fall into the dismals when it had been her choice to rescue her granddaughter. Not that she had *truly* had a choice. She could *not* allow Louisa Maria to go unprotected into a world about which she knew nothing.

Calling up all her determination, she set aside the doldrums and returned her eyes to the newspaper. One more article and she'd read the letters. Then, assuming Anna was still happily reading, she'd scan the advertisements. Occasionally there were personals at which one could chuckle. And she could waste a few moments marveling at the extravagant claims made by sellers of tight lacing or bottles of miraculous medicines that would cure anything or creams which promised to remove all signs of aging from one's skin!

The letters provided a modicum of amusement. There

had been a series recently from two men set firmly on opposite sides of the fence on the issue of the benefits of electricity in healing various illnesses and physical disabilities. One man insisted the new electricity would prove to be a cure for all man's ills. The other claimed it was just one more means of separating the gullible from their money, one more way of putting coins in the pockets of the unscrupulous.

Her ladyship had followed their arguments carefully and it was her considered opinion that neither man was correct. Very likely the invention would be useful in some particular cases, and absolutely useless in others. Lady Dewsbury-Morgan had lived long enough that she firmly believed there was no such thing as a miracle cure-all or, as some called it, a panacea for all ills—but also long enough to have seen great changes in the world. She did not scoff at this electricity merely because it was new.

Soon she'd finished everything but the last resort. All that remained were the advertisements and Lady Dewsbury-Morgan sighed softly. It would take no time at all to peruse them. And then what would she do with her day? For a long moment she stared into space and then, a bewhiskered old gentleman approaching with the obvious intention of wresting the precious paper from her hands, she turned her eyes back to the advertisements.

A few minutes later, her ladyship gasped. She reread the item. Read it a third time. And then, looking all around the room, seeing that no one was, at that instant, watching, she tore the piece from the paper, rose to her feet, and insisting the reluctant Anna move herself, she went to the door and out onto the pavement.

"But I am not ready to leave," insisted Anna, clutching her reticule and parasol, the now-empty basket on her arm. "I was in the middle of a scene. I will never discover how it comes out!"

"Some things are far more important than how some

silly little fictional ninnyhammer manages to mess up her life still again."

"But you do not understand. The hero was about to rescue her."

"And how many times do you suppose he'll have to rescue her in the full three volumes? I do not understand how you can bear to read those adventure stories. Especially when we have, in our own home, two real-life examples of the species."

"*Two* heroines? Why, whatever can you mean?"

"There is your daughter, madam, and there is Miss Ruthven. That, the last time I counted anything, adds up to two young ladies escaping unwanted marriages."

Anna sighed. "Miss Ruthven is so frighteningly competent that I cannot think of her as a heroine in a romance, someone who is escaping a terrible fate."

"Nevertheless, that is exactly what she is. Betrothed in her cradle! Indeed, she is correct that it is a most Gothic thing to happen to a girl in this modern age. Now when *I* was a girl . . ."

Lady Dewbury-Morgan continued her diatribe all the way back to their rooms. Not that it was so very far. They had chosen them with the thought in mind that they would not wish to be far from the shops.

". . . but perhaps," she finished as they turned into their street, "our Miss Ruthven will find she, at least, is out of the woods."

"What?"

Lady Morgan had not approved of Babs running away from her home and guardian merely because she objected to her marriage. And she'd no understanding of why her own daughter had objected to wedding the most marvelous young man in the world. She put her hand on Lady Dewsbury-Morgan's arm, stopping her.

"Whatever can you mean?" said Lady Morgan, her usual complaint when she didn't understand something.

"You'll see," said her ladyship, shaking the detaining hand away. "Come along." She took a moment to catch her breath and added, "I think I shall actually miss her!"

Again Lady Morgan attempted to stop her ladyship but this time she was unsuccessful. "Miss her? Miss Ruthven?"

It occurred to Lady Morgan that if the fourth member of their ménage was to leave them, there would be no one to do the baking and, although she had felt the soups and stews they ate day after day far beneath her, she had to acknowledge—when they might no longer exist—that they were far tastier than anything she herself could manage to produce.

"I wonder if we can find the pounds necessary to hire a cook housekeeper," mused Lady Dewsbury-Morgan— a thought that relieved her companion's mind of her most pressing concern!

Two

"But of course you are coming with me!" said Babs.

After reading the advertisement, Babs had begun an exchange of letters with the man who had been her guardian. She was convinced she was free to return home, but unhappy about leaving her new friends behind. She stared, rather pensively, around the poky little parlor.

"I have become very fond of you—" *You* was such a nicely ambiguous term which need not include all three women. "—*especially* I hold Louisa Maria in affection. Besides, if you had not rescued me, then where would I be? I owe you a great deal."

"You know very well that is balderdash. You admitted you'd the means to return home," chided Lady Dewsbury-Morgan.

"Yes, but I did not *wish* to return home," said Babs, grinning a rather wicked grin. "Now I do. And I am offering you a home for as long as you are willing to remain there."

Lady Morgan disapproved of such generosity on principle and, besides that objection, she was convinced the redheaded chit was far too coming. One might, in fact, if one were so bold as to state the truth, call her—*oh, such a horrid word*—fast. "You should ask your guardian for permission," said Lady Morgan.

"It is my house and I am of age. I need no one's permission to fill it with whomever I wish to invite." She turned to Lady Dewsbury-Morgan. "Come now, you cannot enjoy living here and I know you've not a great deal of money. No——" She held up her hand. "——do not poker up on me! Pride is a sin, you know."

She said the last with such a droll look of extravagant horror her ladyship could not take umbrage and was even forced to stifle a chuckle.

"So? Is it settled?" asked Babs in coaxing tones. "We will all go?"

"You are certain your guardian has broken the engagement? That he will not change his mind once you are back where he can argue with you?"

"My Uncle William writes that my cousin is as much against our marriage as I am. Although he was only a little over twenty, he thought it was a ridiculous decision at the time our parents concluded the arrangement— and he says he stayed away so long, hoping that if he did not return betimes, I would sensibly have wed another."

"I see." Lady Dewsbury-Morgan fought a losing battle with her pride. She looked to where Sissie sat staring into the fire, her hands folded in her lap, her mind somewhere where no one seemed able to reach it— except very possibly this strangely independent young lady whom no one could accuse of not having a mind of her own. Her ladyship drew in a deep breath and slowly let it out. She nodded. "Very well, Miss Ruthven, we accept your kind invitation."

"Excellent. Shall we pack? If I have not lost track of the date, the traveling carriage will arrive sometime around midday, day after tomorrow. I know that none of us have a great deal to do to ready ourselves to leave, but, however little, it takes time to do it properly. Especially since we must do it ourselves. I have concluded one thing from this adventure," she said, rising to her feet.

"And that is?" asked Lady Morgan, thinking that perhaps the hussy had learned that the men in her life knew best.

"I will be far more appreciative of my servants in future. I hadn't a notion of all they did to make my life comfortable and enjoyable. Well, I did, of course, since I was taught to manage my home, but it didn't *mean* much to me, if you understand me! Louisa Maria, come along now. We must pack."

Very gently Babs tugged Louisa from her chair and led her down the hall and into their bedroom. As she packed for the both of them and talked to Louisa she wondered just what she had done to insult Lady Morgan. The woman actually seemed to dislike her, and Babs was not used to being disliked. She found she didn't care for the sensation.

"You'll have a room all your own," she said to Louisa. "And you'll like the rose garden. It is sheltered against the wind and the sun finds it even on the coldest days, so one may walk the paths with no fear one will take a chill. Not that it will be cold for months yet, being only high summer, of course . . ."

She rambled on as she shook out gowns and folded them and laid them in the portmanteau. Shifts followed and then stockings. There were all too few of everything. The Morgan women had been allowed only an hour to throw their belongings into portmanteaus and a couple of ancient trunks before they were to leave the baronet's house forever. They would, all three, need extra of everything.

"I have a sewing woman who will make you up more gowns," said Babs to Louisa, planning ahead. "And there are materials just lying there, useless, up in the attics, so you need not feel it is charity. Not—" She glanced at Louisa Maria who stared at nothing at all and didn't appear to be listening. "—that you will, of course."

Babs sighed, and a trifle depressed by the chit's continued refusal to speak, silently continued her work.

Matthew stared at his cousin, a scowl marring his brow. *"Et tu, Brute?"*

"I am not a traitor, Matt," said Quentin earnestly. "It is simply that I cannot believe you are pining away for that milk-and-water chit. You are blue deviled because she jilted you, not because you loved her."

"I was, *am,* very fond of Louisa." Matthew sighed. "But you are correct about my bad humor—although it is neither because I loved her deeply nor that my pride is hurt." He stared morosely into the fire his valet had laid against the damp and, after a moment, lifted a foot to push a log into place with the toe of his boot. "Neither the one nor the other."

"Then what is it?"

Matthew cast a glance from under his lashes toward his cousin.

"I know that look." Quentin folded his arms and frowned. "What game are you playing?"

"But don't you see?"

"If I did, I wouldn't have to ask, would I?" asked an exasperated Quentin.

"But, my best of cousins, it is so simple."

"If it is simple, then why do you have difficulty explaining?"

Matthew chuckled. "Very well. You know I didn't wish to come to town this season. And you know why."

"Your father said you were to wed or else, and *you* said you weren't ready to be bracketed." Quentin's frown deepened. "On the other hand, you took one look at the Morgan chit and went headlong to your fate like the excellent son that you are."

"I feel a trifle guilty about that." Matthew frowned. "I wish that I knew they were safe."

"Guilty?" asked Quentin, pouncing on the word.

"Guilty. If I hadn't pushed the chit, she'd still be hiding behind palms and peering up at suitors from under her lashes, very obviously wishing the lot of us to the devil."

"Wishing you . . . well, she did jilt you, of course . . . but . . ."

"But, you would ask, how could any sensible young woman give up the opportunity to be my bride? Think what I could bring her. Two houses and a healthy dress allowance just to begin? And then—in the distant future one hopes—the title of countess, Lady Amrington, and the estates that go with the title? And that doesn't mention that my sterling self would be part of the contract?"

"Don't say that last with such scorn. I know of several ladies who would gladly wed you if you hadn't a penny to your name."

"I will bet you a monkey none of them is without a penny to *her* name!"

Quentin smiled one of his tight little smiles. "You would win, of course. I don't know of any *tonnish* lady who would cut off her own nose by wedding where there was no money at all."

"You know several," contradicted Matthew. "What of the Worthington chit? Or even my cousin who is determined to have her vicar? Or . . ."

"I believe I said a lady of the *ton*. You will not pretend Mabel Worthington has the least interest in frills and parties. She will be quite happy in her cottage with her poet."

"She will until forced to kill and clean a chicken for the soup pot."

Quentin barked a laugh. "And my sister? Will she balk at wringing the chicken's neck?"

"You know very well she would not." Calder sobered. "Not that she will find it necessary to go to such extremes as that, of course. Amy is up to anything. I hope my uncle gives in, because I do not think she'll be happy with any other man." He sighed. "Which brings us back to happy-ever-afters for me, does it not? Do you recall meeting this female about whom our aunt writes?"

"You haven't explained why you pursued the Morgan chit."

"Because, my all-knowing cousin, she is nothing like my mother."

Quentin frowned. "Your mother?"

"Peace. That is what I crave in marriage. Quiet. A gentle lady who will not make all around her a living hell."

"I don't recall it being that bad . . ."

"I do."

Matthew's mouth compressed and his eyes had a bleak look Quentin had not seen for ages. He threw off the mood always roused by thoughts of his long-dead mother.

"Now," Calder repeated, "what do you recall of Miss Ruthven? If the chit lives in my aunt's neighborhood then we must have met her back when we'd spend the occasional summer holiday with her."

"Miss Barbara Ruthven?" Quentin pursed his lips. "I am certain we met her. As I recall, you and she very nearly came to a pulling of caps."

Calder started forward in his chair. "Good Lord! You cannot mean that redheaded hoyden who scared the birds, making them wild as bedamned!"

To say nothing, he thought, *of stealing my brand new gun and hiding it so I could not find it.*

Quentin nodded. "I don't know why you objected so strenuously. It wasn't as if it were a shooting party or that we were attempting to fill a game bag to bursting. We were too young. Didn't we return to school only a week or so later?"

"Game birds are not to be frightened into abandoning their nests," said Matthew, speaking rather portentously. "You know that as well as I."

"They are if you object to someone hunting them."

Matthew frowned, his heavy brows pulling together into a single bar above his eyes. "Do you think that was it?"

"You didn't listen to a word she said, did you? Not surprising, of course. You were too busy *yelling* at her to hear anything *she* said."

Matthew laughed. "Very likely. I had not yet learned to control my temper."

"And have you now?" asked Quentin overly politely.

"Stubble it, or you'll find out!"

The two men laughed quietly together and fell silent. Very nearly half an hour later, as if they had never stopped speaking, Quentin said, "But you have no choice, Matt. You know your father will not cease his nagging until you are wed. Your dear Aunt Hermie says this Miss Ruthven is wealthy, not bad looking, and intelligent." He chuckled when Calder grimaced. "Better that than the empty-headed little featherbrain your last bride proved to be." He scanned Lady Blackstock's letter once again. "In fact, except for this bit about the girl being a trifle headstrong, she sounds perfect."

"If Aunt Hermie thinks her headstrong, she must be iron-willed and stubborn beyond belief."

"An overly independent lady, you think?"

"What a diplomat you would make, Quent. Let us call a pig-headed pig a sow, shall we?" asked Matthew in sour tones.

Quentin remained silent and Matthew glanced his way.

"You asked about my temper, did you not?" asked Matthew softly. "I apologize. That last was out of line."

"*Far* out of line." Quentin grimaced. "Very well, if you'll not consider Miss Ruthven, what do you mean to do? Your father has a temper too, has he not?"

Calder smiled a derisory sort of smile. "He has. But, Quent, I am bereaved, am I not? I was very fond of my little Louisa. Am fond of her. Quite attached, in fact. I need time to mourn her loss, do I not?"

"Is that the line you've written him?"

"Something of the sort. Not so maudlin."

"You did feel some affection for her, I think," said Quentin, thoughtfully.

"Yes," said Matthew quietly. "I did."

Quentin knew his cousin well and realized for the first time that Matthew had been more deeply hurt by Miss Morgan's jilting him than he would ever admit. "Then—" He spoke tentatively. "—you will write your aunt and tell her you are not in any state to consider a substitute?"

"No." Matthew sighed. "I have written her that we will join her a week from Tuesday."

Quentin sat forward in his chair and twisted around to stare at his cousin, starched collar points making it impossible to see him in any other way. "Then what have we been discussing?"

"My selfish and maudlin desire to remain free of shackles?" asked Matthew lightly.

"Ah. That was it."

Understanding each other in the easy way of long-time friends, they again fell to musing, Quentin wondering just how deep his cousin's emotions had gone for the runaway bride and Lord Calder idly wondering what sort of woman the odd boy-like girl, Miss Ruthven, had become.

That his aunt liked the young lady was, in some ways, *not* a plus. The lady was utterly scornful of quiet little mice like

Louisa. And Louisa had suited him in a number of ways. Not the least of them was the fact she'd never say boo to a goose, never argue with him, and *never, ever* be the sort of raging harridan he remembered—with a shudder—his mother to have been.

Memories of cowering behind the nearest shelter, a chair or the newel post or some such thing, of pounding heart and tightly closed eyes, of shivers up his spine, all those things still, every now and again, flitted through his nightmares. Calder had no desire whatsoever to replicate his father's marriage in his own. He had hated it when his parents got into one of their roaring battles. *Hated* it.

What, he wondered for the first time, *did they fight about?*

He could no longer recall—assuming he'd ever known. But whatever it was, he was determined his own marriage would be peaceful, which meant he'd not be happy married to an independent sort of woman. Certainly he'd no intention of wedding a woman who might turn into a termagant.

No, he decided, *my sweet little mouse suited me right down to the ground.* And then he felt his ears redden and he hoped Quentin did not notice. *What a coxcomb I sound,* he thought, chagrinned to realize there was such an exceedingly selfish reason for choosing and wooing shy little Louisa Maria Morgan. *But I was—am—very fond of her,* he insisted to himself. Still another thought flitted through his mind. *Is there anything wrong with wishing a quiet life?* He answered himself. *No. There is not!*

"You appear awfully preoccupied with something, coz. What troubles you?"

"Hmm?" Matthew realized Quentin had asked a question. "What?"

"I asked, what troubles you?"

"Troubles me? Not one single solitary thing." *Three or four things, perhaps, but not just one.*

Quentin was a good friend and trustworthy, but the notion he might confide in him concerning the sudden insight he had had into his own character appalled Calder. _But I was fond of her. Am! I mean, I am fond of her. I wonder where she is? I wonder if she is all right . . ._

"Well," said Babs, staring at the note of invitation she held in her hand. "I cannot believe it."

"What can you not believe," asked Lady Dewsbury-Morgan.

"Lady Blackstock is holding a dinner party. We are invited to attend."

"So what is so surprising about a dinner party?" asked her ladyship as she carefully spread more of the excellent plum preserves onto a second slice of toast.

"Lady Blackstock never entertains—unless one considers a hunt breakfast or a rowdy after-the-races sort of thing, something that happens more or less by accident, to be entertaining. That she means to give a formal dinner is the surprising thing. Ah! I see. Her nephew and his cousin are visiting. I recall—" Babs scowled at those memories. "—when they used to stay with her when we were all much younger. Now she wishes to re-introduce the visiting lions to the local lions." Babs' scowl deepened. "I suppose we must go."

"Go?" asked Lady Morgan. She entered the breakfast room just in time to hear that last.

Babs explained. ". . . but it will be a dead bore. She will invite every hunting-mad soul she knows and I will have to bite my tongue until it bleeds in order to remain polite."

"You don't hunt?" asked Lady Dewsbury-Morgan. She finished her toast and lifted the edge of the tablecloth to wipe her mouth.

"Mother Vivian," whispered Lady Morgan shocked. "The napkin!"

Her ladyship looked at the side of her plate to where a neatly folded square of linen rested. "Ah yes. I will never become used to the new-fangled things." But she picked it up, shook it out, and carefully wiped the butter from her fingers. "Well, Miss Ruthven? *Do* you join the hunt?"

"Ride to hounds?" Babs shuddered. "I hate it. I know one cannot allow vermin to destroy one's poultry as they are apt to do if not kept down, but to chase a fox all over the countryside and then to allow the dogs . . ." Again she shuddered, her mouth compressing. "To answer your question, I do not hunt."

"I have noticed you do not serve pheasant or other game birds. I merely thought you disliked the stronger flavor."

"I've no objection to eating them if someone else serves them. They are, after all, unlikely to fly off the table and return to the wild. But I cannot like sending someone out to deliberately shoot them and bring them in for my enjoyment. We raise creatures specifically for the table. We do not need to harm innocent wild creatures as well."

"I once heard an argument that, if we did not kill the foxes and if we did not kill our wild birds, then the foxes would eat the wild birds and everyone would be happy."

Babs grinned. "I will remember that. An excellent argument for when I next find myself standing up to some rabid hunter and, er, disagreeing with him as to the value of hunting." She frowned. "Which I am very likely to do, if I must spend an entire evening with the sort of people Lady Blackstock will invite to her dinner."

"It is very wrong of you to do so," said Lady Morgan, her tone sharp.

"Do you think so?" Babs asked politely. "In what way is it wrong to argue for one's beliefs?"

"You should not argue with your elders. Or with the

men who run this world. It is not your place to think they might be wrong."

Babs eyed her. "Sir George did you no service if he taught you to believe he could never be in the wrong."

"I agree," said Lady Dewsbury-Morgan before her daughter by marriage could speak the words obviously on the tip of her tongue. "My son was allowed by his father to grow into the worst sort of bully. I should never have allowed it."

"*Allowed* it!" Lady Morgan stared at Lady Dewsbury-Morgan. "But it is a father's duty to decide how to rear his children."

"It is a mother's duty to see he doesn't *ruin* them instead of *rearing* them," said Lady Dewsbury-Morgan, "and I failed in that duty. You suffered. Louisa Maria suffered. I suffered, watching what he did to the two of you. I apologize, Anna. You were such a bright-eyed hopeful bride. It did not take long for him to turn you into a dull, frightened rabbit. Do you even recall what you were like before you married Sir George?"

Lady Morgan blinked. One could see how fearfully she looked into the past, how tentatively she drew forth one or two memories, how shocked she was to realize how very much she had changed. "But surely . . ."

"You would say," interrupted her ladyship, "that my son was right to correct your ways? Nonsense. He is, as I have said, a bully. He is also selfish and I fear he has a rather terrifying need to control everything around him. With you and Louisa Maria he succeeded." She huffed, a derisive sound. "Once he was in his teens he tried to change *me*. Fortunately, I was too set in my ways to oblige him."

"He used to say you were irritatingly pig-headed," murmured Lady Morgan and then looked fearfully at Lady Dewsbury-Morgan. She relaxed when the older woman barked a quick sharp laugh.

"Pig-headed? Is that the worst he said behind my back? My dear Anna, you should have heard the things he said to my face whenever I would not bend the knee to his wishes."

Lady Morgan's expression revealed confusion. "But, didn't it bother you?"

"When I was saying worse to him? Not at all. I'll not take from another a right I take for my own!"

Babs laughed. "Very proper of you," she said. "I will return a note that there will be five of us. My uncle will wish to attend, the three of you, and myself." She frowned. "I wonder if my cousin will have finished whatever it is that keeps him in London and have come into the country by then. Perhaps I should say he, too, comes and then I will be very sorry if he does not and upsets her table." Babs stood. She grinned. "Not, of course, that that would bother Lady Blackstock. Very likely she'd not notice. I have heard that she waves her guests toward the dining room, telling them not to stand on ceremony, but to sit wherever they wish, that it is all nonsense, this business of going in two by two according to rank and will ask why one should not assure of having congenial dinner partners by choosing with whom one will sit."

Once again Lady Morgan looked appalled. Even Lady Dewsbury-Morgan appeared a trifle dumbstruck at Lady Blackstock's carelessness where proper manners were concerned. "I very much hope she does not do so on this particular occasion," said the latter just a trifle icily. "Where would we be if just anyone could do just anything he liked? There are *reasons* for the rules of proper behavior."

"Since she has sent out a proper invitation," soothed Babs, seeing the elderly woman was seriously upset, "surely she will abide by proper forms on this occasion."

Her ladyship nodded, was about to say something more, when a commotion in the hall drew her attention.

Babs, already standing near it, opened the breakfast room door.

"Well," she said. "I guess that settles the question of how many go to Lady Blackstock's. This must be my cousin who has just arrived."

Three

Babs walked into the hall from the breakfast room. At the same time, her guardian entered from the west wing. He came from the ground floor suite she had contrived for him to use when his joints grew too painful, in damp weather, to manage the stairs. They both stared at the bronze-skinned, dark-haired man who stood near the door directing several liveried servants as they unloaded the coach in which he'd arrived and the one that followed it.

"James Ruthven, you might at least ask if you can bring all that litter into my niece's hallway!" barked William Ruthven, his grizzly brows drawn tightly together. "In fact, I thought you meant to go to your own place."

"Have you seen The Oaks?" asked James mildly, turning and approaching his uncle, his hand extended. "It is in no shape for man or beast," he added as they shook hands. "I've an army of workmen there seeing to everything from replacing the roof to installing a modern water closet. In the meantime, I mean to impose upon Cousin Barbara. She will not toss me into the cold." He looked around, saw Babs, rightly assumed she was who she was, and asked, "Will you, cousin?"

"No, of course not." She glanced at the bundles, crates, and trunks. "I've a storage room that remains dry year round and which stands nearly empty. Would you object to having this—" She gestured at the growing piles. "—put there? It cannot *all* be clothing or private papers which you will need during your stay."

A rustle drew Babs' eyes to the stairway landing. Cowering at the turn, attempting to hide behind impossibly thin spindles, was Louisa Maria. She stared with huge frightened eyes at the chaos below. Babs immediately climbed up to her and pulled the panic-stricken girl up and into the comfort of her arms.

"It is only my cousin come home from India," she said quietly. "James will not harm you. And you know that my guardian's bark is loud and unruly, but, as I have said before, he will not bite you. Do all those strange men upset you?" Babs gestured at her cousin's servants. "Neither will they harm you."

Louisa searched Babs' eyes, looking deeply into them. After a long moment she relaxed a little.

"Are you hungry? Shall I take you to your grandmother, who is in the breakfast room?" Louisa made no sign, either for or against, and Babs, as was her habit, made the decision for her. "Come along now. Don't regard all this bother." She urged Louisa down the remaining stairs. "Now we will slide right alongside the stairs until we are beyond the clutter. That is right. And here we are at the breakfast room. See? We have arrived and all is well."

She turned Louisa Maria over to Lady Dewsbury-Morgan and her mother and returned to the hall. "Logan," she said to her butler, "you know the storeroom to which I referred. See that all that is not needed by my cousin is taken there and stored properly. Cousin? Would you like to see your rooms at once or would you prefer to join us in the breakfast room?"

"Neither. Instead, you may tell me about that child," said James, taking her arm and drawing her over to where William Ruthven stood leaning on his cane. "Uncle?" he said. "I hope I find you well." When the proprieties were attended to, the three turned down the hall to William's rooms.

"Well may you ask about that child who is not a child and who is not right in the head. Your cousin has filled her house with total strangers, James," groused the crotchety old man, "and insists they be allowed to live here forever."

"As I have told you, Uncle William, they saved my bacon—"

"You need not be vulgar," barked William.

"—and I owe them a favor. I also like them. And I believe I am helping poor little Louisa Maria toward a recovery. For that reason alone I would continue to house them, feed them, and, if necessary, clothe them."

"It is Sir George's duty to see to them."

"Sir George has repudiated them."

"Then," said James, pacifically, "he must have had good reason."

"His reason," said Babs, her voice harsh, "was that he attempted to force Louisa into a marriage she did not wish and was embarrassed when she could not go through with it. She was at the altar when she refused to say her vows. He is the sort who cannot bear to be crossed."

"I see," said James, nodding. "You have a fellow-feeling for her."

Babs frowned, not seeing his point.

"You," he explained, "had no wish for *our* arranged marriage."

She grinned at his gentle teasing. "But I do not own such complete idiots for relatives as does poor Louisa. *My* relatives have seen the sense in what I say."

"I wonder if our uncle would have come around if it were not that I too do not wish to fulfill the contract. You are not at all the sort of woman I would wed, Cousin Barbara!"

"I haven't a notion if you are the man for me, but I certainly wasn't about to stay here and discover the answer *after* the knot was tied, as my guardian insisted was the proper thing to do!"

When William growled, she stuck her tongue out at him. He grunted—half a laugh and half disgust. She grinned.

James, watching this by-play, smiled and shook his head. "You, my dear cousin, are a minx. But you have not explained the young lady's behavior."

Babs sobered and then sighed. "I cannot explain it. Nor can the two doctors we have consulted, one in Reading, who is an idiot, and our own good doctor here, who is a sensible man. Before her father washed his hands of her she spoke perfectly sensible English—if not always sensibly! Now she will not speak at all and half the time it is as if she does not even hear one. She seems to live in a world outside this one."

"Poor child," said James.

"Yes, and I will not have her hurt still more. She will have a home with me for as long as she needs it."

"And that termagant, her grandmother?" asked William, a growl in his voice. "That . . . that . . . wet rag she calls Mother? Or *would* if she said anything at all."

Babs laughed. "I like Lady Dewsbury-Morgan. She may have a bite to her tongue, but she is not boring." She sobered. "Lady Morgan?" she asked, her tone more thoughtful. "Perhaps when she has been away from her husband for a time, she will become more like the woman Lady Dewsbury-Morgan says she was before her marriage."

"I have known women who have been so firmly suppressed by their husbands that they can no longer think for themselves," said James, speaking before his uncle could say anything else he might regret. "Is that her ladyship's problem?"

Babs nodded, her eyes twinkling. "She has acquired the obviously foolish notion that the mere fact someone wears trousers instead of skirts puts him in the right, no matter what idiot thing he says or nasty thing he does. I cannot understand it."

William chuckled but shook his head at the same time. "No, of course *you* cannot understand it." Then he frowned. "I should never have hired that tutor when your governess said you needed more than she could give you. Then, like a fool, I agreed to teach you to manage your property, forced to acknowledge—" His voice took on an exceedingly dry note. "—that I will not always be here to do it for you—" The tone changed back to normal. "—so you should know sufficient you could see you are not cheated and that everything is done properly."

"Did she actually suggest that you might die?" asked James, half amused and half appalled.

"She did. That she was thirteen at the time, was no excuse."

Babs gritted her teeth. "He will never ever allow me to forget what I freely admit was a truly tactless remark. That I needed to know what I was taught is, I suppose, no excuse, but until I raised that particular argument, I could not make him agree that I should—" She lowered her voice. "—bother my little head about such things."

"I assume that at that time, he thought I would manage such things for you."

"Perhaps . . . but I *wanted* to learn and I am glad I did." She laughed. "As things stand, it is a very good thing," she said, her eyes gleaming with humor, "as I am unlikely to ever find a man I wish to wed."

"You are, what? Let me think. Nearly twenty years younger than myself, which makes you about . . . twenty-five?"

"Twenty-six, cousin. High on the shelf and destined to

lead apes in hell." She shrugged. "Better that than to be made over into a poor little squab like Lady Morgan."

"Barbara," chided William, "you know very well that there are very few men of Sir George's stripe. Most marriages jog along quite well without either side suffering to any great degree."

"Yes, and as to that," said Babs tartly, "I would jog along *more* than merely *well* and not suffer at all. I do *very* well alone. It will require an exceptional man to make me believe that I can continue to enjoy life half so well if yoked to him."

The day of the dinner party arrived and, dressed in their best, the party from Merrywood Hall drove to Blackstock Manor, riding in James' new traveling carriage, the only one available large enough to accommodate six in comfort.

Upon their arrival, they were pointed in the right direction by Lady Blackstock's excuse for a butler and joined the company. Lady Blackstock's long low drawing room ran the length of the house so that there were windows looking both east and west and, just then, the sun shone directly in through undraped windows, casting long shadows over the scratched and unpolished but still beautiful parquet floor.

Blackstock Manor, not so large as Merrywood Hall, was more than adequate for a lady who was totally uninterested in how or where she lived so long as she had a well-run stable full of excellent horseflesh, a superior local hunt, and a man who knew how to protect her birds. When younger, her ladyship had traveled each year to Scotland and participated in the deer stalking, but age had made that pastime less enjoyable and she no longer made the journey. She was tall, thin as a rail, iron-hard, and gray-haired.

And blessed with an over-loud voice.

She used it to welcome the Merrywood party. "Come in! Come right in," she boomed. "You've met most everyone I think. Or—" Her eyes narrowed. "—or, perhaps not? Who is this?" She stared hard at James Ruthven and the three strange women.

After introducing the Morgan women, William Ruthven said, "This, Lady Blackstock, is my nephew, James Ruthven. He has finally returned, as you see, from India."

"The bridegroom," growled her ladyship and stared, narrow-eyed, very nearly glowering, from James to Babs and back.

"We have agreed to disagree," said Babs with a demureness that fooled no one—except perhaps Lady Blackstock. Babs thought even that unlikely. There were no flies on her ladyship.

Her ladyship nodded once, making her turban slip down onto her forehead. She rearranged it as she roared, "Well, that's all right then. Come along and meet the company. Do you hunt?" she asked James as she pulled him toward a group of men.

"I have hunted tiger in India, but the sport, in other forms, has not come my way to any great degree." James had been warned that there would be little conversation other than hunting and, an amiable man, was willing to make the effort.

Calder stood with Quentin some distance away. "So that's to be my bride," he said in a near-whisper.

"That's our aunt's intention," said Quentin and then, spying the other women in the Merrywood party, he straightened, swore softly, and glanced at his cousin. "Matt . . ."

Matt was also swearing but in an entirely different tone. "The gods are with me," he finished, his expression one of satisfaction. He started across the room toward where Louisa Maria stood between her mother and grandmother.

Lady Dewbury-Morgan was first to see him. She too swore, but silently and only one pungent word. "Anna. Take Louisa over to those chairs. Quickly."

Lady Morgan, trained by her husband to obey, did so without question, and Lady Dewsbury-Morgan set off on a course to intercept Lord Calder. "Good evening, my lord," she said, standing firmly in his way.

"My lady," he said, attempting to peer around her.

"Don't approach her."

"Don't . . . ?" His thick brows rose a trifle. "But she's my fiancée," he said softly, catching and holding her ladyship's gaze.

"She *was* your fiancée."

"I cannot recall putting a retraction of our engagement into the papers," said Lord Calder, his forehead wrinkling as if he were in deep thought, and his exceptionally thick brows forming the usual, unwittingly threatening, bar above his eyes.

"You feel it was *necessary* to retract it?"

Babs, seeing the two in an overly tense conversation, joined them. "Hello, Lord Calder. It's been a very long time since I last saw you. Did you ever find your gun?"

Red touched Matt's cheekbones at the memory. "Yes. Or rather my aunt's groundskeeper found it."

"I am sorry to hear it," said Babs.

"You are still so much against hunting?" he asked, recovering himself.

"I am."

"And yet my aunt, who is addicted to the hunt, invites you to her home and, not only does she invite you, but you accept?"

"Surely it is not so particularly astonishing," said Babs and deliberately widened her eyes. "If I were to eschew the company of every person who enjoys one form of hunting or another, I would have no society at all."

He found himself chuckling at the wry tone that was combined with a bland expression. "Yes, I see how that could be." He glanced at Lady Dewsbury-Morgan who waited silently but obviously impatiently. "Will you excuse us, Miss Ruthven? Lady Dewsbury-Morgan and I have a few points of interest only to ourselves which must be discussed."

He offered his arm to her ladyship and was about to turn away when Babs spoke in a thoughtful tone. "No."

He whipped his head around to stare at her.

"I do not believe I will excuse you," she added gently.

"What?" He blinked.

"Miss Ruthven," said Lady Dewsbury-Morgan, "you do not understand."

"Nor does anyone else—" Babs still spoke softly. "—although I believe there will be a great deal of speculation as to the whys and the wherefores. That, you see, is why I interfered," she explained gently. "You are drawing attention to yourselves."

Calder looked around the room, saw his aunt smiling and nodding encouragingly, saw curiosity on various and sundry faces, and realized he could not settle the question of Miss Morgan while the whole of his aunt's coterie of friends looked on. "I see. Thank you, Miss Ruthven, for . . ." His voice trailed off; he was unable to think of a proper way of phrasing what he wished to say.

"For restraining us," said Lady Dewsbury-Morgan with a certain asperity, "from adding to the scandal already surrounding us. My Lord, with Miss Ruthven's permission, I will drive out on the morrow. On our way here I noticed a pleasant-looking river with a humpbacked bridge spanning it. It is not far from Merrywood. Perhaps you will agree to a meeting there, about ten?"

"It is actually more a canal these days than a river, but I

know where you mean." He heard his aunt's rather ramshackle butler's slurring voice announce, ". . . Cook will be that upset if everyone don't come to table on the instant."

"I suppose," said Lady Blackstock in her over-loud voice, "that we'd better do this properly. Now everyone, you know the order. That's right. That's right," she repeated encouragingly, nodded, prodded one youngish man who appeared a trifle shy into offering his arm to a another neighbor's daughter. She saw that her one nephew, Quentin, escorted both Lady Morgan and her wisp of a daughter, but shrugged. She didn't care that her table might be upset by the solecism and allowed it to pass without comment.

On the other hand, she was exceedingly upset to see her other nephew escorting Lady Dewsbury-Morgan rather than Miss Ruthven who went in on her guardian's arm. She sighed and accepted the escort of the only remaining man, an elderly rake. The dissipated earl was home on a repairing lease and, as the highest ranking man present, escorted his hostess, as was proper.

Once everyone was seated, Lady Blackstock glanced around her table, saw that that odd East India man had seated himself on the other side of the little Morgan chit and was speaking softly to her.

Farther down the table, Miss Ruthven had her guardian on one side but had failed to avoid, on the other, an admiring young man who was hunting mad and so newly admitted to adult society as to be unlikely to know of Miss Ruthven's feelings on the subject. Her ladyship felt Miss Ruthven deserved him on two counts. She *should* be enjoying Calder's spirited conversation and she had *no business* disapproving of the hunt.

On the other side of the table, Lord Calder had Lady Dewsbury-Morgan on one side and the wife of one of her hunting friends on the other. That didn't make her ladyship happy, either.

Lady Blackstock sighed lustily. Calder, it seemed, was going to be difficult. He had not appeared unwilling to meet Miss Ruthven when they'd spoken about her earlier. So why was he balking at doing the pretty now she had contrived to get them into the same room in a perfectly innocent manner? Had she not done everything to insure that no one suspected it was the opening move in a plot to acquire Miss Ruthven's person and property for her nephew's benefit?

Her ladyship lost herself in trying to think up reasons for Calder's rebellion . . . until her ladyship's butler prodded her—*twice*—and she recalled she had a duty to her guests.

Her butler, unlike most servants, was quite willing to put himself forward whenever he perceived it necessary and, if her ladyship had not responded to his prodding would, very likely, have *ordered* her to pay attention to her guests.

Four

It had been a very long time since Lady Dewsbury-Morgan had had an opportunity to drive herself anywhere.

Her husband had not seen the sense in it, a mere woman at the reins, and besides, it was beneath his dignity. *A coachman,* he had informed her, *will drive you and you will sit behind him, as is proper.* Her ladyship grimaced at the memory.

Her son's reasons for forbidding it were somewhat different. What they boiled down to was that not only was he too selfish to provide her with a proper lady's phaeton and horse, but if she had had them, then she would have been free to go where she pleased without his saying yea or nay and he was not the sort of man to put up with such behavior on the part of *anyone* living under his roof, let alone a mere female.

Therefore, it had been a long time and she rather wondered if she retained the skill. So, obviously, did Miss Ruthven's head stableman. He looked her up and down with a sapient eye and, without asking, harnessed a nicely placid old mare to the gig. "You'll have no trouble at all with old Bess," he told her in a kindly tone.

She didn't.

In fact, by the time she reached the road and turned onto it with a deftness of which she was rather proud, she wished she'd a slightly livelier beast between the poles.

Her ladyship arrived at the rendezvous before Lord

Calder and pulled to the side. A farm cart hauling bags of grain to a mill situated upstream passed her. Lady Dewsbury exchanged a few words on the pleasant weather with the elderly man walking beside the huge workhorse as she settled down to wait.

The day *was* pleasant. A lark sang overhead, bees buzzed in a mass of poppies beside the road, and the sun was warm on her old bones. She almost hoped Lord Calder would forget their appointment. She'd no desire to ruin such a nice day with controversy—but there he came, riding a high-stepping gray with a long tail and flowing mane. Just the sort of animal she'd have chosen herself a decade earlier!

Oh, very well, she amended crossly, *two decades.*

Assuming, of course, that she had been *allowed* to choose a riding horse for herself, which would *not* have been the case.

"Good morning, my lady," said Lord Calder.

His odd brows, thick and dark, looked menacing, and her ladyship wondered if they were the reason her immature granddaughter had feared the man. "It is a good morning," she agreed. "If you would be so kind as to help me down, I believe I would enjoy a walk alongside the stream."

Lord Calder tied his horse to a convenient sapling and came to the gig. He let down the step and offered his hand.

"Easy now," he said when her grip tightened. "There. Which direction would you care to go?"

She set her cane and looked both ways. "I see the mill upstream is working. It will be noisy and very likely dusty. Shall we go downriver?"

Matthew was agreeable and they set off along the broad path that paralleled the water. "You see?" he said, pointing out a slowly moving over-laden flat-bottomed boat. "I said it was a canal. There is quite a lot of barge

traffic along here." He glanced down at her and added,
"As you very likely noticed earlier, the millrace is off to
the side and they've put in a lock which they seem to
have done in any number of odd places where none ever
before existed. Small barges can now navigate the stream
with some ease."

"I see." She pinched his arm. "But that is not the topic
I wished to discuss with you."

"You would not find it easier to ease into our discussion?" he asked, a tinge of humor in his tone.

"No. I want it done and over. My granddaughter is not
. . . well."

His brows rose. One could not say they arched, because they didn't. They were merely elevated straight
bars somewhat higher above his eyes than normal. "She
seemed much as usual last evening. Did she eat something which disagreed with her?"

"It has nothing to do with eating or with last night.
She has been . . . unwell since she left the church that
day."

This time he heard the hesitation. "Unwell." It was
half a question.

Lady Dewsbury-Morgan drew in a deep breath. "If you
must have it with no bark on it, she has spoken no word
since that day. Not one."

"And you blame me?"

"I set the blame precisely where it belongs. Directly on
her father's back. My son," added her ladyship, her voice
harsh, "has wanted the *entrée* to the *ton* since he was old
enough to know he didn't have it and that I do despite
my marriage to his father. To a far lesser degree than formerly, but I *do* have it. He became obsessed with making
himself a place within the ranks of the upper ten thousand and thought he had brought it about when he was
awarded the baronetcy. He was enraged when he discovered he was no more respected or wanted than when

a mere mister. I sometimes wonder," she added in a more restrained tone, "if he didn't become slightly unhinged on the subject—especially I thought it possible when he decided he would achieve his goal if Louisa Maria were to marry a titled man."

"So he told you to present her."

Lady Dewbury-Morgan nodded, her mouth a straight firm line. "Yes." She walked on a few paces, her cane stabbing the packed earth with each step. Finally she sighed. "I admit I was not displeased. I hoped she would marry a good man and take the place in society I'd lost. Such egoism! I must, it seems, blame myself as well as her father," she said mournfully. She drew in a breath and continued. "Louisa was the proper age. I had seen that she was properly trained and taught all she needed to know—but I'd no understanding of how very shy she is or how nervous she becomes when forced to meet strangers. I thought she'd begun to get over it. And *then* . . ."

"Then?" he asked when she stopped abruptly—both speaking and moving.

She started forward again. "And then your eye fell on her."

"Ah."

"My son was ecstatic. So was Anna. His wife, you know." She recalled that Lord Calder had been engaged to Louisa. "Of course you know." Again she paused, but this time Calder let the silence go on. Then, sadly, her ladyship said, "Louisa Maria never learned how to tell anyone that she doesn't want to do something she is told to do. She was told to attract you."

Those brows drew together, making one thick line across his forehead. "What I recall is that she seemed to blow hot and then cold."

"What she did," said Lady Dewsbury-Morgan dryly, "was obey every direct order—and avoid you when not specifically told otherwise."

"I see."

"Do you? Do you truly see that she is—more than shy? She is frightened half to death of any man who comes anywhere near her. Last night was an ordeal for her. She fell asleep the moment we were settled in the carriage and was carried, deeply asleep, up to her bed. She had not yet roused when I came to meet you. She was worn to a thread merely by trying to maintain a proper poise the whole of one evening—and that amongst a group of country nobodies!" Lady Dewsbury realized how snobbish that sounded and grimaced at her own attitude before, somewhat accusingly, she finished, "Worst of all, *you* were there. She nearly lost control when she saw you."

"I feel a great deal of affection for her and still wish to wed her," said Calder slowly. "But I do see she will be difficult to win. Why do I not try courting her more gently now I know more about her?"

Lady Dewsbury-Morgan sighed. "I don't know. I don't know if she will ever feel comfortable with a man. With any man."

They strolled on in silence. And then, a fish rising, they stopped, both of them, and watched, wondering if it would rise again. It did.

"It would be like casting out lures for that fish, would it not?" asked Calder thoughtfully.

"No. Not at all."

Her ladyship spoke firmly and he turned a surprised look her way.

"That monster is a wily old devil," she explained, "and has learned a great deal about lures or he'd not have reached such a great age. Louisa is younger than her years. She doesn't understand them. Lures, I mean. She might be caught, but would it be because she was attracted to the lure, or would it be merely an accident that she happened to bite down when the hook was in place?"

"No girl reaches her years and remains that naïve!"

"Think you not? But, for Louisa, that is it exactly. She has not matured as other girls do and does not . . . not—" She cast a look at Calder and spoke words she would never have spoken to a man if there were not the need to protect Louisa. "—does not feel those things a man and woman feel for each other when they would find pleasure in each other."

Lord Calder cast a startled glance her way at such straight speaking and then stared at the placidly flowing stream. "Perhaps I can teach her to feel those things," he suggested.

"And perhaps not." Lady Dewbury-Morgan came very close to losing her temper and *did* lose control over any sense of propriety. "Lord Calder," she said, "surely you do not want a cold fish for a wife, which I very much fear my granddaughter would be! Doing her duty by you, of course, but dreading each and every time you came to her bed. I know you cannot want that. Why will you not leave Louisa be?"

"I am very fond of Louisa!" he said, turning lowering brows her way.

"Yes. I am sure you are fond of your favorite dog as well," she said with more than a touch of acid in her tone.

He laughed. "Well, yes I am, but I assure you it is not the same."

"Mere fondness is not enough. It will take a great deal of love for a man to be as tender, as *patient* as he must be with Louisa. I do not think you feel that love or are capable of that degree of patience."

For a moment it seemed as if Lord Calder might agree but then his jaw tightened and he shook his head. "I mean to have her," he said. "She is perfection itself."

"*Perfection!* You are a fool."

"She is my choice. I very much want her."

"She doesn't want you."

"I will teach her to want me. I will not rush her. I will have all the patience in the world with her," he said grandly, believing his own words as he spoke them.

Lady Dewsbury-Morgan sighed as she considered how to convince him. "She won't speak. How can you have any sort of relationship with her? How, if you do succeed, could she manage the duties your wife will have, overseeing your establishments and playing hostess at your parties? You have not thought!"

"She spoke perfectly rationally before that day in the church. I believe she will again once she discovers no one will punish her for playing the jilt."

Lady Dewsbury-Morgan turned sharply and studied his profile. "You are not seeking revenge, are you?" she asked, her tone urgent.

Calder turned, a look of surprise raising those brows and widening his rather deep-set eyes. "It never crossed my mind."

"Then you will not be overly pressing and you will, if she continues to . . . dislike . . . you, go away and leave her alone?"

Calder hesitated before responding and then answered her question with another. "Shall we give it a couple of weeks and then discuss this again?"

She sighed. "Very well. I suppose that is more than I had hoped."

He chuckled. Then he stiffened as if he'd thought of another interpretation of her words. "Perhaps you'd explain that?"

"It was not an insult. It is merely that I was uncertain if you'd even show up this morning and, if you did, if you would have any understanding at all of Louisa Maria's feelings. Or, for that matter, if you would care."

He frowned. "I don't suppose I do understand her, but I comprehend that there is a problem—a serious problem—with which I must deal and that it is not a problem which will be easily solved. Nevertheless, she is exactly the sort of woman I have dreamed of wedding. Therefore it is a problem I wish to solve. I will do my best to do so."

"Very well. As I said, it is more than I hoped." They turned back toward the road. After they had gone a few yards she asked, "My lord, why did you come here? How can you have known that Louisa Maria was here?" She considered. "I am stupid. Your aunt revealed our presence in the neighborhood."

"My aunt said nary a word about you or yours. She has it in her head that Miss Ruthven and I will suit. At the time she wrote and demanded I come try my hand, I had spent weeks searching everywhere for you ladies. I had given up . . ." He frowned, an unhappy rather than angry expression. "Still, I must wed and, when my aunt wrote . . . well, at that point it made little difference whom I wed, so, reluctantly, I came. Last night I was reminded why I almost told Aunt Hermie no, why I almost did not come. I knew, somewhere in my mind, that Miss Ruthven is an impossible match."

"You are wrong about that and your aunt is correct. Miss Ruthven would suit you right down to the ground."

"You don't know me very well."

"Do I not?" Lady Dewsbury-Morgan had lived a long life and thought she knew a thing or two, but there was always the possibility she might be wrong. A trifle diffidently she asked, "Will you, then, explain?"

"Miss Ruthven is an exceedingly independent lady. She has a mind of her own and will be neither led nor guided. I cannot see that making for a happy and contented and, above all, *peaceful* home life."

"Peace. Contentment." She frowned. "Peace and contentment imply boredom. Utter ennui."

He blinked. "What do you mean?"

"That that is what you will have if you marry my Louisa

Maria. She will bore you into screaming fits within a very few weeks. I doubt very much if Miss Ruthven would ever bore you. Not if you were wed for fifty years."

"Believe me, there is a place in this world for boredom," he said dryly.

Again they strolled in silence. "I am trying to remember," murmured Lady Dewsbury-Morgan. "Your mother . . ."

"I'll not speak of my mother," he interrupted, his voice harsh and those distinctive brows locked together.

"*You* need not, but *I* mean to do so. She was very lively. Perhaps at times one could even say volatile. A *very* independent lady, if I recall correctly. My lord, surely there is a happy medium somewhere between my mouse of a granddaughter and your mother who was, if nothing else, never boring!"

"Is there?" The brows raised up a notch. "I doubt it. In this case, a little is as much as a lot. Because of my mother's little ways, I've a great dislike of controversy. If you think back to last night, you will recall that practically the first words out of Miss Ruthven's mouth were contentious in the extreme."

He scowled. The loss of that gun, his first, and a rare gift from his father, was one of his least happy memories. He had never forgotten that a mere girl had managed to steal it and hide it so he could not find it. It was not to be borne! That redheaded termagant needed someone to teach her a lesson.

"Um?" he asked, jolted from his thoughts. "You asked? I fear I was lost in reflection."

"I asked when you think you will visit Louisa. I feel I must prepare her."

"I don't know. I haven't a notion what my aunt may have in mind for my cousin and myself so I don't know when I'll be free. Shall I send a groom with a message for you?"

"Excellent. Thank you. Please do not forget."

He forgot. Upon his return to the manor, his aunt talked him into walking her acres with her and, tired from what she called a little stroll, it went out of his mind. He and Quentin entered his carriage directly after dinner with nary a thought to sending a message on ahead.

Soon after their arrival at Merrywood, Babs had discovered that Louisa enjoyed doing the flowers—but only if Babs accompanied her when they confronted the gardener who objected to having his beds raided merely so his employer could enjoy bouquets in her home.

On the day after Lady Blackstock's dinner party, Babs had located Louisa Maria and they were headed for the gardens sometime after Lady Dewbury-Morgan drove onto the road. As she neared the door to the cutting gardens, she discovered the girl was not following in her wake as was usual.

"Now, where did she go?"

But it was obvious, was it not? Oh, not the *where*, exactly, but the *why*. The last few days Babs had noticed that Louisa grew more nervous each time they faced Old Growlie. Not that that was his name. It was Knowly, but since he growled at all times about all things, everyone except his youngest helpers, who did not dare, called him Growlie.

"Oh very well," said Babs aloud, suspecting Louisa was not far off. "I will tell you when the flowers are in the wet room and you can do them whenever you are ready—or not at all, for that matter." She thought she heard a sigh of relief from behind the music room door, smiled even as she shook her head at such timidity, and continued on toward the gardens and her daily confrontation with the gardener.

Not twenty minutes later, James Ruthven strolled down the hall toward the same door, which was convenient to the stables as well as the garden. James meant to ride into the town beyond the village where he would find newspapers other than the ones his cousin paid to have delivered with the post. He was passing the music room when, from behind the closed door, he heard the sound of music.

Slowly, carefully, not wishing to disturb the harpist, he opened the door. There, across the room, a dark silhouette against the bright sun-lit windows, sat Louisa Maria, her head bent and her hands on the strings. She was deft and the music delightful. James slid into the room and sat in a straight-backed chair, one of the row of gilded rout-chairs set along the wall.

The music ended and Louisa Maria's hands pressed against the strings to deaden the vibrations. She didn't move. After another few moments, when she neither began another song nor looked up, James clapped his hands softly, startling her into glancing his way.

"That was beautiful, Miss Morgan. Astonishing, really. I do not believe I've ever heard another young lady play anywhere nearly so well. You have practiced a great deal, have you not?"

After a moment she nodded, one short sharp nod.

"Do you know *Greensleeves?*" he asked quietly. "My mother used to sing it and it was a favorite of my father. I would very much enjoy hearing it."

Again there was a long hesitation and then, not looking at him, she set her hands to the strings and played the ancient melody.

"Delightful. Thank you," he said, still speaking softly.

She didn't look at him, but he was satisfied. Not only had she nodded in response to his question, but she had actually played the requested song. It was communication. And it was enough from a young lady who suffered in such a strange way.

"I hope you will play for me again sometime," he said, rose, and opened the door. "I am riding into town. Is there anything I may get for you?"

She didn't respond.

James had not expected her to do so, but, experienced disappointment nevertheless. He left her there and continued toward the door to the gardens. As he reached for it, it opened, and Babs faced him. "Ah. Cousin," he said. "Were you aware our little Louisa is an impressive musician?"

"I have learned she has a great talent for producing truly lovely bouquets but I was unaware of any other. She plays? I wonder if the pianoforte can possibly be in tune . . ."

"It was the harp."

"Hmm. Perhaps she was able to tune that herself . . . ?"

"You are not musical?"

She grinned. "I hadn't the patience to sit still and practice. So I don't know if I am or am not."

"As I understand it," he said, a trifle pensively, "it is unnecessary to force those who are truly musical to their practice. They *wish* to do it."

"Then that is proof I am not musical, is it not? Are you?" she asked, experiencing a touch of curiosity about this man she was supposed to have wed.

"Actually, I am—or perhaps the truly musical would say, I wish I were," he said, his ears reddening. "I wonder if little Louisa would play duets with me."

"What do you play, cousin?"

"The violin. I took it with me to India and there, where I often had days and days with little occupation, I set myself to improving myself." He frowned slightly. "I play without making mistakes, but I do not have that . . . that lightness of touch, or that depth of understanding

that is required to make a great musician." The regret
faded from his features. "But I enjoy music and perhaps
Miss Morgan can bear to play with me. We will see." He
asked, for the second time, if there was an errand he
could run while in town and was told no. He nodded
and, after holding the door for Babs' entry, left.

Babs found Louisa in the music room still sitting by the
harp, her hands in her lap. She stared out the window.

"The flowers—"

Startled, Louisa jerked stiffly upright and then turned.

"—are in water. You can do them when and *if* you wish
to. It is not a duty you must do regardless of how you feel
about it, but something you may do if you will enjoy it."
Babs changed the subject abruptly. "James tells me you
play. Perhaps after dinner you would play for all of us?
James is a violinist. He hopes you will condescend to play
duets with him, although he does not feel he is nearly so
good a musician as you."

Babs' eyes narrowed as she noticed a faint touch of
color rise into Louisa's cheeks and a faint sparkle in her
usually dead-looking eyes. It was the first sign of pleasure
that she had seen in the chit. Perhaps compliments
would help her to feel more secure? Babs made a mental note to compliment the child whenever there was
reason to do so.

"Well, I must see to the accounts," she said mournfully.
"My land steward comes later this morning and I must
check them before he arrives."

She closed the door and went down the hall, wondering if Louisa would remember to do the flowers . . . not
that she *had* to do them. It was *not* a duty. But the child
seemed to gain some pleasure from the task, and pleasure seemed to have been lacking in her dreary life, so
Babs hoped she would remember. . . .

Five

"This is a mistake, Matt," said Quentin for the third time since entering the carriage for the short journey to Merrywood.

"Will you stop playing Cassandra, predicting doom and disaster? We merely make a neighborly call. What can possibly be wrong with that?"

"I don't know, but I feel it is a mistake."

"You can remain in the carriage and pretend you didn't come," said Calder impatiently.

"Oh no. You would never tell me what actually happens, so I will see for myself."

"See what sort of fool I make of myself?"

"Something of the sort."

Matthew punched Quentin's arm, half jokingly, half seriously. They rode the remainder of the way in silence.

Beneath his usual sangfroid, Lord Calder was nervous. His aunt, when he said they were visiting Merrywood, had responded in her penetrating voice, "Good," she had said. "Excellent. Give Miss Ruthven my best wishes."

There had been no mention of the Morgan women. In fact, after one brief but loudly stated demand that her nephew not play the fool with the little Morgan, she had referred in no way to her arrival the preceding evening with the Merrywood party.

"Very nice place," said Quentin, as they pulled up the

drive toward the Hall. "Miss Ruthven's guardian has done well by her, has he not?"

"What do you mean?"

"As I understand the story, she inherited posthumously and has been in a guardian's care practically from birth; an uncle, I believe. The condition of the house and land says he's done well by her. That is all."

"You haven't been listening to my aunt, Quentin. According to dear Aunt Hermie, Miss Ruthven took the reins into her hands nearly a decade ago."

"But . . ."

"Yes?"

Quentin did a quick calculation. "But she cannot have been so much as sixteen at the time?"

"True."

"But . . ."

"Close your mouth. You'll catch flies."

Quentin's mouth snapped shut.

"A very independent lady," added Matthew, his tone dry. "Not at all the sort of woman I wish to take to wife. She is too argumentive. Now *you* have quite different standards. Perhaps you should pursue her."

Quentin ignored his cousin's suggestion. "You don't want a wife, Matt, you want a doormat."

The door to the carriage opened before Calder could reply to a tone so stern it surprised him.

But Quentin is wrong. What I want is peace. And quiet. A home free of contention and loud voices.

He wanted a woman who knew her place, yes, but a doormat? Someone he could wipe his feet on?

Nonsense.

Never.

No.

"Matt?" Quentin peered into the carriage. "Have you changed your mind?"

Hadn't Lady Dewbury-Morgan said something similar

when she'd attempted to convince him Louisa was not for him? What was it she had said? That Louisa would bore him? And that it would take a great deal of patience to overcome the chit's shyness, her fears? But he was a patient man. Of course he was.

"Matt, either get out or I'll get back in."

"Hmm?" Calder realized with a start he was making a spectacle of himself before the servants. "Have we arrived?" he asked with feigned innocence.

Quentin didn't believe his cousin's tacit excuse for sitting mumchance, but the servants standing about *would* and that was important in the scheme of things. Servants gossiped and, given the oddity of their situation, vis-à-vis the Merrywood household, the less gossip the better. The two tall young men walked in the door where Miss Ruthven's butler awaited them, pretending he didn't know who they were.

He did of course. Country gossip had been thorough and he not only knew their names, but their relationship to Lady Blackstone, to each other, and to the world in general. Nevertheless, cards were placed on the silver tray extended for that purpose. He glanced at them, nodded, and said, "My lord. Mr. Riverton. Please follow me."

To their surprise, he led them away from the open doors to the salon and down a hall. Overhearing Quentin's softly questioning words to his cousin, the butler said, "The family is in the music room."

Just then they heard the harp and Lord Calder stopped the man. "Do not announce us. We do not wish to disturb the performer."

The butler nodded, opened the door silently, and stood by while they entered. He gently closed the door and returned to the hall where he sent a footman to the kitchen with orders to send up a more elaborate tea tray than usual since there would be company.

Lord Calder found a chair next to William Ruthven who glanced at him. The two men exchanged nods.

Quentin, on the other hand, didn't move from the doorway. He was struck very nearly dumb by what he heard. Miss Morgan's touch on the harp was so very lovely, so sure, so wondrously melodic . . . Quentin had never, not even to his cousin, revealed the depth of his love of good music—or what torture it was to listen to poorly trained young ladies who were, invariably, asked to play to entertain guests. The picture she made, bent to the harp, was one he thought he'd never forget.

Lady Dewsbury-Morgan was placed so that she saw the men enter and approved that they did not interrupt yet was annoyed that his lordship had not sent word of their intent as he'd agreed to do. James Ruthven saw Lord Calder seat himself and poked his cousin who was seated to his left. When she looked at him, outrage at his presumption not far from the surface, he pointed, his hand hidden in his lap. She groaned softly and nodded.

Lady Morgan also noticed Lord Calder's entry and straightened in her chair, a pleased look on her face— about which, when she noticed it, Lady Dewsbury-Morgan became suspicious. Surely Anna would not persist in promoting the match!

Quentin noticed none of this, rapt in his appreciation. Calder, although noticing most of the reactions, ignored them. He pretended great interest in Miss Morgan's performance, but wished she played a piano instead of a harp. If it were a piano he could stand beside her and turn the music pages while making evident his appreciation. That was how it was done in the circles in which he moved, a recognized gambit in the progress of a proper wooing.

He no sooner had the thought, however, than it occurred to him that this would be anything but the usual wooing. He suspected that if he were to do anything so normal as to stand near and turn her music, that Miss Morgan would instantly freeze into an iceberg of the sort that was towed each summer from northern seas and up the Thames so that the polite world could enjoy eating ices at Gunter's. She would very likely be unable to play a note!

The song ended and Quentin clapped enthusiastically. The sound brought Miss Morgan's startled gaze to meet his. She instantly scanned the others, noticed Calder, and—obvious to all—she cringed.

Calder closed his eyes, the brows drawing together. How could the chit make it so obvious she was not pleased to see him? The girl needed lessons in manners and he was just the one . . .

He brought his thoughts to a screeching halt. *Not a lack of manners. Fear. Fear of him. Of any man. Remember that. She is not insulting you in particular,* he told himself.

James Ruthven picked up his violin from a table near the harp and moved toward—but not too near—Miss Morgan. "This morning you played *Greensleeves* for me. Do you think we might attempt to play it together?" he asked, drawing her attention. *"Greensleeves,"* he repeated softly when he perceived she was only partially aware of him. "We can pretend the others are not here and play for ourselves alone," he added when he saw she was staring at him, her eyes wide with strain. He smiled gently. "Shall we?" he asked and lifted the violin to his chin.

James played a few phrases. He lifted his bow and quirked a brow. Slowly Louisa lifted her fingers to the strings. He smiled and saw her relax a little more. He set the bow to the strings, nodded, and began again. Her notes came hesitantly, tentative, unlike her usual sure touch—and then, feeling the lovely old song grow, she played as she always did.

James watched her bent head, let his phrasing match hers and was quite pleased with what he felt he'd accomplished. She played with him. Surely, it was a first. In fact, when they finished, she looked up and, very shyly, smiled. James felt blessed. The child had nodded to him earlier that morning and now she smiled at him. Surely, soon, she would also speak.

But the smile disappeared faster than the sun under a cloud. James sighed. "Thank you, Miss Morgan. I enjoyed that a great deal," he said, attempting to draw her attention back to himself and away from Lord Calder who stood beside her.

"It was lovely," said Lord Calder quietly. "Thank you," he added.

"Yes," said Quentin, the spell the music had cast drawing him toward them. "You play exceptionally well, Miss Morgan. I hope to be allowed to enjoy many future performances."

Miss Morgan didn't raise her eyes to look at any of the men, her head bent and her fingers tightly wound together in her lap.

"Perhaps we can practice some other duets," said James, scowling at the Riverton cousins.

"Perhaps, someday, I can sing with the two of you," suggested Quentin eagerly, his excitement preventing him from noticing anything beyond the music. "I would very much like to join you—if it would not be an imposition," he added, finally realizing how dreadfully upset Miss Morgan was. He turned when Babs arrived at his side. "Miss Ruthven, we asked the butler not to announce us so that we would not interfere with Miss Morgan's lovely music," he said.

Louisa looked up quickly, saw that Lord Calder still stared at her, and dropped her gaze back to her lap. The skin around her knuckles whitened, she clasped her hands so tightly together.

"Please remember that I enjoyed your music, Miss Morgan," said his lordship softly and walked away to where

Lady Dewsbury-Morgan stood. "I think," he said to her, "that it will take even more patience than I believed."

"But not less than *I* thought. Why do you persist?" she demanded.

"Ah, my lord," said Lady Morgan, interrupting, "it is so good to see you again. Such a handsome young man. I am very glad to see that you have not taken my daughter in dislike for her foolishness."

Lord Calder stiffened. "Foolishness?"

"Bridal nerves, of course," said Lady Morgan coyly.

"Nonsense," said Lady Dewsbury-Morgan. "If there is foolishness here, then Anna, it is *you* who perpetrate it. Come along. I see Logan is bringing in the tea tray. Do you think there will be any of those jam tarts Cook does so well?"

Calder controlled lips that wished to twitch as he watched Lady Dewsbury-Morgan very literally force Lady Morgan from his side. He turned to survey the company and his gaze met Miss Ruthven's.

She walked across the room to join him. "Will you take tea?" she asked, gesturing toward it. "I can have Logan bring in ale or wine—or brandy—if you would prefer."

"You wish me to drink up and go, is that it, Miss Ruthven?" he asked bitingly.

She blinked. "I doubt it would have crossed my mind," she said with only a trifling touch of acid, "but since you mention it, perhaps it is not such a bad idea."

He sighed. "Sorry. That was called taking the offensive before your opponent can get in the first punch," he said in a far milder tone.

She smiled, her eyes brightening. "You have surprised me. I would not have thought you could make such a graceful apology for rudeness. But since you have managed it, I must be equally polite. Shall we begin again?" She repeated her offer of refreshment in almost exactly the same words as before.

"Tea would be agreeable," he said and offered his arm.

They approached the tea table where Lady Dewsbury-Morgan was pouring and Quentin was handing round.

"No milk or sugar," he said. "One, please," he added when the dish of thinly sliced lemons was indicated. He chose several tiny sandwiches from a large plate, added one sugar biscuit, and took plate and cup and saucer to a chair near where Miss Morgan sat holding her tea and staring at nothing at all. He didn't speak to her. Merely sat there, relaxed, slowly drinking and eating and saying nothing at all. He had hoped if he did not bother her in any way she might relax—but she did not. After a time he rose to his feet, nodded to her—not that she saw—and once again joined Louisa's grandmother who was talking softly to Babs, who was glaring at him.

"What have I done now?" he asked, sighing.

"Why do you not leave that poor child alone?"

"She is not a child. And she is my fiancée."

"She is not."

"I have not sent a notice to the papers breaking the engagement," he said, holding Babs' gaze with his own.

"Then you should."

"I do not wish to lose her."

"You cannot bear to think a mere wisp of a female might have the gall to reject you!"

"Can I not?" He considered. "I think you are wrong. One cannot feel rejected when one was never properly accepted."

"But you did not know you'd not been accepted. You believed you had. I am told you were so certain of it you stood before the altar ready to take your vows."

"That is a tactless comment, my dear Miss Ruthven," he said sharply. "Tactless in the extreme. Surely, avoiding mention of that humiliation is the least a hostess can do when faced with the humiliated one."

"As I said, you were rejected and cannot bear it," insisted Babs, scowling just as fiercely as Calder.

"You will believe what you wish to believe, Miss Ruthven. I cannot prevent you. But I am very fond of Miss Morgan and I hope I can convince her I am not such an ogre as she seems to believe. If you have any affection for her, then why do you not help me?"

She gasped. "Well! That is turning the tables, is it not? And why should I help you when I do not feel you would be good for her?"

He blinked.

"I cannot do what I feel is wrong," she persisted.

"No, of course you cannot," he snapped. "And you are one who must always know what is best for everyone, are you not?"

"For someone who does not like controversy, my lord, you are very good at it," said Lady Dewsbury-Morgan mildly. She stood beside the pair who stood very nearly toe-to-toe, their identical glares burning into each other. She looked from one to the other, amusement giving animation to her features. "As I told you, Lord Calder, she . . ."

Afraid of what her ladyship might say about Miss Ruthven and her suitability, Lord Calder interrupted. "You told me a great deal," he said abruptly and looked round for safe harbor. "I see my cousin has finished his tea. We must go now or we will lose the moon. Thank you for a delightful evening," he said to Miss Ruthven, with only a touch of irony.

"And no thanks to you for making it so," she retorted. "Oh," she added, impatience in her tone, "do come down out of the boughs. You are my neighbor's relative and I will not be on the outs with her. Come. I will walk you to the door and wait with you while your carriage is called."

They collected Quentin who had been talking music

with James while Miss Morgan sat nearby and pretended she was not listening.

"Miss Ruthven," said Quentin as they approached the front door, "I told Matt it was a mistake for us to come here this evening, but I was wrong. So very wrong. If you've no objections, I mean to come again in the morning and James and I will practice one or two duets."

"Why should I object?"

"It is your house and James is merely a guest here, or so I understood him to say. We could, of course, meet at my aunt's if . . ."

"No, of course that will not be necessary."

"I was unaware you enjoyed music to such a degree," said Matthew, eyeing his cousin suspiciously. "Not to the degree you would ride nearly eight miles merely to practice."

"But then *you* are *not* particularly fond of music, are you, Matt?" asked Quentin. "You would have no understanding of what drives one who is."

"The hope of hearing Miss Morgan practice?" asked his lordship.

"Oh yes. I would enjoy that immensely. But I wish to join in with one or both. I would like to produce music to match theirs."

Calder realized his cousin showed far more enthusiasm than was usual for him and certainly more than the socially bored young man-about-town should show. It struck him that Quentin truly wished to experience the music and was not looking for a way of edging his way into Miss Morgan's awareness, had no desire to steal her affections. He sighed. "I see I must apologize once again. It is becoming a dead bore."

"You will find that practice makes perfect. I don't know about you, Lord Calder," said Babs, smiling, "but I've always found practice boring. It is only after one becomes adept at a thing that one may enjoy it."

He bit back a laugh. "Enjoy the act of apologizing? I think not. Even *with* practice. It is one instance where I hope I am *not* required to practice a great deal. Ah. Our carriage. Good evening, Miss Ruthven. *Parts* of it have been very enjoyable!"

"Hmm. I see you are looking for another occasion for which you must practice your apologies."

"Oh no. Surely one need not apologize for the truth."

It was Babs' turn to laugh and she did so. Calder heard her delightful laughter—surprisingly deep-voiced and liquid—in his dreams that night.

Thinking about it when he woke the next morning, he decided she had an irritating sort of laugh and that he must remember not to provoke it. Having so decided, he proceeded to think of several responses he might have made to points she'd made the preceding evening that might, with only a little luck, have roused her chuckles again and again.

Six

"Of course you will enjoy fishing," said Babs, blinking her eyes. Louisa had, in her mute way, made it obvious she had no intention of trying her hand at it. "And if not, well—" Babs thought quickly. "—then bring a book and sit on the blanket. You can read while I fish."

Louisa nodded and went to retrieve the novel she was currently reading.

Babs watched the girl climb the stairs. She waited near the door, the picnic basket and fishing equipment in the hands of a footman who would carry it out to the gig for her.

That, she thought, *is the most Louisa has said since I've known her.* And then it occurred to her that the girl hadn't actually *said* anything. Somehow, she had communicated exactly how she felt and what she wanted—or in this case, didn't want—with surprising ease.

"Going somewhere?" asked James, entering the hall just then.

"Louisa and I are going fishing. I've had Cook pack us a basket, so very likely it will be late when we return."

Louisa joined them and James saw the book. "May I see?" he asked gently.

Louisa hesitated, but then, obediently, held out the volume.

"Ah! I have heard of books like these. Is this one a very wicked Gothic?" he asked, smiling.

Louisa shuddered slightly, a tiny smile tipping her lips just a trifle.

"I see. I hope you do not suffer from nightmares," he teased.

Louisa smiled just a trifle more broadly, but the smile faded abruptly and she moved slightly, putting herself almost behind Babs. Babs looked at James who frowned and then she turned at the sound of steps. "Ah. Good morning, Mr. Riverton," she said. "You have come for your practice with James?"

"Yes." Quentin hefted a case, which obviously held his music. "I hope I am not too sadly out of voice. Oh. Miss Morgan." He greeted her and ignored the fact Louisa moved still further behind Babs. "Will you play with us this morning?"

Louisa reached out and jerked the back of Babs' dress. Babs turned, a questioning look in her eyes. Louisa flicked her gaze toward the door, a pleading look in her expression.

"Yes, very well. Mr. Riverton, Louisa and I have made other plans. We hope you'll enjoy practicing with James."

Quentin did his best to hide his disappointment.

"If we manage to perfect something we will perform it the next time we have an evening together—not that it will be anywhere near so well done as Miss Morgan could do," said James.

Louisa flicked James a glance, her cheeks gaining a hint of a rosy glow that reminded Babs that compliments were a good thing where the girl was concerned.

"You two run along and enjoy the day," said James in an avuncular tone. "The weather is particularly nice and one should not waste it."

Louisa edged toward the door. The gig appeared just then and the girl very nearly ran out to where it waited. Babs sighed. Then she said all that was proper to

Quentin Riverton, nodded toward her cousin, and moved gracefully to her side of the gig where she took the reins from the groom. The man climbed on behind, and, setting the horse in motion, Babs drove to where the groom must open and then close the first gate on their way to the river—or, as one should say, the canal—which was the eastern boundary of Babs' estate.

"Are you certain you will not fish?" she asked, when the groom walked away with the gig to where he would un-hitch and tether the horse where it could graze. When Louisa indicated she would sit under a nearby willow and read, Babs shrugged, assembled her gear, and strolled a lit-tle upstream to where she knew a granddaddy of a fish lived among the roots of a huge old horse chestnut.

An hour passed quietly. Babs drew in her line for the umpteenth time and prepared to cast it out again when she saw a punt round a curve downriver. The poler looked familiar. She frowned. "Surely not," she said, a faint sharpness to the words. "Yes, it is," she said a mo-ment later and frowned still more deeply.

"Good morning," called Calder, a surprised note in his voice. "You *fish?*" he asked.

"Why should I not?"

He poled into the bank and set the pole firmly to hold the punt in place and then turned, balancing easily, to confront her. "If you are against hunting, then why are you not against fishing?" he asked, trying to keep even a hint of controversy from his voice.

"I am not *totally* against hunting. Just hunting for mere sport."

"Hmm. Then if I were to take a gun out for a brace of pheasant for my dinner you would not object?"

"Only that a brace would be unlikely to feed every-one," she said, smiling mischievously.

He barked a laugh. "Are you attempting, then, to bring home enough fish to feed *your* table this evening?"

She sighed. "I have yet to catch anything at all, so if that was my goal, I am unlikely to achieve it."

"You sound aggrieved," he said, chuckling.

"I like fishing. But I enjoy it more when I manage to catch something. So far I've not had so much as a nibble."

"A day or so ago, perhaps a mile upstream, I saw a huge fish rise." Calder recalled why he had been walking along the stream and his heavy brows lowered.

"You regret telling me that?" she asked. "Do you have it in mind to catch it yourself?"

"What?" He blinked, considered her words again, and nodded. "I might, at that. It has been ever so long since I last wetted a line and I've likely forgotten the skill. But why do you ask?"

She shook her head impatiently. "If it is *not* that you would poach in my stream, then why did you frown? If I were Louisa," she added, speaking softly, "you would have frightened me half out of my wits."

"Did I frown?"

"You did."

"I was unaware of it." He frowned again. "Are you suggesting that she finds even my expression upsetting?"

"Your every frown must have set her heart beating— and not pleasantly. But she is sitting just there and I do not think we should discuss her when she might overhear."

"We should discuss her behind her back, perhaps?" he asked, the first hint of a bite in his voice.

"You are correct," said Babs equally sharply. "We should not discuss her at all." She began wrapping her line. "I do not mean to keep you. Good day."

"Going upstream to find that fish?" he asked, wanting, for reasons he didn't understand, to keep her attention.

"No," she said, her tone overly polite. "I am hoping you will take the hint and go so that I may return to my fishing right here." She grimaced. "Not that I am likely to catch anything now you've unsettled anything within a mile of me."

Calder, told to go, perversely decided to stay. "I've a basket lunch. I will share it with you," he said, glancing to where Louisa's head was bent low over her book.

Babs growled softly.

His eyes narrowed. "You would forbid me?" he asked equally softly.

"If you are determined to ruin our day, I cannot stop you."

"Come, you must be feeling a trifle peckish. All this good fresh air, the magnificent sky above, the larks singing—what could be more delightful than sharing a bite to eat?"

"I fully intended to share a bite or even two. With Louisa."

"You, too, have a basket? Wonderful. Let us combine our gustatory delights." He tied up the punt, lifted his basket, and stepped ashore. "Come," he said when she didn't move. "I have bested you. Put a good face on it."

"It is not my face I am worried about," she said, biting the words off. "Oh, very well. I will have John get our basket and pull our cider from the water." She raised her voice. "John . . ."

The three were soon settled, the food and drink spread out so that everyone could reach it.

"I enjoy the informality of al fresco dining," said Lord Calder, rather surprising Babs who had thought him the complete town beau.

"Why in particular?" she asked.

"It is not so obvious when there are only the three of us, but, in a larger picnic group, one is allowed to speak to anyone about anything, not merely to one's dinner partners as one does during formal dining. I know only one couple where one need not mind ones p's and q's." He smiled.

"What have you recalled?"

"Merely one occasion where everything that could go wrong went wrong. A dozen of us were guests of the Mc-Murrys' and I believe everyone there would agree we had the best time of our lives."

"Your hostess must have felt a deal of chagrin," said Babs, although her opinion of the ramshackle military couple was far different.

"Nonsense. The little devil laughed."

She grinned. "I knew it!"

He smiled in response. "You are a bit of a devil yourself, are you not?"

"You are edging toward the need for another apology," she said, smiling.

"Am I? Then I had best retract, had I not?" All the while he and Babs spoke nonsense, he kept an eye on Louisa. He was not pleased to see how little she actually ate, moving her food about her plate. "Are you not enjoying the food, Miss Morgan?" he asked politely.

Louisa raised startled eyes to meet his, turned bright red, and hung her head.

"My dear, I was not scolding you," he said softly.

Again she glanced at him, but only for a moment. The red turned to white.

"You are frowning again," said Babs accusingly. "*Louisa,* he is not angry with you. He is *concerned* about you."

Louisa sent a disbelieving look toward Babs.

"She speaks the truth, my dear." Lord Calder turned a questioning look Babs' way.

She raised her brows and shrugged, unsure why she'd explained to Louisa when she truly did not want the girl wedding Calder. He was *not* the husband for her and *he* needed a strong woman who would fall in with his every whim—and enjoy them—but who would argue for her own wishes and not back down. Otherwise, she feared he would, as did far too many *tonnish* gentlemen, turn into the tyrant Louisa thought him.

Louisa poked her fork at a bit of fruit. She slid it to the other side of her plate. Finally she looked at Babs.

"You need not eat if you are not hungry, Louisa," said Babs.

Immediately Louisa set her plate aside and folded her hands in her lap, but she did not look up.

Lord Calder frowned at Babs who stared back.

Do you, she thought, *really wish this child for a bride?*

His mouth tightened. He nodded, as if he read her mind.

She pursed her lips and shook her head.

He nodded again. Once. Firmly.

She shrugged—and wondered if they had actually communicated or if they had been indulging in two quite separate silent conversations.

"Tell me," she said, searching her mind for an innocuous topic, "about Almack's. I have heard *such* tales."

"You had a season, did you not?"

"Yes, but we did not attempt to get vouchers to that most exclusive of clubs. I might have been accepted, thanks to my fortune, but I doubt my birth is well enough to have made it easy."

"I suspect you would have been bored to tears by it," he said. She continued to look expectant. "Do you truly wish to know?" She nodded and he went on to explain about the patronesses and their excessively rigid rules. "I can't think when I last attended. Not since . . ." He broke off abruptly and glanced at Miss Morgan who instantly stiffened into rigidity. "Not since I met Miss Morgan at a ball and found in her my ideal woman."

Louisa, for the first time, looked up with something very like a glare in her expression.

Babs chuckled. "I think Louisa is telling you you don't know her at all if you think she is your ideal."

"Is that what she said?" he asked, staring at Louisa's bent head. "I thought perhaps she was disagreeing with my assessment of Almack's, that perhaps *she* would like to attend the assemblies." The faintest shake of the head answered him. He sighed. Softly. "No? Then I must assume that Miss Ruthven is correct?" he asked. The faintest of nods and then tension stiffened Louisa's shoulders, as if she awaited reprimand.

"He will not beat you!" said Babs quickly. "Calder!" The word was a demand for his reassurance.

"Beat Miss Morgan!" Matthew was shocked and turned to Louisa Maria. "Of course I will not beat you. Why should you think it?"

Louisa didn't particularly relax.

"She has been taught that she must not disagree with any man. With *you in particular,* she must not be other than you, or any man, wish her to be—but when you suggested it was about Almack's that she disagreed, she said no, and when you suggested I was right, she said yes. Of course, she is fearful of retaliation."

"There is no 'of course' about it. If your father, Miss Morgan, was the sort to lay his whip about your shoulders, no wonder you fear a man coming anywhere near you. I am not the sort to beat a female. I would never harm a hair of your head." And then, just when he was beginning to make her believe him, his unruly tongue got the better of him. "Miss Ruthven's, perhaps, but never you."

Louisa raised wide fearful eyes to stare at Babs who patted her hand. "He is jesting, my dear. He finds me exasperating, but he would not beat me."

Louisa did not appear to be reassured.

Calder's shoulders slumped. He straightened them. "I see I must watch my every word, Miss Morgan, if I am not to upset you. I will try."

Try how you will, thought Babs, *you will not succeed.* She was certain of it. His quick-silver tongue would betray him again and again. She realized she enjoyed the give-and-take, the banter, even the arguments, although there had been no *really* serious disagreement. Yet. Very likely a serious argument would not be at all enjoyable.

She searched her mind for another innocuous topic, found one, and started a conversation that continued until they finished eating—Louisa even managed to nibble almost the whole of her serving of a very nice pudding—and then Lord Calder rose to his feet.

"It is time I was returning. I believe my aunt means to invite you all over for an informal evening of music and conversation. She learned of Quentin's interest, you see, and that he thinks very highly of Miss Morgan's playing. I hope you will indulge us, my dear," he said softly to Lousia. "You are very good."

She lifted a quick look that managed to reach, perhaps, his chest, before looking back down. She nodded once.

"Does Lady Blackstock have a harp?" asked Babs.

"I think not, but we will arrange to have Miss Morgan's transported to Blackstock Manor. It can be done quite easily."

"Very well." Babs rose and followed him to where his punt was tied. "You will not believe it," she said softly, "but Louisa responded to you in quite an eloquent manner."

"Eloquent?" He looked his disbelief.

"She managed to communicate her thoughts with some ease, did she not?"

"Did she? I fear she *speaks* a language I do not comprehend. You seem to understand her pretty well. Why will she not speak words? She has, as I recall, a very pleasant speaking voice, soft and musical and pleasing to the ear."

"No one knows why she will not speak. She has, so far as we know, said not one word since she left the church that day."

"Ah. Humiliating me again, are you?"

"Only if you insist on feeling humiliated. I merely made a statement of fact."

He grinned. "You are a worthy antagonist, Miss Ruthven, never without an answer."

"Antagonist?" She scowled. "You now owe me another apology!"

"Why do you think that an insult?"

"Because, coming from someone who does not like controversy, it must be one!"

He studied her, his brows slightly pulled together in a faintly bemused expression. "You know, it is quite strange . . ."

"Yes?"

"I had not once thought of what we were doing, the banter, you know, that it was controversial."

"Then instead of insult I will feel flattered. I must get back to Louisa, my lord. And you said you needed to return to your aunt?" Babs stepped back and watched him release the punt and step down into it. "I was unaware Lady Blackstock owned a punt."

"Oh yes. Quentin and I used it when we were still in school. It has been out of the water for so long I was a trifle fearful it would have developed leaks, but my aunt, who never thinks to order anything, appears to have had it kept in proper condition." Suddenly, at a new thought, he barked a laugh. "Or perhaps there is someone among her employees who likes to punt and has kept it up for his own use?" His brows rose into that heavy straight line indicative of a query. They lowered, then rose again. "Do you suppose that Miss Morgan would care to go for a boat ride sometime? And you, of course," he added almost as an afterthought.

She laughed lightly. "I would enjoy it, but I cannot answer for Louisa. Good day. Oh, and thank you for sharing your picnic. Please tell Lady Blackstock's cook that I enjoyed that pâté a great deal and would very much appreciate if she would tell my cook the way of it."

Lord Calder saluted and poled out into the center of the stream where the gentle current straightened the punt and, giving the natural movement of the water additional force, he poled off downstream toward home. Babs watched him until the curve took him from sight. She shook her head, wondering at her feelings. They were such an odd mix of elation and chagrin and like and dislike she could make no sense of them.

Turning, she glanced to where Louisa sat. The girl had picked up the picnic, putting everything into the two baskets—Calder had forgotten his—and had her book back on her lap. Babs wondered if she should have a talk with her about Calder, explaining that those brows merely looked threatening, but were rarely that in truth.

She was not surprised to discover she'd no desire to explain it. "So I won't," she muttered and, picking up her fishing gear, she went back to trying to entice her old enemy from under the chestnut's roots.

Seven

Sir George Morgan reread the letter from his wife, disbelief widening his eyes. *It is unnatural the way Mother always finds her feet, never stumbles, is never in the wrong. I cannot bear it. She is a witch, that is what she is,* he thought.

For two days Sir George fumed.

Then he plotted.

Finally he ordered out his brand new carriage with his brand new arms emblazoned on the door panels in gaudy colors that could not possibly be missed by anyone he passed. He entered it with his meek little valet clutching a fat leather purse stuffed with far more money than they were likely to require if they took six trips between London and the southwest of England.

The two arrived the following day right at dinnertime and, perforce, Sir George was invited to dine with the family by Mr. James Ruthven, who happened to go through the hall just as Sir George introduced himself to the Ruthven butler.

"I was unaware, Sir George, that you were expected. I haven't a notion where we will find the others."

"No matter." Sir George was displeased with Ruthven's tone, which, coolly polite, he considered insulting—but he was on his best behavior until he discovered exactly what was going on and so ignored it. "Just send a servant to find my wife," he said with false joviality. "Need to talk to her."

"No, no. Come along. It is not long until dinner and everyone will soon gather in the summer salon."

"I want to talk to my wife," said Sir George stubbornly. "Alone."

"Your wife?" The new voice was one he knew well. "But you have no wife. You repudiated her. In public."

"Mother." Sir George scowled. "Can't hold a man to what he says when in a temper."

"Can I not? I think I do, actually," Lady Dewsbury-Morgan said musingly. "Mr. Ruthven, have you been properly introduced to my . . . son?"

The pause before Lady Dewsbury-Morgan acknowledged the relationship infuriated Sir George and his face turned bright red with the effort to restrain the words hanging from the tip of his tongue.

"Sir George," said James Ruthven, nodding solemnly. He tried to remember what he had been told by Babs about this man. Something about him attempting to force that mute little Louisa into a marriage? "Perhaps," he said tentatively, "we should find your wife?"

"That's what I said." Sir George gritted his teeth. "I want to talk to Anna."

"Did Anna write you?" asked Lady Dewsbury-Morgan sharply, suddenly realizing how her son had discovered where they were.

"And if she did?"

"That utter fool! To have escaped you and then to have asked to walk back into the trap!"

"*You* can do as you like. Go to hell in a handbasket for all *I* care," shouted Sir George. "But I *will* speak with my wife and that immediately!"

"George?" asked Lady Morgan, scurrying into the hall, her eyes wide and her skin white. "Truly I hadn't a notion you'd arrived. Oh, it is so good to see you," she gushed, going up to him and staring, pleading, up into his face, her own evincing a tense and worried expression.

"Utter fool," repeated Lady Dewsbury-Morgan, her cane striking the floor with each step as she moved across the hall and into the salon. James hesitated and then, quietly excusing himself, went up the stairs to his room.

Lady Morgan bit her lip, drew in a deep breath, and suggested she take Sir George up to her room for a little talk. "I've so much to tell you," she said breathlessly. "You will be so pleased."

Sir George growled, but his expression grew more benign as he remembered what his wife had written in her letter. "He's here?"

"Not *here*," said Lady Morgan—and then before he could explode, added, "but just a few miles away. He is staying with his aunt. A very odd lady, I thought. Hunting mad . . ." She prattled on as she led the way up to her room.

"Done very well for yourself, have you not?" he said bitterly after looking around the large and airy bedroom that, for reasons he did not understand, seemed far more comfortable than the room he'd designed and furnished for himself. Miss Ruthven could not have spent a fraction of what he'd spent and yet . . .

He strolled from one thing to another, looking at the pictures on the wall and the bibelots set here and there on tables and dressers and a lovely delicate glass vase that rested on a windowsill. Irritated by what he didn't understand, he deliberately allowed his old-fashioned coat tails to swing around and hit it, knocking it from the sill to crash to the floor.

"Oh dear. Do see what I have done," he said in a falsetto voice that was, his wife knew, the prelude to a vicious scold.

Hurriedly, Lady Morgan spoke before he could begin. "We must plan. I think his aunt wants him to wed Miss Ruthven and not our sweet little Louisa."

Sir George, about to rant and rave about her leaving him, closed his mouth. "Miss Ruthven?"

"Our hostess. An heiress."

"So is our Louisa Maria."

"But Miss Ruthven is a lively creature." Sir George, she knew, disapproved of lively females and, hurriedly, she added, "Too lively. Very much the hoyden, actually."

"Then there is no problem. Calder won't want a hoyden to wife. He wants a doormat. Someone he can rule and who will not complain or set herself up against him in any way."

Lady Morgan felt her skin paling and wondered if she would faint. Was Lord Calder a man after Sir George's manner? She had not thought so. She had thought him a strong man who would protect her daughter. A man who, after a time, might not mind having that daughter's mother in his household—so long as she was not too demanding or too much in the way. But if he were another like Sir George . . .

"Oh, what have I done?"

George's eyes narrowed. "What *have* you done?" he asked in a suspiciously mild voice.

"What? Oh. Hmm . . ."

"A rabbit. Just like a startled rabbit," he said, stalking her. She backed up as he approached, his mouth spreading into a grin that was not echoed in his eyes. "Feel you made a mistake writing me? Think you should have left well enough alone? Well, you did write," he said, "and you'll come home where you belong. And we'll get our Louisa married to that man and he will do his duty by me and—" Suddenly with no warning, he swung his open palm against her cheek, knocking her to the floor. "—that is just the beginning. How dare you run off and leave me to the mercy of those ill-trained servants who are eating me out of house and home and can't even provide a decent meal or make my bed without creases or brew proper morning tea or remember to iron my newspaper or—" He looked around wildly for inspiration, but found none. "—cook a proper roast?" he finished, more or less repeating himself.

"But you cast me out!"

"Nonsense. Merely angry. Shouldn't have been fool enough to believe me," he growled. And then he began to rage that his mother was correct and he'd married a fool and that he should never have picked out such an simpleton and that she didn't know what was what and never would . . . and on and on.

Out in the hall, appalled, James Ruthven listened to the tirade. *Little Louisa's father is a monster,* he thought. *A monster. No wonder she is frightened of her own shadow.* His jaw tightened.

"Well," he muttered, "the man won't be allowed to bully Louisa into marrying Lord Calder. Not if she doesn't want to wed him. I'll see to that."

"What did you say, cousin?" asked Babs, coming along the hall just then.

"What? Oh. Louisa's father has arrived. Listen."

The voice, which had softened for a moment, rose again. And again there was the sound of a slap. The two in the hall heard it and stared at each other.

Babs' face tightened. She started toward the door, ready to open it and demand that Sir George cease and desist.

"They are man and wife," said James, his hand on her arm. "We've no right to interfere."

"It is my house," said Babs.

"Still . . ."

The door opened and a heavyset man, his back to them, stood there with his hand on the knob. "Cease your bawling and wash your face. You don't want your fine friends to see what a useless spineless creature you really are."

He turned, saw James and Babs glaring at him, and scowled. "Well?" he blustered.

"Not at all well," said Babs, scornfully. "Not from what *I* heard." She pushed past him into the bedroom and shut the door, leaving James to deal with Sir George. "Lady Morgan?" she said softly, moving to where that lady lay across her bed, sobbing. She put her hand on the lady's head but got no response. Going toward the washstand, she noticed the broken vase and made a note to send a maid up to clean it up—and then changed that to a footman. She wouldn't put it past a man of Sir George's stripe to molest the maids!

She brought back a damp cloth, insisted Lady Morgan sit up, and then, gently, she washed the lady's face. "There, now. Is that better?"

"I thought he'd be pleased. I thought he'd be happy. I thought . . ."

"You have known the man for a very long time, Lady Morgan," said Babs gently, "and should, by now, have realized that it is impossible to please a man of his ilk."

"Why? What is wrong with me?" Lady Morgan, one side of her face red from the slaps, stared at her hostess in bewilderment. "Why can I never please him?"

"Has it never occurred to you he doesn't *wish* to be pleased?" asked Babs gently. "That he *enjoys* making you unhappy? *Enjoys* hurting you? You cannot change him."

Anna got a stubborn look about her mouth. "He is my husband. He promised to care for me. He should . . ."

"Oh *shoulds* and *oughts* and *if onlys!*" Babs' patience was rapidly disappearing. "Have you never learned that one cannot dream dreams and find the world changed into them?"

"But he is . . ."

"He is a monster," interrupted Babs. "It is a pity you did not know that before you wed him, but there is only one answer now that you have. You must leave him.

Which you *have* done. I do not understand why you want him!"

"He is my husband," said a wide-eyed Lady Morgan, as if that were explanation enough.

Babs sighed. "It is dinnertime. The gong has rung. Are you able to come down or should I have a tray brought up?" *By a footman,* she reminded herself.

Lady Morgan blinked. "Of course I will come down. Why would I not?"

Babs looked at the reddened cheek. The nose and eyes that gave evidence of her ladyship's tears. She shrugged. "In that case, shall we go?"

The meal was uncomfortable. Babs placed Sir George by herself, his wife just beyond him, and put Louisa as far away as possible and between James and her grand-mother, protecting the girl as long as she could from her father's intentions—whatever they might be. Although she thought she knew. He had come to close the trap around Lord Calder.

She recalled that Calder was willing to have the trap closed and wondered why she was thinking up plots to save him from it. But even if *he* did not need saving, *Louisa* did. And save Louisa she would!

As soon as the women left the dining room, leaving the men to their port and nuts, she found paper and pen and wrote a quick note, which she ordered taken by a groom to Blackstock Manor.

"From Merrywood, Matt?" asked Lady Blackstock.

"Yes," said Lord Calder, frowning. "I cannot make heads or tails of it."

"Let me see."

He handed Miss Ruthven's note to his aunt.

"Seems clear enough. You ain't welcome. Not for the time being. You will be told when you can come again."

"Yes, Aunt. I read that. My question, my dearly beloved but oblivious aunt, is *why.*"

"She's had enough of your company for awhile? Is tired of jousting with you? Wishes a repairing lease while she *repairs* her ramparts and digs a deeper moat to protect herself from you?"

"Very funny, Aunt Hermie. Quite the wag, are you not?" He read the note still again and shook his head. "I guess the only way to discover what she means by it is to ask her." He rose and headed for the door. "I don't know when I'll be back," he said.

"Nephew, you come back here. *This instant.*"

He turned, but continued backing toward the door. "Why?"

"There is nothing wrong with the gel's cockloft. She'll have a very good reason for forbidding you the door. You just wait until she sends along another note telling you you are again welcome and then you can find out why she sent the first one."

"But I don't believe I can manage to contain my curiosity. Not even for a day or two."

"Nonsense." Lady Blackstock's eyes narrowed. "But if you cannot, then send Quentin. Or do you think he too was forbidden entrée?"

"There is no mention of Quent."

"Then send him." When Calder hesitated, her ladyship snorted. "Matt, don't be a fool. The gel will, I tell you, have her reasons and they'll be good ones. If you must discover the truth of the matter then either write a note demanding answers or send Quentin."

"I'll write her," he said after a moment—and then grinned. "And I'll send my note to her by Quent's hand!"

"Good." And then she frowned. "There might be ink in that little office my housekeeper uses." Lady Blackstock's frown deepened. "Or perhaps you will find a pencil?"

This time Calder laughed. "I've been here before, Aunt. I knew to bring my traveling desk."

He winked at the lady who found using a pen very nearly an impossibility—not because she could not read and write, but because she hated sitting still for any time at all—except on the back of a horse. Lord Calder eased himself from the room and left her laughing one of her full-bodied laughs at the joke on herself.

Calder met Quentin in the hall. "I forget occasionally why I like our aunt so well."

"What is it this time?"

Calder explained the little joke about the ink, which wasn't nearly so funny in repetition, and went on to ask if Quentin meant to ride over to Merrywood later in the day.

"I thought we were both going," said Quentin.

"I've been forbidden the premises."

"What?"

"Yes, I thought that would surprise you."

"Why?"

"I don't know. That's why I wondered if you were going. I mean to write Miss Ruthven a letter asking for an explanation and, since it is not proper that I write an unmarried young lady, I hoped you would deliver it to her in secret."

Quentin agreed to do so and Calder went on up to his room where he got out his writing materials, set them on the table by his window, and then stared at the sunlit gardens below. It crossed his mind that his aunt needed a new gardener, the wild tangles of shrubs and bushes and weedy flower beds indicative of her current lack of one.

The thought faded as he wondered how to begin a letter to a lady he'd no business writing to. On the other hand, young ladies were not supposed to write to gentlemen, as this one had done when she sent that provocative note!

He shrugged and set pen to paper:

"Mea culpa," he wrote. *"I haven't a notion of what I am guilty, but of something, that is certain, so I will admit it—whatever it is—and apologize. A million apologies. Will that, you think, gain me a step toward that perfection of which you once spoke?*

"Now, having apologized, although for what I know not, I wish an explanation. What have I done? Why am I forbidden the sun of your countenance—and the quieter, starlit features of another among you?"

Calder reread what he'd written and bit down on the end of his pen, pondering how to close his missive. Again he shrugged.

"Leave me not in suspense, oh sunlight in a gray day, but send me reassurance that my apologies will gain me what I most desire in all this world."

He ended it with *"Your servant in all things"* and signed it with the heavy black slashing signature that, once seen, was never forgotten.

Babs, reading it, chuckled. "Your cousin has a way with words, does he not?"

Quentin's brows, of more normal design than Calder's, arched.

Babs ignored his silent question as to what was in the note. "We mean to adjourn to the music room and I hope you will honor us with a song or two, Mr. Riverton."

"Happily," he said and, realizing he would get no hint of why his cousin was not to come to Merrywood, he joined James who was discussing music with Miss Morgan. Or, perhaps one should say, he was speaking of music and Miss Morgan, her hands folded in her lap and her head bent, might or might not be listening.

They had no sooner decided that they would, all three, perform *Greensleeves* when they heard Sir George's loud blustering voice approaching the room. James glanced down at Miss Morgan, saw that she had gone quite rigid, her knuckles becoming a greasy yellowish white, she clenched them so tightly.

For a moment Quentin didn't recognize the voice. Then he did. He swore softly.

"Exactly," said James, his voice dry. He moved so that Miss Morgan was half hidden by his body. Quentin, seeing what he did, also moved, the two of them shielding her—but both knew it would not answer for very long.

"I will not allow him to harm you, Miss Morgan," said James softly.

She glanced up at him, casting him a quick disbelieving look and Quentin, seeing it, wondered if she thought he could not or was surprised by the offer.

James continued talking about music and again Miss Morgan looked up at him, this time a rather wondering look in her expression.

Quentin responded rather at random, his ear cocked to listen to the blustering going on behind them.

"Mother, I tell you I'll not have it. They will come home with me. Now."

"They will not. You have publicly denied them. They are no longer yours to order about."

"You are wrong. Anna is packing."

"Anna is fully adult and I cannot stop her from what she would do, but I can stop you taking Louisa. I am her legal guardian and it is up to *me* what she does and where she goes."

"Pooh. Can't be. Don't have guardians for chits when their father's still alive."

"But you denied she was yours. Before witnesses," said Lady Dewsbury-Morgan firmly. "I have been given guardianship in your place."

"Who?" Sir George's voice had become louder with each word. Now he very nearly screamed, "Who did such a thing? I'll have his guts for garters!"

Louisa Maria winced and started to shake.

"Where is she? Where are you hiding her? She's mine to do with as I please!"

James reached a hand to Louisa's shoulder, holding her when she began to slip to the ground in a faint. "Here," he said softly to Quentin. "Sit beside her and hold her up."

Once he'd seen that the girl was no longer likely to swoon, James turned and stalked to where Sir George waved his fist under his mother's nose.

"Lower your voice." When James had Sir George's surprised attention, he added, "If you cannot behave like the gentleman you are supposed to be, then you may leave my cousin's house." He spoke with such ice in his voice that he froze Sir George. "A gentleman," continued James, "is a woman's *protector*. His duty is to give her *aid* and *comfort*. He is not to make her so *unhappy* she very nearly faints from *fear* of him."

Sir George turned purple. "Who the devil are you? What right have you to tell me how to go on?"

"Someone must," said James, "since you seem not to have acquired the knack of it."

Sir George was so angry he sputtered. Then he roared, "I'll see you drawn and quartered!"

"Yes, just the sort of medieval threat someone of your ilk would make, is it not?" said James calmly. "It is the nineteenth century. You cannot behave like a tyrant. Certainly not to the women in your life."

"You . . . You . . ." Sir George seemed to swell to the point of bursting.

James allowed his eyebrows to arch but said nothing.

"You . . . You . . ."

"Oh go away," said Lady Dewsbury-Morgan. "You are a dead bore, George. That I am forced to admit you are blood of my blood is an abomination."

Sir George turned disbelieving eyes on his mother. "You . . . You . . ."

"I have papers," she said, a warning in her tone. "If Anna is fool enough to go with you, then on her head be it. But you will *not* take Sissie." She turned on her heel and moved away—hiding the fact that the argument had unsettled her nerves a great deal. One reason she had not done more to change her son was her hatred of loud voices. She wished she'd not been such a coward.

"I want my daughter!" Sir George looked wildly around the room, saw where Louisa Maria cowered in her chair, and marched over to her. "On your feet, Sissie. You're coming with me."

James tapped Sir George on the shoulder. "Are you hard of hearing as well as everything else?" he asked mildly. "She stays with her grandmother."

"She's mine!"

"You denied she is yours. It is too late to change your mind." James hoped that was the truth. He also hoped it was true that Lady Dewsbury-Morgan had been given guardianship of the chit.

"Blast you!"

"No, it is you who are blasted, Sir George, and right out of this house." James had had enough. "Your carriage will be at the door in half an hour. I suggest you help your wife finish her packing."

Sir George cast him a baffled look. Then he glared at his daughter. "Well, Sissie? What have you to say for yourself? Are you going to stay here with strangers or are you coming home where you belong?"

Louisa Maria began shaking. Her hands trembled to the point she could not keep them in her lap.

"Well?" he demanded.

"Miss Morgan has spoken no word since she left the church that day," said Quentin, speaking for the first time. "I doubt your yelling at her will change that."

"You . . ." Sir George turned his anger toward Quentin and suddenly, as if a candle had been blown out, his expression changed to one of curiosity. "Don't I know you?"

"Perhaps. But that is not relevant. Your daughter cannot answer you. She does not speak."

"Nonsense. She speaks perfectly. I saw to that. Elocution lessons," said Sir George proudly.

"Nevertheless, she does not speak."

"Well, Sissie? Not a word for your old papa?" he asked in a falsely jovial tone.

Louisa Marie ducked her head still farther.

"Come now. Tell your papa you'll come home!"

One tiny shake of her head and her shoulders hunched as if she feared she'd be beaten. For half a moment James and Quentin feared she would be, but James cleared his throat and Quentin moved closer and Sir George relaxed.

"I said it once and I was right," growled the baronet. "You, Louisa Maria, are none of mine!" He turned on his heel and stalked from the room.

James and Quentin stared after him and didn't see Miss Morgan raise her head and stare admiringly at James.

Eight

Babs, meantime, frowned over a blank sheet of paper, wondering exactly how to respond to Lord Calder's missive. She wished she had his easy facility with the written word as she had when speaking. Unfortunately, when it came to putting her thoughts on paper, the training her governess gave her in proper letter writing seemed to get in the way.

There was another reason she took her time about the chore. Once she had finished she would be required to return to the salon where that awful Sir George would be making life difficult for everyone. She knew she would have to tell him to leave and did not look forward to it. He, she feared, would not leave peacefully.

A tap at the door brought her head around. She frowned, wondering what disaster had struck. "Yes?"

The door opened and James put his head in. "You are needed. Two of your guests are about to depart and, as hostess, you should be there to wish them a good journey."

"Two?" *Not one or three?*

"Sir George has talked or bullied, I know not which, his wife into returning to London with him."

She rose to her feet, concerned. "Louisa?"

"She and her grandmother stay."

Babs let out the breath she'd not known she held. "Just how did you manage that?" she asked.

"What makes you think I managed anything at all?" he asked, blandly.

She chuckled. "I am beginning to know you. You have taken the little Louisa under your wing and there is no way you would allow her to return to that monster's care."

"Not that one can call it 'care,'" he said, his voice harsh.

She nodded. "Very true." Then she sighed. "I do not look forward to the next few minutes," she said.

"I and Mr. Riverton, along with any number of servants, will see Sir George leaves quietly."

If not quietly, Sir George did leave, and left behind his mother and his daughter.

Mr. William Ruthven had returned to the house an hour or so before Sir George and his wife left it. Disliking what he knew of the man, he had played least-in-sight and gone into hiding, telling his niece he'd reappear when the monster was gone. Now, hearing what was afoot, he came to where she and James discussed Sir George with Quentin.

"You should," said William, "have recommended they stop for the night in Stains before crossing the heath."

"Why?" asked Babs, who was exceedingly pleased to be rid of them.

"I heard a rumor that there is a gang of bridle-culls working it."

"Highwaymen? Surely not," said Babs, frowning. "It is years since there were any engaged in that business."

"Still, that's all they talk about in town. According to what I heard, there were two attacks in the last week."

"So recently? Perhaps that explains our ignorance?"

"It is true that no one has been into Stains until I'd reason to see my solicitor. Didn't get back until half an hour before dinner and Logan was kind enough to warn me that Sir George was on the rampage—" He looked at James with this news since Babs already knew it. "—so I had a tray in my study and only just learned they've gone."

"What do you think?" she asked, turning to James. "Should someone ride after them and warn them?"

"Surely Sir George will hear when they stop, as he must, in Stains to change horses . . . ?"

"But if he does not?" she asked, worried about Lady Morgan and the Morgan servants. Sir George, so far as she was concerned, could take his chances! "Lady Morgan . . ." she began, her voice trailing off.

James sighed. "Very well. I will ride after them."

"I will ride with you," offered Quentin. "It is likely that Sir George will not thank you for the information and may do so in an insulting manner. You may be glad to have me along."

"What is *most* likely," said James, his voice once again like ice, "is that he will continue on merely because we tell him he should not."

"If it were not for Lady Morgan, I would say we leave him to his fate, but since she is with him—" Quentin spoke wearily. "—I suppose we had better try to catch them up."

"I will send a note to Blackstock Manor, explaining where you've gone and that you may be late," said Babs, smiling at the two men. "And thank you. If you did not go, I would worry about them until I knew they'd arrived safely in London."

Babs' note to Lady Blackstock included an invitation to her ladyship and her two guests to join the Ruthvens for a small dinner party the following evening . . . which tacitly informed Lord Calder he would, by then, again be welcome at Merrywood. Then, having invited the Blackstock party, she was forced to write several more invitations—to the vicar and his wife, and two of her nearest neighbors. It did, after all, require a number of guests if it were to qualify as a party!

James and Quentin discovered where Sir George changed horses and were disturbed that the baronet, when his wife timidly suggested they stay at the inn until daylight promised safety, had pooh-poohed the danger, insisting it was a tale the innkeeper put forward in order to increase his trade. His coachman, hearing the news, also argued in favor of remaining where they were until morning, but he was told not to be such a weak-kneed lily-livered spinster and, grimfaced—according to one hostler—the man had taken up the reins and set out.

"Only half an hour ahead of us," said Quentin as they too rode up onto the heath on the road to London with the sun fast headed toward the horizon.

"We will catch them up before dark and if Sir George will not turn around I suppose we must accompany them as outriders," said James, urging his mount to a canter.

They went in silence, riding hard for nearly twenty minutes, at which point they heard shouts and a gunshot. Another shot and then a third immediately following reached their ears as they kicked their horses to a gallop. A scream echoed above the sound of their horses' pounding hooves . . .

. . . and then silence.

"Hold on," shouted James, a gun in one hand, cocked and ready. "We're coming."

Quentin, startled by the sight of the pistol, wondered where it had come from.

They heard swearing from near the coach they could now see through the dusk. It was pulled to the side of the road and leaning in one window was a rank-rider. Another highwayman, the one swearing furiously, faced them and, as they neared, pulled his horse around and galloped off over the wasteland. The last pulled his head from the window and swung his gun their way. James aimed, pulled the trigger, and with a cry, the man tumbled to the ground, his horse stepping on him in its attempts to pull loose, but the reins were wound around the man's wrist and it could not get free.

Another scream from inside the carriage and James called out, "Lady Morgan, it is only us. We will take care of you and see you safe."

The driver climbed down from the front of the coach, mopping his forehead with a wildly-colored handkerchief. "I thought we were all goners," he said, when Quentin pulled up beside him and looked at the mayhem.

On the driver's seat, Sir George's valet sat shaking like a leaf, his skin pale and his mouth set in the rictus of a silent scream. The coachman followed Quentin's look and grimaced. "Yellow-livered prig, that one. He'll be all right." He nudged one fallen man. "Sir George got that one first. And then that one over there." He pointed. "He was a bully and a hard master, not fair in his ways, but he met this disaster bravely, I'll have to give him that." He said it with obvious reluctance.

James, on the other side of the coach, had opened the door and found himself with an armful of sobbing womanhood. Lady Morgan had tumbled into his arms and would not let go. She trembled so hard he feared she'd shake herself apart.

"Now, now," he said rather helplessly. "It is over. You are safe." He continued in much the same fashion until, finally, she seemed to come to herself and, tipping her head back, stared at him. "You are safe," he said once more. "We came up just in time."

"No, no. Not in time," she said and began sobbing again.

"Now, now . . ." he said helplessly.

"Sir George is *dead*. What am I to do? My husband is *dead.*"

James frowned. Surely the woman wouldn't mourn the man, cruel and harsh as he'd been. "Hush now. We will return to Merrywood and you will have his mother to tell you how to go on."

"Mother Vivian!" She reared back and glared. "*She* won't care. She won't care a jot. She has never understood. She thinks she doesn't need a man. But one does. *I* do . . ."

James saw that a touch of temper was just the thing to stop her tears. "Oh, surely you do not mean that. He was her son. But did you *want* that ogre for husband . . . ?"

Lady Morgan lifted her chin, a stubborn set to her mouth.

"Oh very well—" James pretended to give way. "—but I think you will appreciate having the women about you at such a time. Now we must get organized. You return to the coach and . . ." He was startled when she shook her head vehemently and backed away. "Why not?"

"Ride with . . . sit there beside . . . share the . . ." To his horror, she began weeping again. "You cannot expect it of me. My sensibilities. It is too much. I *cannot.*" She cast a fearful glance toward a dead man and then toward the open carriage door, her skin turning a dirty ashen color.

James finally perceived the problem and sighed. One of the highwaymen's horses stood, hoof cocked, just along the road and he went to get it. "We will tie Sir George to . . ."

But Lady Morgan shook her head violently. "So disrespectful. You cannot."

"Then," he said, only faintly exasperated, "what would you suggest we do?"

"Perhaps—" She looked at him from under her lashes. "—you would allow me to ride before you . . . ?"

James was not happy with the suggestion. Riding any distance in such a manner would be exceedingly uncomfortable. On the other hand, if he did so, they could put the other bodies into the carriage along with Sir George's and not leave them alongside the road. He agreed and, the plan made, they were soon ready to turn the carriage and return to Stains.

James got a room for Lady Morgan at the inn, hired a maid to stay with her, found a doctor, who gave her a dose of laudanum when she swore she'd not sleep a wink for the horror of it all, and, finally, was able to turn his attention to the local magistrate who had waited, more or less patiently, for her ladyship and her megrims to be shut away so the men could get on with the business surrounding the death of the three highwaymen.

They ended the evening with a brace of brandy bottles that James, Quentin and the magistrate managed to finish before stumbling up the stairs to rooms of their own.

And while they drank and talked, the brand new widow dreamed, not of the horror she'd gone through, but of strong arms holding her and broad shoulders on which she could lay her head, and a darkly tanned skin ruined by an eastern sun. She woke much refreshed and very unhappy when none of the men, particularly a certain one, joined her for breakfast.

Or for lunch.

It was mid-afternoon before James and Quentin mounted their geldings for the ride back to Merrywood, Lady Morgan unsuccessful in her effort to coax them, especially The One, inside with her. Neither had a head that would have withstood her prattle, and neither wished to insult her, and, besides, both believed the fresh air might finish the job a long sleep and a sip of the hair of the dog had begun. They hoped that, by the time they finished their slow journey to Merrywood—a wagon carrying the sad burden of a closed casket following the Morgan carriage forced them to a staid pace—they would feel normal once again.

They returned barely in time to wash up and change their clothes, only to discover that the planned dinner had been hastily cancelled, honoring the proper forms surrounding a death in the family.

Lord Calder, reading the note sent to Lady Blackstock, frowned. Sir George was dead! If Louisa Maria felt she must mourn her father for the year prescribed by society's dictates, then she would not wed during that period. Would Lady Morgan insist on proper forms? Or, since she seemed in favor of his marriage to her daughter, would she allow a quiet wedding with only family and no bride visits or any of the other folderol common to a wedding in the circles in which he traveled?

"What is it, Matt?" asked Quentin.

"What? Oh nothing important." He frowned as he realized one could hardly call a death unimportant.

"Sir George is no great loss," Quentin said when Calder explained. But his cousin still frowned. "Want to talk about it?"

"I was wondering what my father would say to a wedding postponed for such a reason."

"Knowing your father," said Quentin with sympathy, "I doubt he'll be happy with the notion you must wait a year. He wants you wed and filling your nursery."

Lord Calder recalled Lady Dewsbury-Morgan's lecture on the sort of wife Louisa Maria would make. Once or twice he had wondered if he truly had the patience to teach her to enjoy his attentions. He sighed.

"Not such a bad thing, filling one's nursery," teased Quentin.

Given his thoughts on the subject, his lordship wondered if that would be true.

"Not with the right woman," added Quentin—and did so with no hint of a jest in his tone and with a rather odd look in his eye.

Lord Calder had no desire at all to speculate as to its meaning. Instead he turned on his heel and walked off. One might even say he stalked off. Why did everyone conspire to convince him Louisa was not the woman he wanted or needed. He did need her. He needed peace and quiet . . .

. . . and boredom.

Boredom.

A vision of Miss Barbara Ruthven filled his head, and, quickly denying he wanted anything to do with a strong-minded woman, he brought his mother to mind in order to reinforce that decision. He remembered *her* wild behavior, *her* tempestuous and contentious ways, conduct that made life a misery for everyone around her. He would *not* endure a marriage of the sort his father had endured. He would *not.*

But once again, traitorously, Miss Ruthven sneaked past his defenses and into his mind . . . along with an even more traitorous reaction from his body.

No.

He wouldn't have it. A grim look about his jaw, he headed for the stables, tacked up his horse himself when the groom was a trifle slow in leaving off his work to do it, and rode off toward Merrywood. His temper grew rather than dissipated with the exercise and, by the time he handed his gelding to one of the Merrywood grooms, he was absolutely furious. It was all her fault. If she had not hidden the fact Sir George had arrived at Merrywood, then everything would be in train for a proper wedding . . .

. . . and there she was. Hoyden. Witch.

Lord Calder hurried across the lawn toward the arbor into which Miss Ruthven had disappeared. She reappeared just as he approached.

"Lord Calder," she said, smiling. The smile faded. "What is wrong?"

"*You* are wrong." He came very near to snarling it. "How dare you take it on yourself to interfere between me and Sir George? How dare you decide it was your place to keep me from him? How dare you keep Louisa Maria and me from a proper we . . . ?"

"Stop."

Astounded she had the nerve to interrupt him, he did stop, his mouth still open on the unfinished word.

"In the first place," she said, "it had nothing to do with you. I mean, asking that you not come to Merrywood when I knew Sir George had just arrived. The man was in a temper. He was impossible. He actually hit his wife and I feared he'd hit Louisa Maria. Especially if he discovered you were nearby, assuming he had not been made aware of it by Lady Morgan." She cocked her head. "Now I think of it, he probably did know."

But Calder was still assimilating an earlier comment and ignored that. "He hit . . . ?"

"*She* appears to be used to it," said Babs, "but *I* am not. I cannot understand why she went off with Sir George. He threatened Lady Dewsbury-Morgan with the law if she did not hand Louisa Maria over to him, but her ladyship stood firm, and he left with Anna. And then, stubbornly, foolishly, he insisted on continuing toward London when it was far too late in the afternoon and he had been told about the highwaymen."

Lord Calder refused to be mollified. "A fine excuse," he sneered. "If you had not interfered, the man would still be alive. It is your fault he is dead."

"Nonsense. No one is responsible but that pig-headed bully's own stupid, stubborn, idiotic self!"

Lord Calder reached for her. "Don't argue with me. Don't raise your voice to me!"

Suddenly, bursting from the arbor, Miss Morgan ran toward them, her parasol at the ready. She laid it about Calder's shoulders. "You will not! You will not harm Miss Ruthven," she said, her long unused voice cracking.

He grabbed the parasol just as Babs reached for and hugged Miss Morgan. "Louisa, you spoke!"

The girl's eyes widened. A look of terror filled her eyes and she jerked from Babs' loose embrace and ran toward the house as if a devil were on her tail.

"Now what was that all about?" asked Babs.

"I don't know," said his lordship, frowning, his brows a straight thick line above his eyes. "Do you sometimes wonder if she is quite right in the head?"

"She *spoke* . . . and then ran off as if a boggard were after her . . ."

"A *what?*"

Babs blushed. "A goblin. One of the maids is afraid of them and will not step foot outside once the sun is down. She is convinced they are all around us, but what they'd do to her if they caught her—well, she isn't certain."

"You asked?" he asked grinning.

"I was curious. I wonder if Louisa is afraid of such things."

"More likely to be afraid of her father," said Calder slowly.

"But he's dead."

"Worse!" He grinned sardonically. "Now she must worry about his ghost?"

Babs chuckled. "Still, why would she, at that particular moment, have fallen into a panic. *She'd just spoken.*"

Calder pursed his lips, frowning. "I have just remembered something. That day in church, her father said—" Calder spoke slowly, trying to recall the sense of what was said. "—she wasn't to speak again until she was ready to speak the proper words."

"Proper words?"

"The oath that meant," he said dryly, "she accepted me as her spouse."

"So—she is in a panic that she spoke but isn't willing to wed you, is that it?"

"That is my guess."

"And you still want to wed her?" asked Babs, disbelieving.

He sighed. "Yes." He stared off into the future. "Well, I think I do . . ."

"But then again, maybe you do not," she said, a touch caustic in her speech.

"Maybe . . ."

"My lord," she said, touching his arm, "you do *not* want to marry her. Believe me. It will not do. If only you were to tell her so, perhaps she could be happy again."

"Happy. The mere *thought* of wedding me makes her unhappy?"

"Yes."

When she added no more, he barked a laugh. "Well, I guess that is straightforward and simple enough even I can understand you."

"So you will tell her?"

The ironic smile twisting his mouth faded. "No. I won't. I am still unconvinced she has any conception at all of what she wants or doesn't want. I still think I can convince her she wants me."

"You, Lord Calder, are a fool." Babs turned on her heel and stalked off across the lawn.

Calder frowned and then followed. "Fool I may be, but at least I know what I want."

"You don't."

"I do too!"

She turned and he very nearly ran her down, stopping abruptly and clasping her shoulders to keep her from falling backwards when she realized how near they were to bumping into each other.

"I want peace," he said more quietly. "I want contentment. I want a quiet home life and I do *not* want a woman who is always arguing with me or raising her voice to me or causing scenes in public if she does not get her way or raging at me or deliberately ruining something I like because she is angry with me or . . ."

Babs stopped his words by the simple process of laying her fingers across his lips. "Hush now. Of course you do not wish that sort of woman for wife. But you also do not wish a woman who will be so fearful of rousing your temper she will spend the whole of her life tiptoeing around you, avoiding you whenever she can, and yessir, nosir-ing you until you are so tired of it you cannot help but do exactly as she fears and explode at her!"

The picture she drew was so vivid that Calder shut his eyes against it. "No, of course I do not want that," he agreed.

"But that is what you will get if you wed Louisa Maria. Or anyone like her. Don't you see?"

He sighed. "I see only one solution."

"You will tell her you do not wish to wed her," said Babs, smiling.

He grimaced. "I suppose I will. In the end. But the solution to which I refer is that I wed no one, which means I shall have to put up with rows with my father who is determined I wed and do so immediately. *I do not like rows.*"

It occurred to Babs that his father's attitude was rather strange. "Why is he in such a rush? You are not so very old, after all."

He swallowed, his distinctive brows drawing together in a pained look. "My brother. My older brother. He was at the siege of Burgos."

"Was."

He nodded. "He took a ball to the lungs."

"I am surprised he was allowed to join up."

"He had wanted nothing else since he was a child and, as he pointed out to Father, I exist."

"So you inherit."

"I never thought it!" The sharpness in Calder's voice softened. "Henry was . . . special. I looked up to him, admired him. It was bad enough when people suddenly started calling me by *his* courtesy title, but now our father has become obsessed with getting himself grandchildren. Preferably lots of them. And preferably years ago!"

"It must have been terrible for him when his heir died—even if he knew it might happen. I see why he wants you wed."

His lordship nodded, staring off into space.

Babs bit her lip, eyeing him, a sudden vision of herself filling her mind. The picture of carrying his babe in her arms was very nearly more than she could bear. Having lots of children. Children to fill the Merrywood nursery and the grounds and the woods and the fields. Happy children. Playful children. And not *lonely* children as she'd been lonely, despite the wonders of the whole of the Merrywood estate about which she played and, later, learned to value and to care for.

And then, inside where it didn't show, she laughed. Very likely if she were to bear him all those children, all the boys would look like her, delicate-boned and red-headed while all the girls would look like him with thick dark hair and thick heavy brows.

And why not? she thought. *Lord Calder, you do not know it, but I think I am going to convince you I am just the wife to keep you happy.*

She couldn't say that, of course, and wouldn't just at this moment even if she dared, not when he was settled into melancholy at the thought of defying his father and, simultaneously perhaps, enjoying the prospect of eternal bachelorhood!

"Well," she said, drawing his attention, "however that may be, perhaps you might like to join us for potluck. We eat in less than an hour, I believe." Country fashion, they usually dined in midafternoon. Only when there was company did they eat at a more fashionable hour. Babs cast a knowing eye toward the position of the sun and nodded. "Less than an hour. Do join us," she coaxed.

He seemed to come back from a long way away. "No," he said. He modified that to something less abrupt. "No, thank you. I think I'll ride the long way back to Blackstock Manor. I've a deal of thinking to do."

"How you'll tell Louisa you'll not continue to wish her to wed you?"

"How I'll tell my father I do not intend to wed at all," he retorted. "Telling Miss Morgan will be easy by comparison!"

"A labor of Hercules, telling your father?" she asked, teasing.

That drew a smile, although a rather weak one. "Yes. A task that would make even that ancient hero blench."

"Hmm. You are faced, then, with a truly heroic feat. I will admire you from afar while you get on with it."

"You will not," he said still more dryly, "admire the explosion which will erupt once he knows."

She laughed—but he did not.

"You wait." His tone was wry, self-deriding. "You'll discover the truth of what I say when the top rises off Blackstock Manor," he added, then, saying his goodbyes, returned to the stable, riding off across country toward the village rather than toward the manor. He did indeed have thinking to do—and the task of the building up of his courage. Calder did not like brangles. He had not liked them since he was a child.

And now he was about to deliberately step into the middle of one with his father.

He did not look forward to it.

Nine

Babs was staring in the direction in which Calder had ridden when James, who had been looking for her, found her.

"Cousin," he called when still some distance off.

Babs tipped her head toward him, but her eyes remained trained on the distant prospect. "Yes?"

"Explain to me what you said to Miss Morgan to upset her so."

She turned. "To Louisa? I didn't say anything at all to upset her. Lord Calder, with reason, was angry with me. So angry he actually took hold of my shoulders and, if given time, might have shaken me." She smiled a reminiscent smile. "Before he could, our brave little Louisa rushed to the rescue. She whacked him about his shoulders with her parasol," she added when James frowned.

"Is that all?"

Babs' eyes twinkled. "Actually not. She *spoke.*"

James' frown deepened. "So?"

"So she ran off, obviously in a panic toward the house. Something—" it was Babs' turn to frown "—Calder said makes a great deal of sense, actually." Babs explained about Sir George telling Louisa she wasn't to say anything until she was willing to say the marriage oath.

James was not a slowtop. "I see. Having actually allowed words to escape her, she may fear she has, somehow, accepted him?"

"It seems reasonable. I tried to reassure her, but was not successful. As I said, she ran into the house."

"Where she ran into me. Literally. We were near the music room, so I took her in there. Since she was her usual mute self, I could make no sense of anything except that she was upset. Finally I sat her at her harp and suggested she play while I discovered what was wrong."

"And now you have. James, are you developing a *tendre* for our little Louisa?"

"It would be nonsense on my part. She is far younger than you are and I feel *you* too young for me!"

"I have come to the conclusion," she said musingly, "that sense has nothing to do with losing one's foolish heart."

He cast her an understanding look. "Lord Calder?"

"I wonder . . . but it is ridiculous. I do not even like him half the time and yet, whenever I think of him my heart beats more quickly and I feel—" She turned a look toward him from under her brows. "—very strange."

Unlike Calder, James had brows that would rise independently and now one quirked, a hint of a smile touching his mouth. "Strange?"

"Not at all the way a lady *should* feel . . ." she added pensively.

"But?" he said.

Babs realized she'd said too much and wondered how she could retrace her steps without embarrassment. "You heard that little word even if I did not say it?" she asked, needing time to think of a way out of her dilemma.

"Yes. And, since you have already said, at least *suggested*, much a young lady should not say, especially to a man, even if that man is her cousin, you may as well say the rest."

"I don't believe," she said pensively, "that I have ever claimed to be a lady. Not if one must pretend to what does not exist and pretend what exists does *not.*"

"Do ladies do so?" he asked, startled.

"It has seemed to me they do." Babs felt as if she could breathe again and settled into an explanation that would, she hoped, keep them from any more embarrassing disclosures. "During my one London season I found that no one would speak of the horrors I saw all around me. Hungry, badly dressed children. Women— so many women—selling the only thing they had to sell. Ex-soldiers, maimed in battle and trying to live on a shilling a day, or whatever pittance they are given by our penny-pinching government. And then there were other men, drunk at all hours—and women too. The gambling that went on day and night in all classes." She shook her head slightly. "All of it ignored. I was looked at askance when I spoke of it."

"They pretended none of it existed?"

"That was my feeling."

"And what did they pretend existed when it did not?"

"The family," she said promptly. "Children were never seen. They were cared for by nannies and, later, by governesses and tutors and, the boys, at least, were often sent off to school while still babies—or so *I* judge a bewildered child of only nine or ten to be! Men and women married but rarely saw each other, going their separate ways, following their own interests, showing no affection for each other." She grimaced. "When I questioned such behavior I was informed one did not wear one's heart on one's sleeve, but, in my opinion, the heart was rarely involved."

"Surely you do not speak of all tonnish marriages. All families."

"No of course not. I exaggerate for the sake of the argument. But in far too many cases seemed to me as if . . . if . . . as if the union existed only in the eyes of the law and not in the heart, where a marriage should be made, *should* be *felt.*"

James nodded thoughtfully. "Sometimes, cousin, you surprise me."

His comment brought her from her thoughts rather abruptly. "I do?"

"I wonder if Lord Calder has any notion at all of what he would win if he were to take you to wife."

The compliment, along with relief that he did not mean to ask, again, for explanations of feelings she should not feel, had Babs smiling broadly. *"You* did not want me!"

He grinned in response. "That is still true, but not because you are not worthy of the position of wife." He sobered. "Frankly, I do not approve of marriages between cousins."

She nodded. "Too often the children . . . *suffer?*"

He nodded. "I haven't a notion why it happens, but I too have observed that there are far more . . . marred . . . offspring than when one weds away from one's family."

She nodded. "I enjoy talking to you, cousin, and will always enjoy it I think, but I did not and do not wish to wed you."

He smiled. "Then we are in agreement, are we not? I will see if her music has soothed Miss Morgan . . ."

Babs chuckled. "The one thought following the other, of course."

Two spots of red appeared on James' cheekbones. "Perhaps," he said, smiling a trifle ruefully before walking off. "But I doubt it."

Babs, putting him and their conversation from her mind, turned, and, once again, stared into the distance—although Lord Calder was long gone from view, he instantly returned to her thoughts as if he were not.

Calder rode toward the village, thinking he might stop at the tiny inn for an ale, but, when almost there, he decided he was not in the mood for conversation. Especially not the sort of conversation he would find among those gathered at this time of day for a drink. Or two. Or three. . . .

Instead, he turned down a lane he'd never before explored. The land rose here and, just when he'd decided the lane went nowhere, he reached the top of a rise and stared down into a tiny but perfect valley. A stream burbled through the bottom and, here and there, small groves of nut trees formed islands of cool dark shade. On the far side, somewhat higher on rising ground, was a house. Men crawled all over it—on the roofs, on scaffolding along the walls, and, in the left hand wing, two workmen hung out of windows on the second floor where they appeared to be removing the frames. Very likely rotten wood needed replacing.

Calder, watching, wondered to whom the house belonged. It was a neatly designed house, a comfortable looking house, but the outbuildings should be torn down—assuming they did not fall down all by themselves—and begun anew. Who could have allowed such a lovely home to deteriorate so? He, wishing to avoid his thoughts for an interval, decided to find out.

The man in charge of the work approached him when he dismounted in the forecourt. "Yes, sir? Can I do something for you?"

"You may satisfy my curiosity. I am visiting my aunt, Lady Blackstock—"

The man nodded, acknowledging that he knew the name.

"—and never before rode this way. To whom does this house belong?"

"Mr. Ruthven, sir. Mr. *James* Ruthven, who is just returned from many years in India."

"I suppose that explains it. He was poorly served by whomever was left in charge?"

"As to that, his father lived until just a year or two ago. The old man became—a trifle strange in his latter years."

Calder nodded, grinning. "More than a trifle I would say and for longer than a few years, I'd guess," he said.

The builder merely smiled, unwilling to say more about the father of the man who paid him.

"It is a lovely old house," said Calder, understanding the situation.

That touched a spot in the heart of a man who loved his work. He beamed, turned, and gestured broadly. "'Tis a perfect jewel of a house. Would you care to see it?"

Calder spent a pleasant hour following the man about. He learned far more about flying staircases and old-fashioned wainscoting and the problems of dealing with deteriorating plasterwork than he had ever expected to know—but, surprising himself, he found it interesting.

"There are some bits that remind me of Merrywood," he said at one point. "Do you know Miss Ruthven's estate?"

The man nodded. "The houses were built about the same time. A bit of competition between brothers, if I understand the tale correctly. They were each determined to build the more perfect house."

"This one is not so large, but I would say it won in the perfection stakes."

The builder nodded. "A most satisfying house. Or was. And will be again." He nodded firmly, emphasizing the point.

"I will tell Ruthven I think you are doing excellent work."

"Thank you." They had returned to the courtyard and the overseer, noticing one of his roofers doing something not exactly in the way he liked, excused himself rather abruptly and was already yelling at the fellow as he headed toward a ladder.

Calder collected his mount and decided he had used up all the excuses he could find and must, finally, return to his aunt's even though he had not decided how to write his father the news concerning his decision. He could find no phrasing that would not make his parent furious—and yet the letter must be written.

Perhaps, he decided, *the thing to do is simply tell him I cannot bear to wed. At all. That marriage is not for me.*

After leaving his cousin standing and staring at nothing he himself could discern, James returned to the house and entered the music room where he picked up his violin and tuned it. Then he joined Louisa Maria who was deeply involved in practicing a new piece, one of several James had had sent from London when he learned she loved music as much as he did himself. He found where she played and, hesitantly, joined in. Startled, she hit a wrong chord and stopped.

He smiled, silently encouraged her to begin again, and joined her. For half an hour they worked together to perfect their new duet, but it was not yet to either's satisfaction when the dinner gong sounded.

"We can work on it again tomorrow," he said as he loosened his bow and put way his instrument.

She nodded and waited by the door for him to join her—new behavior on her part since she was more prone to simply go off on her own and not think to await another.

"Miss Morgan," he said musingly as they walked toward the dining room, "I wonder if you are aware that you cannot be forced, by anyone, into a marriage you do not want. It is the law. There is also the fact, harsh as it is to speak of it, that your father is dead and can no longer harm you in any way. There is no reason at all why you should not speak if you wish to do so. . . ."

He opened the door to the dining room. ". . . And does that not smell good?" he said, changing the subject abruptly so that the others would not know of what they'd spoken. "I find I am surprisingly hungry." He rubbed his hands together and, ignoring her, went immediately to his place.

Louisa Maria very hesitantly followed. All through the meal she glanced toward James and then away. Once the sweets were passed, she made it clear she was going to her room and, silently, excused herself.

Babs stared at the gently closed door. "What," asked Babs, "was that about?"

James smiled a very tiny, almost wicked, smile. "I told her no one can force her into a marriage she doesn't wish to contract and that her father is dead and can never bother her ever again, *and* that, if she wished it, there was no reason why she shouldn't speak again."

"And?"

"You wonder if she will? I haven't a notion, but you could see she was thinking about it."

"What," interrupted Lady Morgan, "do you mean no one can force her to wed where she doesn't wish it?"

"It is the law," said James, turning to her.

Lady Morgan's eye widened. "The *law?* You would say parents have no say in whom their child weds? That is outrageous. That is not right. Of course one's parents know best. The young are far too, well, *young* to have a say in anything so important . . ." and on and on.

James listened patiently. When she finally realized he was simply waiting for her to stop speaking, she turned bright red and apologized for carrying on.

". . . but," she added, "I do not understand how it can be."

"I did not say a daughter can wed wherever she wishes—merely that she cannot be forced to wed where she does *not* wish."

We'd Like to Invite You to Subscribe to Zebra's Regency Romance Book Club and Send You 4 Free Books as Your Introduction! (Worth $19.96!)

If you're a Regency lover, imagine the joy of getting 4 FREE Zebra Regency Romances and then the chance to have these lovely stories delivered to your home each month at the lowest price available! Well, that's our offer to you and here's how you benefit by becoming a Regency Romance subscriber:

- 4 FREE *Introductory Regency Romances are delivered to your doorstep (you only pay for shipping & handling)*

- *4 BRAND NEW Regencies are then delivered each month (usually before they're available in bookstores)*

- *Subscribers save almost $4.00 off the cover price every month*

- *You also receive a* FREE *monthly newsletter, which features author profiles, discounts, subscriber benefits, book previews and more*

- *There's no risks or obligations...in other words, you can cancel whenever you wish with no questions asked*

Join the thousands of readers who enjoy the savings and convenience offered to Regency Romance subscribers. After your initial introductory shipment, you'll receive 4 brand-new Zebra Regency Romances each month to examine for 10 days. Then, if you decide to keep the books, you pay the preferred subscriber's price, plus shipping and handling.

It's a no-lose proposition, so return the FREE BOOK CERTIFICATE today!

Treat yourself to 4 FREE Regency Romances!
A $19.96 VALUE... FREE!
No obligation to buy anything ever!

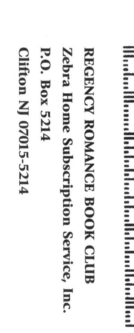

REGENCY ROMANCE BOOK CLUB
Zebra Home Subscription Service, Inc.
P.O. Box 5214
Clifton NJ 07015-5214

"Oh." Lady Morgan appeared to think about that for a long moment. "But that means a picky girl might never wed at all. If they never wished to wed someone suitable, that is."

"True."

"But . . ."

After a lengthening silence, he asked, "You think that it is terrible? To remain unwed?"

"To not have one's own establishment? To have no security? To live as the poor relation on someone's charity? Of course it would be terrible."

"Lady Morgan, it is a terribly impertinent question, but did you *enjoy* being married to Sir George?"

"Enjoy? Of course not. What has enjoyment to say to anything?"

"You do not think one should enjoy one's marriage?"

She blinked. Once. "I . . . don't know, do I? I suppose it never occurred to me one could."

James sighed as he shook his head. "I am sorry."

"Sorry?" She looked up, blinking rapidly. "Why are you sorry?"

"That you should have spent all your younger years," he said gently, "with a man who did not care for your comfort or your happiness."

Lady Morgan appeared to be totally confused by his comment. "But . . ."

"Did it never ever occur to you that he should?"

"No! It was my place to make *him* happy—" Tears filled her eyes. "—and I failed. Always. Over and over. Again and again and again." The tears overflowed. "No matter how I tried, I could never please him."

"Of course not."

"What?"

She looked very much like a startled rabbit and James had great difficulty restraining a chuckle, but, given the seriousness of what he wished to say, he managed to do so. "Sir George," he said, "did not *wish* you to please him. Not really. He was the sort who found his enjoyment in making others unhappy, making them suffer, or in using them to forward some plot—as he did when he tried to force your daughter to wed Lord Calder."

"But Lord Calder was such a catch. Such a *nice* young man. He would never have beaten her. Never."

He was startled into asking, "How can you know?"

"I asked, of course."

James chuckled. "Yes, of course. Why did I not think of that?"

"I *wanted* her to marry him. I still want it. It would be so appropriate, so right and—" She brightened. "—it was what her father wanted and she should do what he wanted."

"Why?"

"Because it is a child's duty to obey her parents," she said, as if that settled everything and she could dismiss everything contradictory that had been said on that subject.

"Is that the only reason you wished her wed to Calder?" asked James gently.

She looked up at him from under her lashes and then down at her tightly clenched hands. "Because I could visit them . . . ?" she said hesitantly in a very small voice.

"I see," said James after a long moment.

She gasped, her eyes widening with sudden understanding. "I am as selfish as Sir George!"

"But with far better reason," retorted James quickly. "You hoped," he added gently, "to escape the burden of your marriage by sharing in her establishment."

Lady Morgan nodded, hanging her head in shame.

"Forgive yourself, my dear Lady Morgan. Anyone would understand why you felt the way you did. You must remember, however, that it is no longer necessary to study how to please your husband . . . He is no longer here to be pleased," he added when she looked up at him, a question in her eyes.

Those big blue eyes widened and, suddenly, a smile broke across her slightly faded features, lightening the whole into something nearer to what she must have looked in her youth. "I had not realized . . ."

"No, why should you? Be happy, Lady Morgan," he said and walked away—and didn't see her looking after him with admiration, perhaps something more than admiration, in her gaze.

Ten

It was some days after James' discussion with Lady
Morgan. Her ladyship had been quite thoughtful and
perhaps a trifle withdrawn ever since. Now she stood before Lady Dewsbury-Morgan, her hands tightly clenched
and her eyes showing defiance.

Lady Dewsbury-Morgan stared at Anna. "What do you
mean, you wish to return to London? Why would you
want that when you are in mourning and cannot go into
company or give parties?"

Lady Morgan pouted. "I don't see why I cannot. Oh,
not large parties, but small intimate dinners with friends
and . . ."

"What friends?" interrupted Lady Dewsbury-Morgan.

Lady Morgan opened her mouth to respond and,
after a short hesitation, closed it. All the Morgan friends
had been her husband's friends and were not, not a one
of them, of interest to her.

"We are better staying here for the time being," said
Lady Dewsbury-Morgan. "I have considered asking Miss
Ruthven if we might not lease the dower house which, at
the moment, is empty. It is a pretty little house, just the
right size for the three of us. We have already made a few
friends in the area, who would drop in for tea or a musical evening, so we would not be lonely even if we must
follow convention and adopt our blacks for the coming
year."

"But . . ."

"You wish to cut a dash now my son is no longer around to prevent it?"

Lady Morgan blushed, adding much needed color to her features. "I never would!"

"Why not?" Lady Dewbury-Morgan chuckled at Anna's shocked expression. "My dear, when I first knew you, you were so *alive* and looking for all sorts of happy diversions. You did excellent needlework—"

"Oh, but George said it was a waste of time!"

"—which was much admired by everyone who saw it." Lady Dewsbury-Morgan sighed. "Another failure on my part. I should have encouraged you to continue with it. My son, you see, could not bear to hear you praised. It might give you confidence in yourself and undermine his control of you. There was also your music. You were forced to give it up for the same reason. And I recall that you liked to ride. How long has it been, Anna, since you last rode?"

Anna's wide-eyed expression of shock remained in place as she thought back to the girl she'd once been. And then her features crumpled and tears rained down. Awkwardly, Lady Dewsbury-Morgan took Anna into her arms and patted her back until the storm passed.

"You'll feel much better now," she said bracingly when Anna finally pushed away and turned her back. "You can forget the years you were forced to behave as if you were always and forever a naughty child in expectation of punishment. Now you can think of the things *you* want to do. But *not* in London," finished her ladyship and left the room before the new widow could argue the point.

Remembering the dower house, Lady Dewsbury-Morgan went to find Babs.

"But are you unhappy here with me?" asked Babs.

"We are more than happy, but we are now free to make plans for the future. The lawyer says Anna has a very nice widow's portion and, of course, Sissie is an heiress and has an excellent allowance while she remains unwed. We will do very well and there is no reason at all we should continue to impose upon your generosity. On the other hand, we enjoy your company and have made acquaintances among your neighbors, so we would be foolish to go elsewhere—at least for the period of our mourning. So, if you could see the way clear to leasing us Woodbine House, everything would work out for the best. I am certain of it."

"I see no reason why you could not lease it—but not instantly. The house has sat empty for years now, and no work done except, of course, to see that the roof doesn't leak and the windows are unbroken. It must be cleaned and I am sure much will need repainting and the gardeners must find the garden and—" She threw up her hands. "—I don't know what else!" She smiled. "Why do we not go look it over? Will Lady Morgan and Louisa Maria wish to go as well?"

The party visiting the dower house was enlarged to include James and, when they arrived unexpectedly, Lord Calder and his cousin. When it became clear that everyone else was going, William was consulted to discover if he too wished the treat.

"Treat? Nonsense. Just an old house. Likely damp," he added repressively. "Tell the ladies they will be much better staying here."

"I thought you were against their coming," said Babs, her eyes twinkling.

"Got used to having them around. Like the gel's music. They should stay here," he finished gruffly.

"Well, they are unlikely to move any time soon, because of all that must be done to ready the house. We will see exactly what that is and set it in motion—" She frowned slightly. "—even if they do not end up leasing Woodbine. Now the notion is in my head it seems a good one. I do not know why I have not thought of it before. Someone should be living in it. It isn't good for a house to sit empty."

William rattled his newspaper in irritation and nodded. "I was remiss—but usually there is some relative who needs a roof over their heads, and when my widowed sister died, I left it for the next indigent family member—and then forgot it when none appeared."

"I am not blaming you, Uncle. But when I think over our family tree, I cannot remember a soul who is likely to want it anytime in the near future, so I will see to doing what must be done to rent it. Very likely to the Morgan women in the first instance."

She went from her uncle to the kitchen where she ordered a large picnic packed and transported to Woodbine and then, finally, rejoined the others. They soon sorted themselves out for the short journey to the dower house.

An hour later, her hand on the long-unpolished banister, Babs returned to the ground floor of Woodbine House. Looking around, she said, "I admit to being pleasantly surprised. The house is in better order than I thought possible. Still there is much to do before anyone can live here. The gardeners must cut back those vines hiding the windows from the sun and trim the overgrown shrubbery. We must have the painters in and the furniture inventoried and replaced where necessary. Lady Dewsbury-Morgan, will you and Lady Morgan put your heads together and make decisions concerning colors and fabrics for new drapery and—" She toed the faded runner going from the front door all the way through the house to a back door. "—worn carpets such as this one?"

"When I suggested it, I didn't think it would be such an expense to you," said Lady Dewsbury-Morgan. "Perhaps . . ."

"No," interrupted Babs, smiling. "Now you've put it

into my mind, I mean to lease the place, so the work must be done. If *you* want the house, then you should have it done up just as you would like. What is the matter, Lady Morgan?"

"But Sir George always makes such decisions. Sir George says . . ."

James put his hand on her shoulder and she looked up.

"Sir George made and wanted. Not makes and says," he said softly. "You can have things just the way *you* would like."

"I forgot," she said, her eyes glowing. Once again color came into Lady Morgan's cheeks. This time it was from anticipated pleasure. "I didn't think."

"There is much which has changed for you and it will take time for you to accept it all," he said and turned to Quentin who was talking to Louisa Maria who, her head bent, listened to him. James moved to join them and found Quentin describing a particular concert of ancient music, which he had attended that spring season.

"I wish I had not missed it," said James, when the younger man ceased speaking. "I used to attend, back before I went to India, but I was so newly home and had so much to see to, that I did not think of it. You will enjoy the concerts when next you go to London for a season, Miss Morgan," he said.

Sudden alarm filled her eyes.

"You must not worry about joining in another season," said Quentin earnestly. "We will see that you do not feel harassed and will make certain that you enjoy it. It will be quite different from your last season. You will have friends to watch out for you."

She smiled gratefully but looked back to James for reassurance.

"Yes, of course. You need only enjoy yourself." James wished he'd not mentioned the season, which had, obviously, alarmed her. He changed the subject. "Do you care for gardening?" he asked. "Shall we explore and see what remains of Woodbine's flower beds?"

The three of them left by the back door and Calder, standing near to Babs, watched them go. He told himself he should join them and keep an eye on his interests, but he had just mentioned the builder he'd met at James Ruthven's house, and how good he seemed to be. He'd recommended that Babs hire him for the work here and could hardly, with politeness, abandon the discussion that ensued.

"I believe it is still several months before Ruthven Hall is returned to what it was," said Babs pensively. "I cannot wait so long."

"The man might hire more workmen and then over-see both sites," suggested Calder. "They are not so far apart it would be impossible."

Babs nodded. "A possibility. I know James hunted out the very best and I *would* like to profit by his efforts. I will speak to him. Now, Lady Dewsbury-Morgan, Lady Morgan, shall we begin again and discuss what must be done? Calder, will you act as our scribe and take notes?" She handed him a tablet and pencil before he could say no and then turned into the main salon. "Now, in here . . ."

Several hours later, they had picnicked and were about to go their separate ways when a Blackstock groom found them. He handed Calder a missive and, stoically, stared into the far distance while it was read.

Calder sighed. "I suppose I should have guessed it," he said.

"What is it?" asked Quentin, hearing a morose note in his cousin's voice.

Babs, who had not felt she could ask, very nearly clapped her hands in appreciation that Quentin had done so for her.

"It is Father. He arrived unexpectedly and is angry I am not there to greet him."

"But how could you know to be there when we had no word he was coming?"

Lord Calder's expression lightened. "Quentin," he said in teasing tone, "how can you suggest anything so logical? You know that sort of argument will not interfere with his sense of irritation. We'd better go. Or," he amended, "I, at least, must go. It has been a very pleasant afternoon, Miss Ruthven," he said and turned to speak to Louisa Maria, but discovered she had disappeared.

"In the carriage," muttered Babs. She wondered at the illogical irritation she felt when he turned from her to Louisa Maria.

"Tell her that I will see her when I can," he said loudly enough that the girl very likely heard for herself. He mounted, took another look at the carriage, and then down at Babs. "I really did enjoy myself—much to my surprise!" He grinned before reining his mount around and trotting down the drive—

—*Which needs a great deal of gravel and smoothing*, thought Calder, *and me without the notebook!*

"He enjoyed following us around and taking down what we said?" asked Lady Morgan who had eavesdropped on Calder's leavetaking. "How strange."

"Why?" asked Babs.

"He is a man. He should enjoy giving orders to be written down."

"Perhaps," said Babs, wondering *exactly* what Lord Calder had enjoyed. She recalled the banter between them, the laughter, the suggestions made in jest and others made seriously. It *had* been enjoyable. All of it. "Whatever *his* reason, I enjoyed it as well. Did not you?" she asked, suddenly turning a sharp gaze on her ladyship.

Lady Morgan looked surprised. "Why, yes! Now you point it out, I see I enjoyed myself a great deal."

The surprised look disappeared and a thoughtful look

replaced it. Babs hoped Louisa's mother was beginning to realize that her world no longer revolved around Sir George.

That evening, James listened to the two older Morgan women discuss the decisions made concerning the dower house. After a short time, he cleared his throat. "It all sounds delightful. Light and airy and very well thought out, though you had very little time in which to do it."

"It will take far longer to choose fabrics—finding the exact colors and patterns, you know—for the window hangings and to re-cover the furniture," said Lady Morgan, her face showing more animation than he'd ever seen. "The chair seats in the dining room are in terrible condition and we can embroider proper covers for them once we are settled there, but in the meantime, they must have new. There isn't a decent bedcover in the house, I fear . . . oh so many things we must do."

James cleared his throat once again. "I wonder," he began tentatively, "if I might impose on some of your time. The inside of my house is ready for the painters. I wonder if you ladies might go over the rooms and make the same sort of decisions for me. I very much like what you plan for Woodbine and would appreciate it if you would give my home the same touch."

Lady Morgan's eyes widened much as her daughter's did when her emotions, either bad or good, had been touched, but Lady Dewsbury-Morgan shook her head. "You don't want me. It was Anna's doing. I never knew she had such good taste. George, of course, didn't approve of a woman having ideas, so I suppose my ignorance is not surprising."

"Then, Lady Morgan, would you drive over with me tomorrow and do what it appears you do so well?"

"But . . ."

"What is it?" he asked gently, when she didn't go on.

"But today was for us. I mean we didn't have to please anyone . . ."

"You didn't have to please some man," he said, putting into words what Lady Morgan could not bring herself to say. He nodded. "But I *like* what you've planned. I believe, if you were to use the same excellent taste in decorating my home, that I would like it just as well. Your idea for painting a bright flower-filled garden on the breakfast room wall, for instance. With the light yellow paint you've recommended for the other walls and white for the woodwork and ceiling—why, it will be light and cheery all year round. It is an excellent notion."

"I once suggested it for our London house and Sir George thought it a stupid idea," said Lady Morgan in a small voice.

"George," said Lady Dewsbury-Morgan, her voice dry as dust, "didn't think of it himself so of course it was stupid. He really did give you a poor opinion of yourself, did he not? I am sorry, Anna, that I took the easy road and did not interfere."

"You *don't* think it a stupid idea?" Anna asked, voicing the question in such a tentative, hopeful manner that James grinned. She immediately looked abashed.

"Don't look that way," he said quickly. "I have already said I like it. I do. It is a brilliant notion. We will find a mural painter who can paint us our gardens, one for me and one for you at Woodbine. My builder will know a good man for the job." When Lady Morgan brightened, he added, coaxingly, "Will you come tell me what else should be done?"

Instantly, she looked worried.

"I believe I will approve whatever you suggest, but I assure you that if I do not I will not berate you but will merely ask that you think up another notion."

She eyed him. Finally, lowering her gaze, she drew in a deep breath, and nodded.

"Excellent. We will go tomorrow, unless you have other plans? Perhaps Louisa Maria will like to come as well. In fact, we can ask everyone and see who would enjoy the drive and another picnic—they can wander about while you and I do our work."

Just then William Ruthven came in and, rather gruffly, asked if perhaps they might have some music before the evening ended and everyone moved to the music room where Louisa Maria and James played several duets and, when it was discovered that William played the pianoforte, they ended the evening standing around it, singing ballads.

"Well," said William, closing the instrument, "that has been quite delightful. Babs, I apologize for suggesting to you that it was not a good idea filling your house with strangers. These particular strangers—" He smiled at the Morgan ladies. "—have been a great boon to us. Good evening," he added, and quietly left them staring after him in some amazement.

"Well," said Babs.

"Yes?" James.

She looked about her, saw Lady Dewsbury-Morgan's wryly raised brow, saw that Lady Morgan looked flustered, saw that Louisa Maria was fussing with the music and paying no attention, and turned back to James. "I have never before heard Uncle William apologize. For anything!"

Lady Dewsbury-Morgan nodded. "He is of the old school which was trained up so that one was not to admit to making mistakes. One ignored them or, if one could not, blustered one's way through, or, if it were *that* sort of thing, fought a duel. I too was surprised to hear him, but then, perhaps it was more an exceedingly graceful *compliment* than an *apology.*"

Babs chuckled. "I believe you have hit the nail quite firmly on its head, my lady. James, were you aware that Uncle William played so well?"

"He played far better when he was younger. Very likely you do not recall it, because I think he had pretty well given it up before I left for India. I think—" He looked thoughtful. "—that was when his hands began to grow a trifle arthritic, he could not bear it that he could no longer play as he once did. His joints, you know, began bothering him a very long time ago."

"I have never known him when he was not suffering from aches and pains," said Babs, slowly. "He never complains, but one knows . . ."

Lady Dewsbury-Morgan nodded. "I know because I've my own pains with which I deal. On days when I ache the worst, I notice Mr. Ruthven does very little, and holds himself in that careful way that one does when one hurts."

"I will make him up one of my tisanes as I do for you when you are most achey," suggested Lady Morgan, surprising everyone that she dared to make such a decision all by herself. "We will see if it helps him."

And that ended what had turned out to be a very pleasant day and evening.

The evening spent by those at Blackstock Manor was less pleasant. Lord Amrington was not so uncontrolled that he lit into his son the moment Calder appeared, but his lowered brows and growling tone made clear his irritation.

Lord Calder was very near to losing his own temper before dinner ended and the three men were left at the table with the port going round. Her ladyship's ramshackle butler caustically suggested that the three not come to blows, and that they were *not* to break her ladyship's best crystal since it was the last in the house, and then he left the room.

"That man . . . !"

"Yes, but he is good for a laugh now and then, Uncle Adam, and since everyone knows him, no one pays attention to his oddity."

"I do," said Lord Amrington, glowering. "He belongs in the stables."

"I believe," said Matthew pensively, "that that is where he came from."

Amrington blinked. Then barked a laugh. "Yes, now you say it, I see it is just the sort of thing your aunt would do." He sobered, the glower returning. "Which is irrelevant. You, my boy, will explain yourself."

Calder sighed, glanced at Quentin, and then down at his glass. "I do not see what needs explaining. My chosen bride wants nothing to do with me. I'll have no other. What is so difficult about that?"

"Nonsense, that's what it is. All nonsense. Why you ever chose that namby-pamby little nobody I never understood. No countenance. No intellect. Nothing at all to recommend her—not even a particularly good body, if that is the sort of thing to draw you." His lordship's glower turned to a scowl. "What is more, none of that is relevant. You *must* marry. You must provide an heir. *At once.*"

"I believe it still requires the usual nine months, Uncle Adam," said Quentin in a misguided attempt to draw the man's fire from his cousin.

"Then, the sooner he begins the better," retorted Amrington. "The heiress sounds an excellent choice. For once I agree without reserve with your aunt. Tomorrow you will drive me over to meet the chit and, assuming she is as advertised, I will open discussions with her guardian."

"You will do nothing of the sort," said Matthew, rising to his feet.

"Will I not?" asked his lordship, a dangerous note in his overly silky voice.

For once, Calder stood firm. "You will not embarrass Miss Ruthven. She is beyond the age where you can arrange a marriage between us without her permission. For that matter, so am I. Besides, she has only recently escaped an arranged marriage. Do you think she will, willingly, enter into another?"

"Not a young thing?" asked Amrington, alarmed. "Your aunt didn't mention she was on the shelf. I am certain she did not."

"She is, I believe, in her mid-twenties."

His lordship relaxed. "Not too old, then. She can bear you half a dozen brats before she puts a stop to such things."

Calder blinked. He turned to Quentin and found his cousin staring at him. "Er . . . puts a stop to . . . ?" he asked, curious.

"You don't think women of our status are willing to go on bearing children forever, do you? Your mother stopped after the third. Wouldn't allow me near her bed in the usual way of things. Not unusual, you know," he added, a trifle embarrassed, when the cousins, the both of them, stared at him. "Why," he blustered, "do you think so many men set up those cozy little houses in the suburbs!"

Lord Calder, for the first time, wondered if his mother had had some reason for her tantrums. Neither cousin could turn his interested gaze from his lordship.

"Not that we didn't, er—" Red spots colored his lordship's cheekbones. "—have our moments, of course. Just not the, er, normal sort of moments," he said, a trifle defensively. When Calder continued to stare, he cleared his throat. "Not proper, discussing such things with you. Your *mother*, after all!"

"*Three* children?" asked Quentin, again attempting to change the charged atmosphere between father and son. "Apologies, my lord, if it is painful, but . . ."

"Not painful. Didn't *know* about it until after she lost the third one. You would have been about two years old, I think," he said, turning to Calder. "She never recovered from that loss," he added, staring across the room at a still-life painting of dead fowl and a rabbit laid on a table with fall vegetables. "Never again was she the lighthearted gel I married. Now there was a *real* woman for you," he added, musingly, "lively and awake on every suit. Ready for a lark no matter when or where." He sighed. "Miss her. Still, after all these years, I miss her." He poured himself another glass of port. "Really do miss that woman," he said dreamily and fell into a brown study, staring into his glass in a moody manner that was new to the cousins.

Matthew caught Quentin's eye and jerked his head toward the hall. Quentin nodded. Carefully, they rose to their feet. Without haste, they moved toward the door. They had it open when his lordship spoke again.

"'Tisn't the end of this discussion, you know," he said gruffly and tossed back his port, reaching for the decanter even before he set down his glass.

The cousins froze, but when nothing more was said, they made their escape.

"He still misses her?" asked Calder when they were well down the hall and wouldn't be overheard.

"That's what he said."

"But how can he? She was a shrew. A termagant. Wild and loud and . . . and *nasty.*"

Quentin frowned. "You know, Matt, you weren't all that old when she died. What? Ten or so?"

"Almost twelve. Why?"

"Well, how much did you have to do with them? With your parents? I mean, you were in the nursery and then the schoolroom and then we were nine and sent off to school . . ."

Calder frowned. "You would suggest that perhaps I've a distorted view of their life together?"

"Just a thought."

"My nurse used to, quite literally, shake in her shoes when Mother went off on one of her tears."

"Which, very likely, you then believed the proper response to your mother's ripping up at your father?"

Calder's thick brows drew closer together. "You are suggesting that my father did not feel that way about her raving?"

"Well, unless I misunderstood, it sounded as if he and she enjoyed the making-up part, so isn't it likely they enjoyed the battle preceding the making-up?" Quentin frowned slightly and spoke his thoughts as they occurred to him. "After losing that baby," he mused, "it is possible, is it not, that she only allowed him to make love to her when she was so riled she lost rational control? That perhaps she . . . perhaps she got angry so she could, without feeling guilty, forget her decision not to have more children?"

Calder looked still more thoughtful and Quentin decided he'd said enough. Hopefully not *more* than enough. It was, after all, not a subject the two of them *should* discuss. They entered the billiards room where they found their aunt knocking the balls around the table and waiting, anxiously, for them to appear so they could have their usual evening game—or two or three.

"Afraid you'd be stuck for hours with your father," she said. "He looked ready for the lecture of the century when I left you to your port like a *proper*—" She rolled her eyes. "—lady should do."

Calder waved away her comment. "Aunt Hermie, what do you remember of my mother?"

Lady Hermione Blackstock straightened and set the end of her cue on the floor. "My sister was wonderful, Calder. You didn't know her when she was herself. She lost . . ." She eyed the cousins, obviously debating whether to speak of something that was usually not mentioned between women and men.

Calder needed information and was unwilling to allow her to use propriety as an excuse to avoid giving it. "She lost a child."

Her ladyship nodded. "It was a girl. She'd wanted a girl, you know, having provided the usual heir and spare. Losing the child . . . well—" Brows similar to Calder's but less thick drew tightly together. "—I think she never got over it. It changed her . . ."

"Changed her. Turned her into a shrew?" asked Calder bluntly.

"What? Oh, no. Whatever gave you that notion?"

Calder drew in a deep breath, wondering where to begin.

"You think because she and your father used to have the most marvelous arguments that your mother was a *shrew?*" Lady Blackstock glared—and, given the family brows, her glares were quite effective. "Nonsense. They loved to argue. They would make up things about which to argue."

"Are you saying they *always* argued? I mean from the very beginning of their marriage?"

"From before their marriage," said Lady Blackstock and chuckled. "They would go at it hammer and tongs and the space around them would clear, leaving them practically nose-to-nose once they really got at it." The chuckle was more a laugh this time. "Everyone predicted they'd eventually come to blows, but they never did. One would say something to make the other laugh and then they'd go off arm in arm." She spoke with a touch of suggestion then. "Looking for privacy, *I* always thought. They'd get that look, you know."

Calder pokered up. Discussing his parent's relationship with his aunt was more than he could manage.

Lady Blackstock, noticing, laughed huge guffaws that shook her frame. "Well, enough said, I suppose. The younger generation is such a mealy-mouthed bunch of whey-faced prudes! Do let us play!"

So they played and were eventually joined by Lord Amrington. "Ha! Still can't make a two-corner shot," he said, watching Lady Blackstock.

"Neither can you," her ladyship retorted. "Can you?" she finished, rather spoiling it.

He waved the glass he carried, slopping a little of the dark red wine. "I can do it in my sleep. Here, Calder, give me that cue. Time I showed you youngsters how to do the thing."

He and his son exchanged what they held and Calder absent-mindedly sipped his father's port as he watched his father clear the table.

Something else I didn't know about my father? he asked himself.

Eleven

The next morning, Matthew strolled into the breakfast room hoping for peace and quiet while he broke his fast. Unfortunately, he found his father there, nursing a large cup of coffee. The older man tipped his head up, stared bleary-eyed at his son, and then closed his eyes as he drew in a long careful breath.

"Bad head?" whispered Matthew.

His father winced. "Want to talk to you," he said. His voice was rather whispery as well. It was nevertheless quite firm.

Feeling sympathy for his father's condition after the previous evening's over-indulgence, Matt suggested, "Maybe later? When you aren't, er, suffering?"

"Can't wait. It's about Alfred."

"Alfred . . . Woodward?"

"Of course Alfred Woodward," said his father testily . . . and then winced. Lowering his voice, he spoke more calmly. "Heir presumptive."

"Alfred! But I thought Quentin . . ." Matthew considered the family tree. "Oh."

"Precisely. *Now* do you see why I insist you wed and fill your nursery? When there were both you and your brother—"

It was Matthew's turn to wince. He disliked remembering that his beloved brother was dead.

"—then it didn't matter, but now . . ."

"I see." Matthew stared out the window behind his father's back.

The older man, in consideration of his throbbing head, had sat so that the sunlight did not fall on his face. But the coffee was having the desired effect, and he was beginning to feel more the thing. "I apologize for last night. I don't often overindulge, but thoughts of your mother . . . well, as I said, I still miss her. I have never met another woman who could stand up to me, who would give as good as she got, who could argue the devil out of hell if need be. She was a wonderful woman, Matt," he finished so simply his son was forced to accept that his own memories were distorted. "I would like it if you could take the time to find your other half, but I cannot allow it. You must wed."

"Alfred," said Matthew and grimaced. "I see. That would never do."

"His hopes were roused by your brother's death, you know. He came to me and insisted I give him an allowance and, frankly, I could see no way around it. Heir presumptive, you know?"

"That . . . *here-and-therian?* We are supporting his . . . ?"

"Vices? That is the best word for it, I think. Yes, we are—although not to any great degree. I managed to keep *his* allowance to a modicum of what *you* received in the same position."

Matthew sighed. "Why did you not tell me this sooner?"

"In the first place, I assumed you knew. Secondly, I avoid discussing that particular blot on the family escutcheon as much as possible. Besides, you had found your little Louisa Maria and, although I didn't like the stable, the mare appeared healthy enough . . ."

"Father!"

Lord Amrington chuckled and then winced. His head was better but not to *that* degree! "There is another point on which your aunt and I agree. Yours, my boy, is a namby-pamby generation that refuses to look a thing straight in the eye. Refuses to call a spade an old fashioned shovel!"

"Nevertheless, to refer to Louisa as a brood mare which is what you mean—it is outside of enough!"

"We will not argue. Instead, promise me you will approach Miss Ruthven and persuade her to wed you."

"She is aware that I am still pursuing Miss Morgan. How am I to twist in the wind and, abruptly, suggest she and I wed?"

"I haven't a notion. If you had done as your aunt suggested and made a dead set at Miss Ruthven, you wouldn't have this problem, would you?"

Matthew's lips compressed and he looked more than a little grim. "I don't see my way. How to instantly change horses in midstream as it were."

"Change brood mares in midstream?" suggested his father, hiding a grin.

Matt felt his ears heat. "Very well. I see that I too do not choose my words well and, at times, am not so delicate as I would wish."

"Just as well you can occasionally slip. You frighten me, you are so perfect."

"Perfect!" Matthew cast his father a look of disgust. "Nonsense."

"Oh yes. Your brother used to say that you were born to be earl and that was another reason I should allow him to do as he wished me to do."

Matt looked at him questioningly.

"Buy him his promotions as opportunity arose, of course," he finished.

"I looked up to him. In my eyes he was the perfect one," said Matthew quietly.

"You were both good boys, but Henry George was army-mad from the cradle." Amrington slapped his hands flat on the table—and winced. "Enough of that.

He is gone and you are my heir and you must accept the fact that you've responsibilities you never dreamed to have. You *will* marry, Matthew, and you will do it soon. Promise me."

"You must give me a little time." He grimaced at the image that came to mind—given the preceding conversation—and then said it anyway: "If I must change saddles from one mare to the other, it cannot be done on the instant."

"But you will begin? Today?"

"Why are you so desperate? Surely a few weeks or months will make no difference?"

Amrington's gaze dropped to his cup and then rose to meet his son's. "Alfred has been gloating. He claims that you lost your heart to the little Louisa and when she would not have you, you claimed you would have no other."

Matthew pursed his lips, frowning. "I may have made such stupid claims in my cups, but no one believed me . . ."

"Except Alfred."

"You mean," asked Matthew, his brows drawn in a bar, "that he has begun borrowing against his future title?"

"I fear it. My solicitor is looking into the situation. And if he is, then the only way to stop him is for you to wed and produce an heir. Preferably three or four."

"If Alfred dies," asked Matthew, "who follows him?"

"His younger brother at the moment, but Alfred is threatening to wed and get himself an heir."

"His brother is in the army and may not survive, but we cannot have a son of Alfred's in line for the title," mused Matthew, frowning. "I fear there is a weakness in that branch of the family."

"Comes from his mother's grandmother. The woman had to be restrained the last decade of her life. Her daughter wasn't exactly all there either, and Alfred's mother! You will recall how impossible that one was."

"Isn't she the one who ran off with the groom and, eventually, died in Venice?"

"In a bordello, yes."

"She did that to herself."

"Yes, but it was uncontrolled self-indulgence that led to her downfall and she passed that on to her son. Alfred . . ."

"Alfred wants his own way," interrupted Matt, "and he wants it now if not yesterday. I remember that in him. He wasn't so very much older than Henry, you will recall."

"I should have wed at a younger age. I should have had more sons." Amrington pounded the table with his fists.

"Hush. Alfred is merely venal, not evil. It is not as if he will attempt to rid the world of me or my heirs." Matthew sighed. "But there is no way out—" He grinned a suddenly mischievous grin. "—unless *you* will find yourself a young wife and produce those sons of which you just spoke?"

His father grinned. "And don't you think I couldn't!" he said . . . but immediately sobered. "Thing is, since your mother . . ." He drew in a deep breath and let it out slowly, looking morose again. "You go get yourself a wife, son. No ifs, ands, or buts. You must wed, and sooner rather than later." His lordship pushed up from the table and stared at his son who, finally, nodded. "I think I will go for a ride and see if that will clear my head. . . ." He wandered from the room, leaving his son to stare at his empty place.

Quentin arrived before his cousin had moved to choose his breakfast and he wondered at the grim tightening of Matt's jaw line. "What is it?" he asked as he served himself from the kippers and then added deviled kidneys to his plate. "Shall I ring for fresh toast?" he asked before Matthew could reply.

"Ring. Not that it will do any good. Our aunt's house is more than a trifle disorganized."

"What a delightfully tactful way of putting it. Are you not eating?"

Matthew rose, filled his plate, and carried it back to the table. "Father was already here when I arrived."

"Still insisting you wed Miss Ruthven?"

"I thought *you* were now heir presumptive," said Matthew, not responding to the question.

"What? Never. Alfred . . ."

"So my father pointed out."

"You knew that."

"No, I didn't. At least I never thought about it. He's so much older than we are and so dissolute that I don't think of him at all if I can help it. I was sure you were in line after me."

"No, Alfred is. Aha! So *he's* why your father wants you wed."

"Exactly."

"You'll have to admit that that makes sense."

"Unfortunately."

Quentin bit back a laugh. "You are for it, Matt."

"Yes."

"Must you sound quite so morose?"

"It's all too much all at once, Quentin. Learning that my father loved Mother, that perhaps she wasn't what I thought her, but merely loud and argumentative because that's the way the two of them liked it . . . I cannot take it in. I still want my nice, placid, undemanding little Louisa . . . and—" He sighed. "—I have about accepted that I cannot have her."

"Miss Ruthven is really a very nice lady, you know. If you could just stop looking at her through distorting glasses."

"Distorting glasses?"

"You have seen them. Those lenses that make things look odd and different from reality."

Matthew smiled but it was weak. He looked at his plate and shoved it away. "I'm not hungry. I think I'll go riding. . . . Coming?"

"Not this morning. Aunt asked if I would help her with plans for an extension to her stables—and don't laugh," he added, although Matt showed no signs of doing so. "I do know a bit about proper stabling. My father is very nearly as horse-mad as your aunt, as you know."

Lord Calder's canter about the countryside brought him, finally, to the path along the river that Miss Ruthven's uncle, along with a few other local landowners, had had dredged for barge traffic. He watched a load of coal. A workhorse towed it, a boy, barely big enough to hold the lead rope, tugging it occasionally to keep the huge animal in motion.

Matt shook his head at the sight. A child that age— what was he? Four? Five?—Working all day every day, rain or shine. The imp grinned up at him as he approached and he realized the boy was rosy cheeked, and not mistreated in any way, which might not have been the case if he'd worked for a harsh master who insisted on a long day's work for little food and nothing but rags to wear.

Lord Calder dug out a coin and tossed it to the boy who surprised himself as much as he did his lordship by catching it. The lad looked at it, looked up at Calder with wide eyes, and then, quickly, shoved the coin away somewhere within his clothing. He bobbed his head, skipped a bit, grinned again, and walked on.

Lord Calder shook his head that sixpence could make

the child so happy, watched him go around the bend, and then continued on up the path. He had about reached the place where he'd once found Miss Ruthven fishing . . . and there she was again, although she was not fishing.

"The barge interfere with your sport?" he asked.

"Yes. Not that there was much sport in any case. It is too hot today and the fish, more sensible than we, are keeping cool in some deep dark pool. They will wait for the sun to go down before coming out for food."

Lord Calder looked around. "Are you all alone? Not even a groom?" he asked and couldn't quite keep the disapproval from his voice.

"This is my land. Who would bother me?"

"Have you any notion of the sort of riffraff who travel on barges like the one that just passed?" he asked a trifle gruffly.

"I know old Neddy. Hid on his barge years and years ago—running away, you know—and he not only wouldn't let me, but tied up and took me back to Merrywood." She glanced around. "Besides, I do have a groom." She pointed to where a man slept, curled up, under a tree not too far distant.

He chuckled. "You always have an answer, do you not?"

"I try," she said, giving him a quick sideways glance.

"You know my father has come to stay with us at my aunt's," he said after a moment.

"You don't sound too happy about it," she said.

He was surprised to hear something very like a wistful note in her tone and glanced at her. "Should I be?"

"I never knew my parents. Either of them. My mother died not long after I was born and my father in a riding accident not long before. I have often wished I were not an orphan so I suppose I resent it when those who do have parents do not appreciate them."

"We rub along pretty well most of the time," said Lord Calder.

"Rub along."

He grinned but wryly. "I heard myself say that and knew you'd not like it. My father isn't one of them, but I know people who would be better off *without* the parents to whom they are supposed to give respect, if not love."

She nodded. "I am not irrational in this respect, because I too know some people who should never have attempted to rear children, but for the most part . . . I think I've reason to be jealous?"

He smiled. "Perhaps."

They were quiet for a time and then, feeling nervous, Calder asked Miss Ruthven if she had plans for the rest of the day.

"Plans? Not particularly. I suppose I should return home soon now, but only because it seems the proper thing to do. Why?"

"I wondered if you would care to come to the manor to meet my father."

Babs hesitated. She was curious about the man who was forcing Lord Calder to honor an engagement he should never have contracted. She did have her groom along, so propriety was not a problem. Still she hesitated.

Finally she spoke slowly. "Why do I not return home and send invitations to Lady Blackstock asking all of you to dinner tomorrow evening? We were forced to cancel the last party—Sir George's death, you know—and this would not be a *formal* arrangement, but merely the two families, and perhaps the vicar and his wife. I feel Louisa Maria needs distraction and, if for no other reason, Lady Morgan must *not* be allowed to fall into the doldrums. According to Lady Dewsbury-Morgan, Anna is beginning to return to the sort of woman she was before her marriage, but every so often she develops a fit of propriety that is most alarming and, occasionally, has gone so far as to insist she must go into deep mourning for that awful man."

"You feel responsible for keeping her from succumbing to propriety?" he asked, tongue-in-cheek.

"That sort of false adherence to strict rules is so hypocritical. Or do you not agree?" she challenged.

"You'll get no argument from me," he said peacefully. "Not on that subject. Miss Ruthven . . ."

When his impulsive words led to no more, she tipped her head, looking at him curiously. "Yes?" she encouraged.

"Miss Ruthven . . . do you truly think it a mistake for me to continue thinking of Miss Morgan as my fiancée?"

"Yes," she promptly responded. "She doesn't want to marry you, my lord," said Babs quietly, wondering where this conversation might lead.

He nodded. "I have known it for some time. I have admitted it to myself, but I have felt such a fool, inadequate, a failure—"

"Nonsense!"

"—that she is so frightened of me. . . ." He paused, then tipped his head. "Nonsense?" he asked.

"Of course it is nonsense. Her feelings have nothing whatsoever to do with you. She is a little mouse because her father made her a mouse. That she found enough courage to *refuse* to wed you is the miracle."

Lord Calder clasped his hands behind his back and twiddled his crop. "I must wed," he said.

"Is there some special reason?" she asked, her heart beating rapidly.

He glanced at her as if he'd forgotten her and then nodded. He explained about his brother, about Alfred, about his father's fears. . . . "So you see," he finished, "it is imperative that I wed and that I not put it off."

"You were so deeply in love with Louisa Maria that you find the notion painful?" she asked a trifle hesitantly.

"What? Love? Oh no. I was *very* fond of Miss Morgan," he said, as he'd said to her before, and then continued slowly—as if thinking as he spoke. "I don't believe I've ever been deeply in love, not as the poets describe it. Perhaps I never will be." He sighed. "I don't seem to have the knack for it."

She stared at him for a long moment and then said, "So there is no real obstacle to finding another bride, is there?"

"A more difficult prospect than you might think." A muscle jumped in his jaw. "Would *you* be willing to accept a man whose bride jilted him at the altar?"

"When the bride was Louisa Maria?" Babs chuckled. "Why would I not?"

He turned to her, gently grasped her shoulders. "Then would you? Would you think about accepting my suit and becoming my wife?" Before she could respond by more than widened eyes, he continued. "Do not answer me now. You need to think about it. I am not a bad catch. I can give you a review of my current situation and prospects, and I think you already know something about me just from the times we have been in company together, so you can, perhaps, make a rational decision about whether we would suit . . ." He trailed off and stared over her head. Then he sighed. "I would do my best to be a good husband to you," he finished.

Babs had been about to turn him down flat, angry that he'd even suggest such a thing in such a way after the things they'd just been saying. Instead, listening to his hurried, rather nervous speech, she grew thoughtful and was, at the last, disarmed by his final comment and the wistful look that went with it.

"You are seriously proposing we wed?" she asked.

"Yes."

Again she hesitated. "I *should* say no. If I had any sense I *would* say no . . . but—"

Calder realized he was holding his breath.

"—I *will* think about it. Please do not mention that we've had this discussion, because there are questions I will have when I've formulated them properly and I see no reason why everyone should watch us come to a decision." She moved from under his hands and leaned to pick up her tackle. "I will send that invitation to your aunt, my lord. We cannot speak of this in company, of course, but perhaps the following day we may meet again? Here?"

"I will be as patient as a man may be while waiting to hear his fate," said Calder, bowing.

Babs, once again wishing she had his easy way with words, curtsied, turned, and walked over to nudge her groom. They were part-way home when she spoke to the man. "You were not asleep, were you?"

"No." After a short silence the groom asked, "You going to marry that man-milliner?"

"John," she scolded, "Lord Calder is not a fop! Not by a long shot! You think so because you've never before seen London tailoring." She frowned. "As to marrying him . . . I might. John," she added, speaking sharply, "I do not want talk of this bruited about. Can you, er, dub your mummer?" she asked, quoting a phrase she'd once heard her coachman use to a young groom who talked constantly. "Can you keep this a secret from absolutely *everyone?*" she added, wanted to be certain he understood.

"I won't go blabbing. You can order me to go with you the next time you ride out so you don't have someone up beside you who *will.*"

"Thank you, John. I do not wish Lord Calder embarrassed if I decide against him—or, for that matter, find *myself* red in the face. If I say him nay it would be better for both of us if it is never known he asked me."

"Pretty lukewarm, I'd say," said John, conversationally. "Don't think he'd be hurt."

She chuckled. "Yes. I suspect that is one of the things bothering me. On the other hand, weddings in the *ton* are often more cold-blooded than they are among the other orders of society."

"Such a marriage isn't for you, Miss Babs," he said loyally. "You hold out for a man who will treat you right."

"I don't think his lordship would beat me or anything like that," she offered.

He cast her a sharp look. "'Course he wouldn't, but that isn't what I'm talkin' about," he finished a trifle mysteriously—at least from Babs' point of view.

But Babs was no longer interested in pursuing the conversation. It had occurred to her once again that she *wanted* to wed Lord Calder, which astounded her when, all too often, she had been uncertain she even liked the man. On the other hand, he was neither vicious nor so self-centered he never thought of others. Except where Louisa was concerned, he even seemed more sensible than many. But still—why did she think she'd like to wed him?

She didn't like the answer that popped into her head. *Of course I have not fallen in love with him,* she scolded herself. *Have I?* After a moment she answered that. *Yes, blast it, I have!"*

Instead of falling into despair as another woman might have done, Babs immediately set about planning ways and means of making Lord Calder fall just as deeply in love with her.

Twelve

Lord Amrington stared rudely at his hostess who, when Babs realized it, raised her chin to him and stared right back. Suddenly his mouth tightened in a repressed grin.

"You'll do," he said just loudly enough that Babs and no one else could hear.

"I wonder if I want to," retorted Babs, wondering if Lord Calder had discussed her with his father.

"Ha! A challenge."

"You like them?" When Amrington nodded, she asked, "Does Lord Calder like them as well?"

His lordship tipped his head. "Well, he has a bit of a reputation for taking on all comers when it comes to curricle racing. Has a team that has yet to be beaten. I'd say that involves challenges."

"And one day," she said in overly sweet tones, "his wife will find herself a widow all because he races?"

"Make up your mind, gel." Amrington scowled. It was not half so impressive as his son's scowl since his lordship's brows were neither so heavy nor so dark. "Either you want a man or you want a mouse. You can't have it both ways." His brow smoothed as he turned from her. "Lady Dewsbury-Morgan! How are you going on?"

The scowl Amrington lost took up residence in milder form on Babs' unlined forehead. She was wondering what she'd done or said to make the man think she wanted his son.

"What did my father say to you that upset you so?" asked Lord Calder, calling her attention away from the older man.

"Upset me? He didn't upset me. Merely offered me a thought which requires a bit of thinking."

"You'll not tell me what it is?"

Her mood lightened and her eyes twinkled. "No. I'll keep you wondering."

"Until tomorrow," he said softly and glanced around to see if anyone was listening to them.

"Or the next day," she said, also looking around. "Or the next. I'll not settle anything instantly when it is the whole of my life at stake." Her cousin walked by them and she raised her voice very slightly. "We have planned to present a program of music after dinner. Does your father like music?"

"He isn't fond of the sort of music the usual young lady produces for the entertainment of guests, but he will enjoy it when Miss Morgan plays." Even as he spoke for Mr. James Ruthven's benefit, Calder gestured in such a way as to suggest that his father's enjoyment of the evening was irrelevant. "Miss Ruthven," he continued more quietly once Mr. Ruthven was beyond hearing, "you will not keep me in suspense for long, will you?"

She widened her eyes, pretending surprise. "But is it important? I made sure you did not care too much, one way or the other."

"Nonsense. Of course I care." His lordship was surprised to discover that it was true. He *did* care. The notion was shocking. Until he understood it, he didn't wish to continue discussing it. "I notice," he said, grasping another topic, "that my cousin is speaking to Miss Morgan. I wonder what he has to say to her."

"They talk music, of course. Or rather he talks and she

communicates by gesture and expression. I have seen her mouthing words, but not aloud." Babs spoke a trifle pensively. "It is sad, is it not? You said her father said something there in the church. James thinks it did something to her mind. It took so much courage on her part to walk away from you when told she had no home and had never been allowed friends to whom she could turn."

"I will never understand why she did it."

"Despair."

"What?"

"She could not marry you—not fearing you as she did. The alternative was equally terrible, but did not include years and years of misery. She chose it and if her mother and grandmother had not found her . . ."

"She feared death less than she feared me," he murmured. "I *wish* I knew what I did to make her believe I was an ogre."

"As I have said before, you did nothing. Her father, on the other hand . . ."

"Yes, you have said that he was cruel to her. Evil, one might say."

"And then—" She cast him a mischievous glance from under her lashes. "—there are your eyebrows." She laughed lightly when the brows rose, a thick black bar above his eyes. "Yes. Exactly."

"My *eyebrows* convinced her I was a monster?"

"My dear Lord Calder, have you never stood before a mirror and seen what they can do? I assure you, they give *me* shivers when you frown, and I am not a little mouse afraid of my own shadow!"

He frowned and she gave a delighted shudder.

"Oh, yes," she said, her mouth barely under control, her lips twitching ever so slightly, as she attempted to remain serious. "Just like that."

"You are a minx," he said, grinning down at her.

"Am I? Perhaps you do not want a minx to wife," she

half-said, half-asked, a pensive expression underlining her words.

"I think I could bear it," he retorted.

"Good. Because," she continued in a tone so serious it rather surprised him, "I am the way I am and I will not change just to please you. If I accept you, you get the bad along with the good."

"I wonder what you consider the bad and if I would agree," he said, a querying note clear in his tone. But they were interrupted before she could frame a reply, the Ruthven butler announcing that dinner was served.

"About time," grumbled Lady Blackstock. "I'm truly sharp set. Not used to waiting this long for my dinner."

Only because he insisted, did she remember to take Mr. William Ruthven's arm and pace her exit from the salon to his slower steps.

"All nonsense," she blustered, when he teased her about her lapse. "All these rules! Do nothing but interfere in what a woman wants to do."

"Yes," said Mr. Ruthven, "but they do maintain a certain order to life. I know you would not," he added when he saw she was about to object, "allow your stables to be run in a haphazard fashion or your horses misbehave, so why allow one's own, er, stable to fall into disarray?"

She cast him a startled look and burst out laughing. "Didn't know you'd a sense of humor, Willy."

"You don't know very much about me at all," he murmured, wincing ever so slightly at the despised nickname.

She eyed him up over her shoulder as he seated her at his right hand before taking his place at the head of the table. "I know enough. *You don't hunt,*" said Lady Blackstock in her blunt, and in this case, accusing fashion.

"No." His brows drew in slightly. "I did. Years ago. But Babs doesn't like it and I hated upsetting her. So, I sold off my hunters and now ride only for pleasure. I heard," he added—

A trifle wistfully, she thought.

"—that, last season, you had several really remarkable runs. Until the wily old fox was finally cornered. After that the runs were nothing to speak of?"

"You heard correctly. I think, if I were Master of the Hunt, I'd have called off the hounds and let the creature go. He was truly a bold old dog of a fox. I admired him."

"Besides," said Mr. Ruthven, grinning ever so slightly, "you would then have had more good runs."

She laughed her overloud laugh. "There is that, of course!"

Talk was sprightly around the table, the food was good, and the company relaxed and even the men anticipated the good music to come. They did not sit for long over the port, but joined the others in the music room where Miss Morgan was nearly finished tuning the harp and Lady Blackstock just finishing her second glass of port—brought at her request by Babs' disapproving butler.

Her ladyship and Lord Calder were, actually, the only ones in the room who did not find the music exquisite. Neither had much of an ear for it and both were preoccupied with other things. Lady Blackstock worried that her favorite hack had thrown a splint and wanted to get home to check it before going to bed. Calder wondered just how Miss Ruthven would reply to his proposal—and planned how to change her mind if she said no . . . *and* wondered why he thought he'd bother. He didn't, after all, really wish to wed her.

Did he?

Of course not. He didn't wish to wed anyone. Still, if she said no, then *could* he change her mind?

What, he wondered, *would she do if I were to court her with flowers and trinkets, and play the cavalier? Would she like that? She is,* he decided, *a trifle stubborn, but surely that doesn't preclude a liking for trinkets and such?*

But stubborn . . . ? He suspected that if she said no, it

would be difficult to convince her her nay should become a yea.

His jaw firmed. *But I'll do it.*

Miss Ruthven was not yet aware of it, but she *would* become Lady Calder and before the summer ended. He mused about their nuptials as a livelier melody played in the background.

We will, he decided, *take a long wedding journey . . . to the Lake District perhaps.*

They could visit his friends. Quentin's recently discovered secret enjoyment of music was more understandable when Matt thought of his own secret love of good poetry, of the hours he spent scribbling verses that, occasionally, pleased him.

The Wordworths and the Coleridges, whom he had met as a student on a walking tour, and with whom he had since corresponded, would be welcoming. There would be delightful hours of discussion of literature and poetry . . . but there were other things to do. They could take out a boat on the lake and perhaps do a bit of fell walking and . . .

. . . and then of course there would be the nights . . .

When that thought registered, Lord Calder felt his ears heat and he cast a look around. He felt a great deal of relief that no one was looking his way—although he had the impression that Miss Ruthven had just turned away her head?

No. Surely not.

Besides, even if she *were* looking his way she could not know what thoughts had embarrassed him . . .

Still, perhaps it would be better to delay such musing until he returned to his own room at his aunt's. Which, not too much later, after Quentin and James had performed a final duet, was possible. In the confusion of leave-taking he had time for only a few words with Miss Ruthven and then the Blackstock party departed.

But he had verified that she'd not changed her mind and would meet him as planned.

Babs went to bed that night with an ache in her heart. Could she bear not to wed him? Bear to lose him? The answer to that was yes and that, although she would hurt for some time, she *would* recover.

Still . . . did she want to lose him? No. So, she *would* wed him.

And then what?

He didn't love her, so she must never allow him to know she loved him. The humiliation if he discovered it! Or, *worse,* the pity. No, she would be forced to keep silence on that subject and hope that he developed some affection for her. Enough, at least, that he would not look for it elsewhere!

That thought almost made her heart cease its beating. Or at least it felt that way. She knew men kept mistresses. It was no secret even from such as she who had no female relatives and only heard the gossip from the neighbor ladies when invited to work parties to sew shifts and shirts for the workhouse or to garden parties when someone had a particularly nice show of flowers and wished to exhibit them to all and sundry. The women talked and, by listening when she did not appear to do so, she had learned a great deal a young unmarried woman should not know . . .

. . . including the information that Sir Marcus and Lord Hammersmith, both local landowners, had longtime mistresses and illegitimate children tucked away where they bothered no one. Their wives appeared resigned—in fact, Lady Hammersmith actually seemed to approve, which Babs did not understand.

So. Could *she* bear it if Calder set himself up a mistress? The answer was a resounding no.

"Then I mustn't marry him," she murmured to the bedpost.

But if she did not . . . would she ever discover what those same women meant when they spoke of what happened between the sheets, some for it and some against, or how even those against it thought it was worth it when they could hold in their arms the infant that came from the pain and embarrassment of childbirth.

"I want a child. No, not merely a child, but *children*. And I can't have them if I do not wed."

Would having her children about her compensate for having a husband who did not love her? Her children would love her. She would like filling her nursery with a great number of children . . . oh, not the bearing of them, of course—not if what she'd overheard was true, although animals she'd observed giving birth did not seem to find it a great burden—but whatever the case, having children to raise and worry about and care for and teach and . . .

"Yes. I *will* wed him. I will have his children. And the children will be enough." She sighed. "They will have to be," she asked the bedpost, "will they not?"

Her mind would not settle. *Would* they be enough? Was there no way to teach a man to love one? Surely it could be done, but how did one go about it? She remembered the way her maid had flirted with the first footman, looking up at him and smiling at him—

"I can do that."

—and giggling . . .

"Giggle? No. Never. I do *not* giggle," she told the bedpost, speaking firmly, just as if it might contradict her. Her lips pressed together. There was no way she could manage a *giggle*.

But the rest?

The smiles and the sidelong looks and the banter? That she could do, could she not? So what else did one do to make a man love one?

"Dare I ask Lady Dewsbury-Morgan? She is a wise old woman . . . but did her husband love her? Did she love her husband?"

Babs was very nearly certain that theirs was not a love match but an arranged marriage and a not particularly happy one. So perhaps not her ladyship. She sighed since she hadn't a notion of any other she might ask. The few young female friends she had were all married and had moved away. It was not the sort of thing one could put into a letter . . . was it?

No it was not.

So. Was there anything she could dream up which she could do to make Lord Calder love her?

The bedpost was not particularly reassuring and she sighed, deciding she would just have to go on as she'd been doing, being herself. After all, it was she herself she wished him to love, was it not? He seemed to find her amusing on occasion and he seemed to enjoy their talks . . . So perhaps she must allow him to see more of who and what she was and then, if she were lucky, he would learn to love her . . .

And then she fell asleep—and dreamed of Lord Calder taking her into his arms and kissing her. It was the sort of dream she had never before experienced and, waking to find the dawn mellowing the darkness, she wondered what, exactly, his kisses would be like . . .

It occurred to her that, if she was to meet him later that morning, she had a great deal to do, and that it was a waste of time to wonder about his kisses since he would kiss her. Eventually.

But not today. She was not ready for such things. Not yet.

She was nearly dressed when a much-surprised maid tiptoed in to do the early morning chores normally accomplished before the room's occupant roused.

"That's all right, Milly. I'll be out of your way in a trice.

Do you think Cook can manage tea and bread and butter for me if I go down?"

"Oh yes, miss. The morning rolls are cooling and she has porridge but I don't think she's started Mr. William's kidneys or Mr. James' kippers. Might be a nice slice of ham if you be liking one . . ." When Babs headed for the door, the little maid gasped. "Oh, miss, should I go tell her you'll be in the breakfast room?"

"You do your chores, child. I know my way to the kitchen. I used to spend a great deal of time there when I was your age and somewhat older. Perhaps I will do the kippers so Cook can fix me a shirred egg!"

"Go on with you!" sputtered the maid, surprised into indiscretion.

"You think I could not?" Babs grinned. "I most certainly could! Should I?" She didn't, Cook having everything well in hand.

"An egg, perhaps? And a slice of ham and toast along with my tea. Why do I not eat right here at the kitchen table like I used to do and you can tell me if there is a problem about which I am unaware."

Before Cook had finished, Babs wished she had not offered to hear complaints. The new knife boy was impossible. Fat little Mary ate more than she managed to help fix for her mistress' table. The chimney sweep had not done a good job on the kitchen chimney and if they weren't careful they'd have a chimney fire,

". . . You just wait and see . . ."

And, finally, there was the new meat man. He was not supplying the best quality meat and he charged far more than the last man so why had they changed?

The last question was easily answered! "We changed," said Babs, "because you insisted the last man was cheating on the weights. But go back to him if you wish. Quality is more important than quantity. As to the chimney, why have you not called the sweep back to do the job properly? I can do nothing about Mary. She is your responsibility, but perhaps if she were not so unhappy, she would not eat so much, so perhaps you might first discover what it is that makes her unhappy all the time, and as to the knife boy . . .

Babs paused, considering the most proper manner of proceeding, then nodded.

". . . ask Logan to speak to him firmly. He is a male servant and therefore he is Logan's responsibility. Report to *Logan* that the lad does not behave. Is that *all*?"

"Only that the gardener says the birds got into the berries," said the cook, bridling that, even if no *words* were spoken to the point, Babs' tone had been a subtle reprimand, "and we'll not have nearly enough for winter preserves." Why had she been scolded for making complaints, when Mistress had asked?

"Hmm . . . Now *that* is a real problem. Maybe the gardener's boys could scout around the neighborhood for wild berries and bring home a couple of bucketsful. I will suggest it to him." She rose from the table. "The eggs were, as usual, perfect. I do not know how you manage to make them so very light and fluffy."

The cook grumbled about how it was not easy, but her mood obviously lightened at the compliment and Babs escaped, aware their meals would be up to Cook's usual high standard as a result of those few simple—but true— words of praise.

As she walked up to her office to bring the accounts up to date, she wondered if it were quite fair to know someone so well one could use their little quirks to manipulate them. But then, if one did not, how did one manage so many different people as one had in a household the size of theirs?

All such philosophical thoughts were put aside when she saw the pile of receipts and bills placed in separate piles at the side of her desk. She sighed, seated herself, and began the work that occupied a great deal of several mornings of each week. She had wanted to learn to manage her own affairs and she had. So now it was her responsibility and one she would not shirk—but there were times, she mused, that it would be very nice to pretend none of it existed and just go off and do as she pleased.

A sharp short laugh followed that last thought. Was that not what she had done when she'd run away? And see how that decision had worked out! James had not wished to wed her, so if she'd remained where she belonged, all would have been well and—she stared at the account book—her responsibilities would not have fallen onto others' shoulders.

She sighed at what had been an error of judgment on her part—but then it occurred to her that if she had *not* run away, she would not have met the Morgan ladies and that would have been something to regret, so perhaps she had not erred?

Lord Calder tethered his gelding on a long rope not far from the path along the stream. He had, as an excuse for going off alone, brought along his aunt's fishing tackle. He waited impatiently for Babs' arrival but finally, feeling some irrtation, decided she had forgotten or changed her mind or that she didn't wish to see him.

Irritation turned to a mild depression. He'd no desire to return to where his father would undoubtedly have another lecture ready to deliver concerning his duty to the title, so, choosing it at random, he tied a lure to his hook and began casting among the shadows along the far bank.

He heard hooves approaching just as a monster fish took the bait so he could not look around to see who came. Instead, he was fully occupied with bringing the creature near his net. Silence kept him company and he knew that whoever stood just behind and to the right was watching the fight as closely as he was himself, but he had no time to check to see if it was Miss Ruthven or some other.

"Well done," said a deep voice, when he netted the fish. "I had no notion there was such excellent fishing along this stream.

Calder turned. "Mr. Ruthven."

"Call me James. It is too confusing, with two Mr. Ruthvens at Merrywood. What are you doing?" he asked sharply.

Calder had completed his task of removing the hook and watched the fish swim away. "He gave me excellent sport. I see no reason to punish him for doing so."

"So you released him."

"Yes. Besides—" Calder's eyes twinkled and his lips formed a tight grin. "—I forgot to ask Miss Ruthven's permission to fish her stream, and I would not wish to be accused of poaching!"

James chuckled. "I see. But there she comes. It is too bad you have already released that monster or you might have asked her now. Do so and the next time you'll feel free to take him home."

"If *you* do not catch him first?"

"There is that. Babs," James added as she, followed by her groom, stopped near them, "you should have seen the fish Lord Calder just netted."

"Did you catch my granddaddy of a fish?" she asked, turning worried eyes on Calder.

"I did not ask to be introduced," teased Calder, "but he was certainly huge enough to be a grandfather many times over. Do not be concerned. I released him."

She relaxed. "Was there a tear in his fin?"

"On the right side? Yes."

"That's him. Hello, James, are you riding over to your property?"

"I thought I would," he said. "Why do you not accompany me?" he suggested, wondering if he were interfering in an assignation and, if he were, what he should do about it.

"Have you seen his house?" asked Babs of Calder.

"Yes. I was exploring the countryside one day and, when I saw the workmen, went down to introduce myself to his builder. An excellent man I thought," he added, turning to James.

James nodded. "I am meeting the Morgan ladies there in an hour or so. Lady Morgan is giving me the benefit of her advice with regard to decorating."

"Did you have a destination in mind for your ride?" asked Calder, casting a glance expressive of innocence toward Babs.

"I did," she said equally innocently, "but I would like to see what has been done at the Oaks. Will you join us?"

Their little game fooled James completely and he relaxed, assured there was nothing between the two that should not be. Calder packed his fishing gear and, very soon, the three rode on together, followed by Babs' groom.

The morning was frustrating. Calder could have no private conversation with Miss Ruthven and discovered that, because he could not, it was exactly what he wanted more than anything.

"I do not like suspense," he muttered to himself.

He was overheard. "What suspense?" asked Lady Dewsbury-Morgan.

"Hmm? Oh—" He felt his ears heat up. "—would you believe the suspense of wondering if I will or will not catch a certain fish again?"

"That you wonder if you will catch a—umm—certain fish, yes," she said and turned away.

Calder stared after her.

"She is sharp as a needle, is she not?" asked Babs softly from beside him.

"You think she has guessed?"

"Perhaps. If she has, I wonder what she has seen."

He smiled at her frown. "We have been careful. She must be exceptionally perceptive to have guessed, so perhaps she has not. Perhaps it is something else."

"You would suggest our guilty consciences gave one meaning to her words while she meant something entirely different?"

"Exactly."

"Hmm. I can think of no other interpretation."

"But then we've those guilty consciences to which you referred," he teased.

"So we do."

Calder swept a quick glance around. "Have you news for me so that we need not again feel guilty?"

"For meeting surreptitiously? I'm afraid not," she lied. "Tomorrow? The same place?"

"Very well."

"Tomorrow, then," she said and walked off.

He heard her tell her cousin she was returning home and thought about joining her, but that, very likely, would give the game away. Especially if Lady Dewsbury-Morgan merely suspected something was going on. He'd no desire to do anything that would tarnish Miss Ruthven's reputation in the neighborhood and riding so far with her—even with a groom following along behind—might do just that. He also wished to protect himself from embarrassment if it became known he was courting her and she had turned him down.

Except he had decided he would not accept no for an answer, had he not? He had. And he wouldn't.

"Looking a trifle grim, my lord," said James. "Anything I can do for you?"

"Hmm? Oh just a sudden thought. Perhaps I will ask

your advice if I cannot come up with a solution myself . . ."

James did not probe. "Speaking of advice, what do you think of that gazebo thing at the end of that garden?" He gestured to where a ramshackle vine-covered summer-house stood.

"I think it interferes with the vista beyond," said Calder after a moment's study.

"Exactly. Down it comes. Lady Morgan thinks it would be a nice spot in which to take tea or to find shade in warm weather when one wished to sew or read out of doors, but I can easily build elsewhere where it will not clutter up an excellent view."

"Will you need protection from the sun for your sewing and reading?" asked Calder a trifle slyly.

James barked a laugh. "I am not yet so decrepit I think to sit by the fire with my needle, but, although I will not be wedding my cousin," he continued in a more serious tone, "I have no intention of remaining a bachelor." His eyes settled on Miss Morgan.

"The wind in that quarter?" asked Calder gently.

James frowned. "I thought about it . . . but soon came to realize she thinks of me as a hero rather than a man. I doubt—" The frown deepened. "—if any man could maintain the role of hero for long."

"You saved her from her father's anger and you told her she need not wed where she had no will to do so. I suspect that is all that was needed to make you her hero forever."

"But I do not wish to play that role in my marriage," said James pensively. "Besides . . . no, I will not suggest that. Time will tell."

"You suspect my cousin has an interest there?" asked Calder.

James cast him a quick look. "You too have seen how attentive he is to her? How gentle?"

Calder nodded. "I have never seen him treat a woman in that particular manner. I hope he has not lost his heart, since I very much fear that Miss Morgan will never overcome her views concerning marriage."

"Perhaps if her mother reweds and she sees not all marriages are like that between her mother and father?"

"Perhaps. But who would wed her ladyship?"

James cast him another look, this one of astonishment. "What can you mean?"

"She is one who takes a pet too easily, too often she is a whiner, and I would not be at all surprised if she didn't, once she did not fear for her skin, become a nag as well."

"Ah. You judge by what you saw in London. She is quickly returning to what Lady Dewsbury-Morgan tells me she was like before her marriage."

"I have not, of course, had much to do with her since the wedding," said Calder politely, half-apology and half-explanation.

"I am living under the same roof and see her every day."

The same roof as Miss Ruthven, too. Calder wondered what it would be like to live under Miss Ruthven's roof, to see her every day, to talk to her whenever he wished . . . to go up those highly polished stairs with her to their bedroom of an evening . . .

"I see she is looking for me. Excuse me," said James, not quite interrupting thoughts very likely better interrupted.

Calder stared after James as the man walked toward where Lady Morgan stood on the terrace gesturing for him to join her, but did not consciously observe them. In fact, he barely knew he was alone, so deep had he sunk in dreams of holding Miss Ruthven, of kissing her . . . and more.

Without particularly thinking about it, he strolled to where his gelding was tethered, ordered the groom hovering near the horses to saddle it, and then, still without

particularly thinking about where he was going, rode off
. . . and eventually found himself crossing the humpbacked bridge where—it seemed a very long time
ago—he had met Lady Dewsbury-Morgan.

"So why am I on the road to Merrywood," he asked
himself as he reined in. "Because I want to see Miss
Ruthven. I want this settled," he told himself and gently
kicked his confused mount back into a proper trot.

But Miss Ruthven was unavailable. She had gone
home only to discover her overseer had need of her. A
problem with the roof on her home-farm tenant's barn
required her decision, so she went off immediately upon
receiving the message to inspect the situation.

Lord Calder, feeling a bit of a fool but nevertheless
deeply disappointed, returned to Blackstock Manor
where he immediately ran into his father.

Thirteen

Lord Amrington studied his son for half an instant and stiffened. "She has turned you down."

"She has not."

His lordship relaxed. "Then what is the matter?" he asked more mildly.

"The matter?" Lord Calder, since becoming an adult, had gotten out of the habit of seeing his father as a source of advice or sympathy. He shrugged. "I was unaware anything was the matter—or perhaps it is merely that I have just had a long ride to no result and am both tired and a trifle peckish. I wonder if that man Aunt Hermie calls a butler could find me something to eat . . ."

He wandered off looking for the fellow who was never where he was supposed to be and was, on this particular occasion, lounging in the small back parlor, his feet set upon a footstool and a newspaper more or less hiding him from discovery.

Lord Calder cleared his throat.

The paper rattled and then, slowly, lowered, the butler scowling over the top. "Can't a man get a moment to himself without someone demanding he do something?"

"I thought," said his lordship mildly, "that *doing something* was the reason my aunt paid you."

The butler sighed, took his deliberate time folding the

newspaper, and putting it aside. He rose to his feet, pulled at a nonexistent forelock, and, sneering, asked, "And what is it I should be doing right now, your lordship?"

Calder's eyes narrowed. "You will come with me," he said.

Another sigh and the fellow followed him from the room to where Lady Hermione Blackstock was studying a racing form.

"Yes?" she asked when Calder, once again, cleared his throat.

"Aunt, I wish to complain of insolence in this man. I think you should either see to training him up to his position or you should give him notice."

Her brows rose. "Insolent?" She looked at the butler who scowled right back. "Jeremy, what have you been up to now?"

"Weren't up to nothing," was the sullen reply.

"*Exactly.* I need something to eat. Since it is his duty to provide for such needs, I went looking for him. I found him sprawled in a chair in the little parlor and reading the newspaper, *the one I could not find when I wished to read it earlier.* He was nasty when I interrupted him, seeming to feel it an insult that I required him to rouse himself to do the job for which he's being paid."

"Let you get way with murder, don't I?" asked Hermione.

The butler grimaced.

"You *are* paid to do a job of work, you know," she said.

"Got too many people here wanting too much work," he retorted.

"Too many days of the year you don't do any, so it won't hurt you to stir your stumps when there is company."

"Bah."

"Maybe you want to return to your old position?" she asked, her voice suddenly coated with ice.

Jeremy, if that was his name, froze. "You wouldn't."

"You think you can do anything you wish and I'll not object?"

"You better not object," he muttered.

"Aunt, has this man means of blackmailing you?" asked Lord Calder sharply.

"He thinks he does, but it is all nonsense. I've found it rather amusing to let him think it, but enough is enough."

"I'll talk! You won't like that."

"Won't I? Why not?"

The fellow gave her a baffled look. "You're a lady."

"So?"

"So ladies don't do it."

"I do it. Have for years and I *am* a lady."

Calder grew more than a bit perturbed. "Aunt . . ."

"I'll tell the tale and you'll be laughed at and shunned and . . ."

"You'll say nothing," said Calder abruptly. "Aunt, what . . ." But he feared he knew. It was not unknown for a lady to take a servant to her bed.

"I like a good prizefight, Matt," she said to her nephew. "Since my beloved Blackstock died and can no longer escort me, Jeremy, here—" She gestured. "—has taken me. Now it appears he thinks he is in a position to do me an injury, which is nonsense."

She had *not* been dallying with the man! Calder breathed a huge sigh of relief. It was not something the ladies of her acquaintance would approve, but they knew his Aunt Hermione was more than a trifle eccentric, and were more-than-likely already aware of her penchant for the fancy and fisticuffs and that Lord Blackstock had introduced her to some of the fighters. He doubted anyone would actually cut her for still attending prizefights now he was dead.

"You," he said to Jeremy, "are greatly at fault. I cannot

give you notice, because I did not hire you, but my advice to my aunt is to get rid of you. A man who thinks to take advantage of the person who pays him is not worth his pay. Aunt? What do you wish to do?"

She pursed her lips, twisting them to one side, and stared at Jeremy who shifted from one foot to the other and back again.

"You are a fool, man," she said.

The butler, if one could call him that, swallowed hard.

"Perhaps I found you amusing because I am too lazy to do anything about you," she mused. His eyes narrowed. "So . . ."

Calder could see the man held his breath.

She nodded. "Yes. I will give you one more chance, but one more step across the line and you are out on your ear, do you hear me?"

Jeremy nodded but there was a stubborn look to him that made Matthew think he would, as soon as he dared, drift right back into his old idle and insolent ways. On the other hand, Lady Blackstock did not particularly seem to care that the organization of her home was chaotic in the extreme . . .

She surprised her nephew, her frown intensifying. "It has occurred to me that Mr. Ruthven might be correct," she murmured.

"Mr. Ruthven?" asked Calder.

"Mr. William Ruthven. He suggested that I'd not allow my stables to be run in a ramshackle fashion and wondered that I allowed my household to behave in slipshod ways. I find I agree and that changes must be made. Jeremy, you will plan out a weekly schedule of the work and bring it to me. If you cannot write, then have Cook jot down your notions for you, but do it in the next day or two."

Jeremy looked baffled. "Schedule of work? What work?"

Lady Blackstock blinked. "Why the work around the house, of course. The polishing and scrubbing and dusting and all that sort of thing. How should I know? You claimed you knew how to buttle. So buttle."

Calder suddenly felt a trifle sorry for the man. "When you have an evening at the inn, do other butlers also come there?"

"Don't have much to do with them," said Jeremy sourly. "Too high in the instep for such as me."

Sympathy faded. "That is too bad. I thought perhaps you could talk to one and get advice from him. That is, I assumed you might if you want to keep your position."

"Don't see why we can't go on as we have," he said petulantly.

"Because now I look about me, I see I have been remiss, far too easy going, far too uncaring," said Lady Blackstock. "This is a nice house. Always rather liked it," she added, sounding rather surprised at herself. "It is wrong of me to let it go to wrack and ruin merely because I've no children to whom I can leave it and haven't much cared what happened so long as it outlasted me. I think perhaps," she said, her eyes narrowing, "that *I* will make up that list myself and then we will see if you can get the maids and footmen to do their work properly." She sighed gustily. "Time I'm done with mourning Blackstock. Didn't much care about anything after he stuck his spoon in the wall, but—well, he died near to a decade ago." She straightened her shoulders. "Time I let him go," she finished, a sad look about her that caught at Calder.

He nudged the butler and nodded toward the door. Gladly, Jeremy escaped. "I don't think I ever really got to know him, Aunt Hermie," said Matthew gently. "Tell me about him." He sat down near his aunt and took her hand in his and, for an hour, listened to her tales of the man she had married, a man who had not only allowed, but had encouraged her odd interest in sport and horses and things women did not normally do. Finally she ran down.

"I see," said Calder, patting her hand. "He must have been an interesting man."

"Interesting? To talk to?" She chuckled. "Never had a word to say about much of anything—except horses, of course. Exciting? Yes! Always! Never at a loss for something to do or somewhere to go." The smile faded. "And now I don't go much of anywhere, do I?"

"You could," he said.

She nodded. "Yes. Funny. Never realized how I just followed his lead all those years. Never thought of things to do myself. Just enjoyed his notions which suited me right down to the ground—and then . . . he wasn't there."

"Time you began thinking up notions of your own, perhaps," he said encouragingly . . . and then wondered if that was, given his aunt's particular penchants, a *not* particularly good idea.

"Used to think I'd like to visit Italy," she said thoughtfully. "Never came to anything, of course."

"Why of course?"

"Blackstock didn't like boats," she said simply. "Anything else and he was game. We even went up in a balloon once. Now there was a treat, Calder," she said, her eyes sparkling. "You should try it sometime!"

"Italy?" he asked, drawing her mind back to it.

She blinked. "I'll have to think about it . . ."

"You might talk to my father. He'd give you advice. He went there on his grand tour and enjoyed it immensely." Calder recalled how often he'd been forced to listen to his father speak of Italy. "I wonder," he mused, "if he might not like to go back." He nodded. It was very likely true that his father would like to return to some of the places he, all too often, droned on about when in his cups.

Droned on? Calder shook his head slightly. It was more that he hadn't wanted to listen to his father's tales because Napoleon had closed the Continent to such travel and he'd felt jealous that it looked as if he'd never, himself, see or do any of the things about which his father spoke. But the war appeared to be winding down, so travel might soon be possible . . . except that his father had a great deal of responsibility to the property and might not feel able to go . . .

Unless I begin taking more of an interest in the estate?

Calder sighed. It was not easy accepting that he'd been more than a trifle selfish in insisting he remain in London with his friends and his frivolous pastimes. The fact was, not only must he wed, but also he must learn what he'd need to know for when his father died, leaving him the estate and title and he *had* to take responsibility. Hopefully far in the future, but the day *would* come. He sighed again.

"What is it, Nevie?" asked his aunt.

"Hmm? Oh, just thinking I've been a selfish man in a lot of ways and it is not only *you* who needs to reform your ways, Aunt. I do too. It's just that it always seemed that if I avoided taking up my responsibilities, then perhaps my brother . . ."

"You could pretend he wasn't dead," she said, nodding. "I guess we both did a bit of that, did we not?"

"We'd better improve ourselves, hmm?"

She laughed and slapped him on the back in her mannish fashion. "We'll just have to get busy and organize our reform. Come along, nephew. We'll begin by strolling through the house and you can point out to me where I've been letting things slide for too long."

"The chimneys," he said promptly, offering his arm. "The bedroom chimneys, at least, badly need sweeping."

"First thing on the list. Now what else?" she asked—just as she tripped over a worn place in the hall carpet.

Calder caught her, saving her from a fall. Once she was righted, they looked at each other, looked at the carpet, looked back at each other and, suddenly, they were laughing so hard it brought Quentin and Lord Amrington into the hall to see what was going on.

The two found it impossible to explain to the others why they found the situation utterly hilarious—especially since Lord Amrington had tripped over that identical spot just that morning and was still a trifle angry about it!

Babs once again had a long conversation with her bedpost. "So," she finished, "do I tell him I'll wed him?"

The bedpost, as bedposts tend to do, remained silent.

She sighed. "I don't think I will. Not yet. Not until we know each other a bit better. That is what I will tell him. I will tell him I do not wish to wed a stranger. That I want to know his interests, want to know how he feels about . . . about . . ."

She recalled her work that day, the accounts brought up to date and the decision to rethatch her tenant's barn. One thing she must learn was whether Calder felt strongly about his responsibilities or whether he was one of those awful landowners who took and took and never put anything back into their properties. She could not wed that sort of man and she didn't know how he felt. She hadn't a notion . . .

"So much I do not know about him," she said pensively. "In fact, other than that our minds seem very much in tune when we banter and jest, what *do* I know?"

She thought about that for a bit and decided she knew he had a sense of humor. And she liked it that he had released her old fish—*not*, as James said, because he'd have been considered a poacher if he had not, but because he knew she would prefer that the fish lived. She knew he had a quick mind and that he respected hers. In fact, he seemed to *like* the fact that she was quick to understand, something some men did *not* appreciate. Too many were happier when they knew their women had to look to them for advice and explanations.

What else? He was awfully slow to sort out his feelings about Louisa Maria, was he not? More hurt in pride than in his affections, surely, but unable to get beyond the fact he thought he wanted a docile wife and Louisa fit the role to a nicety . . . and yet he *had* accepted that she would not have him, had he not? Finally? He no longer plagued the chit with his attentions and that was good.

"But he wouldn't, would he? Not now he has asked another. Me. He could not continue plaguing her, could he?"

Again the bedpost remained silent.

"Despite how strongly I am drawn to him, I don't know him well, do I?" she asked softly. And, deciding that that was one thing she could correct, she turned on her side, settled her pillow and went to sleep.

"But what do you wish to know?" he asked, staring at her, a baffled look narrowing his eyes.

"Your interests. Your beliefs. What you like to eat. I don't know. I just don't feel I know you well enough to wed you," she said, shrugging. She cast her line again and, after a moment, he did too.

"Well?" she asked.

He sighed. "I haven't a notion what to say to you. Perhaps if you were to ask questions . . . ?"

"Very well," she said, thinking. "Yes, very well," she repeated more firmly, recalling one question. "Yesterday I had to see to the roof of my home-farm's barn. We had wind not long ago and the old thatching was damaged. What would you have done about it?"

"Me?"

"If you were in charge."

"Oh. If I were responsible, you mean. Well, it is never good for a building if the roof leaks. The wet gets into the wood and it deteriorates. I suppose I would have ordered in the thatchers."

She nodded. "I did that. After checking the house, I decided it, too, must be rethatched."

"Was it leaking?"

"Not yet, but it was last done at the time the barn was rethatched so it very likely will in the near future."

"So you will go to the expense even though you feel it has some good years left?"

"One bad storm would be enough to do for it, I think. My steward agreed."

"Have you a good man working for you?"

"My uncle chose him and, in my opinion, chose well. We seem to have the same notions about what is right, how much one may demand of one's workmen, for instance." She shrugged and then looked up from where she was drawing in her line for another cast. "Your father must have a great deal of property for which he is responsible. Do you know his land steward?"

"Ouch."

"You do not?"

"You are touching on a point about which I was scolding myself just yesterday. I have avoided learning about the estate because, well, I think I felt it an insult to my brother's memory as well as looking as if I wanted to step into my father's shoes if I showed the least eagerness, you know?"

"I wonder," she said slowly, not looking at him, "if it is

not more an insult that you refuse to keep faith with their responsibilities which are now yours whether you will it or no."

Matt nodded. "That is what I concluded. I had a bit of a talk with my father this morning. Not too involved, but enough that he knows I want to begin my lessons. Although not just yet—" he glanced at her. "—not while the other thing is unsettled."

Babs had cast as he spoke and watched her lure float down past a particular spot on the far side where there was a sunken log. She was thinking about his words when, suddenly, her line jerked taut and she very nearly lost hold of the rod. For a time she was fully preoccupied with landing her fish. A smile twitched her lips at one point. She could see, from the corner of her eye, that his lordship wanted, badly, to take the pole from her, bring in the fish himself, afraid, perhaps, that she would lose him.

"There," she said when he lifted the net up under the fish and pulled him from the water. "Well, my beauty, twice this week you've been caught. You, old man fish, had better be more cautious!" She watched Matt release the hook and look up at her questioningly. She nodded and he let the creature slip back into the water.

"That is going to be one surprised fish if someone else catches him and takes him home for his supper," said his lordship, resettling his hat, which had fallen off when he knelt on one knee to remove the hook.

She grimaced. "It will happen one day. I cannot expect to continue such sport forever. Tell me about your home, about growing up there."

He nodded and they drew in their tackle and put it aside, going to where Louisa sat on a blanket, reading. He spoke of the Amrington's best loved estate, the house and gardens, the woods and streams, the home farm and more distant farms where he and his brother had pretended to help in the harvest . . .

". . . And probably got in the way more than helping," he said, self-deridingly. "Those were good days, when Henry was still alive and Quentin would spend the long summer vacations with us." He grimaced. "Unfortunately, there was another cousin, a little older than my brother, who was often a guest as well."

"Unfortunately?" asked Babs. She saw that Louisa was listening, barely pretending to read her book. Would the chit suddenly realize his lordship was not the ogre she thought him and want him back?

"He wasn't . . . nice . . . even then. He's not someone I'd want to introduce you to."

"Is there any reason why you would have to?" she asked.

"Well, he is my cousin," he said.

Babs realized he meant she'd meet all his relatives once they were married—not that he yet knew they were to wed.

"Worse," he added, "he's my heir."

"Ah."

"Yes. Quite," he replied in a very dry tone indeed.

Louisa looked up and, confused, looked from one to the other.

"Never mind, Louisa," said Babs and smiled. "Calder was merely making a point."

Docilely, Louisa looked back down at her book—but for once, Babs thought her curiosity did not go away.

"What of you, Miss Ruthven? Was your growing up similar?"

"No. I was very much alone, you see. No cousins visiting, either bad or good, and few young people my age in the region. They were older or much younger, leaving me to make my own entertainments."

"And did you?"

"Yes. When I was allowed time to do so. I'd a very good governess, but she eventually decided there was little else of an academic nature she could teach me and insisted Uncle William hire a tutor. Mr. Rowland was here for three years and a strict taskmaster. When he allowed me to escape my schoolroom lessons, my governess would pounce on me to set me to more womanly tasks. Cook, for instance, taught me to make bread and pastry and simple soups and stews. When I was fifteen, she set out the day's ingredients and sat down and waved her hand and said 'you do it,' so I made the whole dinner that day."

Louisa, Babs discovered, was staring at her in disbelief and she laughed. "Do you think it a rather odd upbringing, Louisa? I was also taught a great deal about how my head groom runs my stables. I was not, fortunately, forced to clean out stalls, but I did learn to care for tack and to groom my mare and what to feed her and how much and when to water her. I watched when new animals were broken to carriage work although I have no notion how a young one learns to accept a rider on his back—something I have been told can be dangerous work if not done properly."

"Or even if it is," said Calder, more amazed than ever by the woman he had decided would be his wife. "I broke an arm once, working a rough-broken gelding I chose and bought for myself."

"A showy creature, I am sure," teased Babs, "and always throwing out splints and too short in the back and . . ."

Calder half growled, half laughed. "He was a great mount. Eventually. And lived a long and useful life." He was silent for a moment and Babs, a brow quirked and her lips twitching, silently questioned that. He sighed. "He lived a long and useful life," he amended, "so long as he never saw a cat. I haven't a notion what the creature had against cats, but if one crossed in front of him, or was even sitting placidly in the sun on a wall we passed . . . well, I assure you, that animal taught me to be always on the alert and never ever take for granted that one might ride without care and constant awareness, so, you see he was a good animal and taught me a lot."

Babs nodded. "I had a mare a bit like that once, except it was white. Anything white. I didn't dare take her out when the Queen Anne's Lace was in bloom. She would shy away from every blossom. A sheet hung over a bush to dry would send her into fits. A lady dressed in white? I assure you, if I saw such ahead of us, I turned that mare and headed in another direction!"

"Why did you put up with her?"

"Because she would, when behaving, give me the fastest, smoothest ride I have ever experienced. Unfortunately, Uncle William saw her acting up one day and the next I discovered she'd been sent away. I was *not* pleased."

"Very likely I would have done the same," said Calder. "I would dislike it very much if you were to find yourself with a broken neck simply because you failed to notice a rider with white-topped boots approaching!"

"But it was *my* horse, *my* responsibility, and, if I had broken my neck, then . . ." She looked over the hand placed over her lips, up into his eyes. Calder shook his head. Babs tugged his hand away. "You would say I was foolish to keep the animal. You kept yours."

"Yes, but I was not responsible for the feelings of a guardian who must have worried about your safety and would have felt he had failed his brother if something happened to you."

Babs dropped her gaze after a moment when his held steady. "Yes. Uncle William would have felt guilty and would not have accepted that I was of an age to make my own decisions."

"How old were you?"

She grinned. "I think I was fourteen that summer."

He chuckled. "I can see, I think, where he might not have thought you quite of an age to be rational about your mare!"

"She was such a beauty," said Babs, just a touch of wistfulness in her voice. "Truly, so long as I kept my wits about me, she was not a problem. I am an excellent rider, Calder, and have not gone off a horse since I once attempted a wall with a ditch on the other side of it. And that was not the horse's fault, but my own. I *knew* he was not a strong jumper."

"You had a particular reason for the jump?"

She grinned. "I wanted to get ahead of the dogs and foul the fox's scent! I was dragging a bag full of strong herbs, you see."

"Does that do it?"

"I don't know. It was an experiment. Only I went off my horse and the hunt passed by before I managed to catch my mare and remount."

Louisa gurgled in her throat and Babs looked at her.

"What is it, Louisa?" she asked.

Louisa looked disapproving.

"You think I should not have done it?"

Louisa nodded.

"Why?"

For half a moment Babs thought the girl would respond, but then Louisa gave her a look denoting disappointment and turned away.

"I do wish you would talk, Louisa," said Babs, gently. "You could if you would, you know. There is absolutely no reason at all, now, why you should not."

Louisa stiffened.

"Truly. Your father is dead. He cannot hold you to any order he gave you," said Babs, wondering if that could possibly be the reason the girl did not speak as some who knew her believed.

Louisa stared at her, then glanced at Calder, compressed her lips, and got up. She wandered off, far enough she could no longer hear their words but still be seen, settled where a great number of small daisies grew, and began making a daisy chain.

"I think she very nearly spoke," said Calder softly. "Did you mean to trick her into speaking?"

"She spoke that day she thought you were attacking me. She *can* speak. I know she can."

"You did try to trick her."

Babs' eyes twinkled wickedly. "I suppose I did."

"If she were to speak before she is ready, might it not do more harm than good?"

Babs stared at him. "My lord, that is a very perceptive comment. I am surprised."

"Surprised I can be perceptive?" he asked stiffly.

"Yes. Oh, come down out of the boughs. I do not mean to insult you. You will admit you were not particularly sensitive when you meant to continue your pursuit of her!"

He sighed. "I was not, was I? And I have yet to tell her I will not." He plucked a blade grass and put it between his thumbs, and, blowing past it, produced a whistle. Babs watched, interested. Then she plucked her own blade of grass and attempted to emulate him. Hers did not work.

"How do you do that?" she asked.

"Here. Hold the blade more tautly," he said, taking her hands in his and positioning the grass to better effect. "Now blow gently," he instructed, lifting her hands to her mouth.

Although she felt as if her heart would burst from her breast at his touch, she managed a bit of a whistle.

"Try another grass blade. They don't last very long."

She chose another and again he helped her to hold it properly between her thumbs. This time, expecting his touch to influence her, she controlled her emotions and produced an interesting shriek. She laughed, her eyes glowing. She looked at him, still chuckling . . . and her gaze tangled with his much as her fish line had tangled with a bush earlier that day. Feeling a hint of hysteria at the thought, she wondered if she'd need his help to untangle this knot as she had that one.

Calder's hands tightened around hers. He, too, felt as if he were caught, as if there was no way to break away from her, that, somehow, in that particular instant, they were tied together by lines that could never be broken, by something that frightened him a trifle, a feeling, an emotion, he'd never before experienced and was uncertain he wished to understand.

Louisa made a sound of distress and both Babs and Calder turned their heads to look toward her. She was holding one hand with the other and tears spurted from her eyes.

"A bee sting," said Babs and rose gracefully to her feet. "Get some mud from the river, my lord. It helps remove the hurt." She didn't know whether to be glad or sorry that they'd been disturbed.

Calder nodded and went to the waterside. Once there he found he had to lie full length to reach down the side of the stream to where there was mud. He brought it, returned to rinse his hands, and returned to tell the women he would leave them now.

Babs, glancing up at him, chuckled. "Yes, I see you might feel it necessary to return home," she said. "If your valet grumbles about removing the dirt from your coat, do tell him it was all my fault."

"Nonsense. I will tell him the truth. It was," he explained when both Babs and a watery eyed Louisa looked up at him, "the fault of the honeybee, of course."

Even Louisa smiled a bit at that.

Babs, watching him go, realized she wished he would stay.

I enjoyed our morning together, both the fishing and the talk and—She nodded firmly. Once. —*even the arguments. We have discovered a deal about each other we did not know before and that is a very good thing altogether.*

Fourteen

That evening, while Louisa Maria played a new piece for the family, James Ruthven moved to the back of the room where her mother sat with a book of poetry laid open on a table holding a shaded lamp.

"Lady Morgan," he said softly so as not to interfere with everyone else's enjoyment of the music, "I wish to thank you for all the aid you've given me. My house will look quite delightful when we are done with it."

She blushed, looked sideways at him, and back at the book. She shut it and lay it aside. "I enjoyed it." In an even softer, slightly muffled voice, she added, "I do not believe I have ever enjoyed anything half so much."

He looked down at her, surprised. "That seems a very odd comment," he said, softly, wishing they were alone so it would be less difficult to keep their conversation private.

"Sir George . . ." she muttered and stopped.

"He would have spoiled it?" he asked gently.

She nodded.

"He was not a good man, Lady Morgan. You must not feel guilty for feeling you are better off without him."

She cast him a slightly anguished look. "He *died* to save us from those awful men."

"Yes," said James, but was far from certain it was so. He had discovered Sir George carried a ridiculous amount of money with him when he traveled and suspected his pounds, shillings, and pence had worried the man rather more than his wife's safety.

"They would have killed the both of us," she insisted.

"Very likely," said James and, when he saw she trembled, added, "but it didn't happen. You are safe and must forget all that. Think about what you want to do with your future. You must," he suggested playfully, attempting to lighten her mood, "think up something other than house decorating which you would enjoy. There are, unfortunately, not that many houses available where you can apply your fine touch."

"I have thought," she said, her little chin firming.

He blinked. After a moment he asked, "Can you tell me?"

"I would have *friends*. I would visit them and they would visit me and Sir George would *not* tell me it is a waste of time and all foolishness!"

He chuckled, but hoped her voice had not risen to where the others would notice. "I believe Lady Dewsbury-Morgan said you were a wonderful needlewoman. Will you take it up again?"

She nodded. "I have ordered my housekeeper to find my old projects and send them to me."

"Your London housekeeper?" James wondered that the house was still staffed. Wouldn't her ladyship's solicitor have seen to closing up the house and dismissing the servants? Curious, he asked.

"I told him not to. I wanted to return to London, but—" A wistful look made her almost pretty. "—Mother Vivian thinks we should not."

"You *will* return. Someday. But perhaps you should have him reduce the staff to just a few. Just those needed to maintain the house while you are in mourning and the knocker is off the door?"

She sighed. "I do not feel as if I am in mourning. Not properly." Her jaw hardened. She glanced at him and then away. "I do not really *wish* to mourn." Again she took a quick look at his face. "There. I have said it. You may despise me if you will."

"But I don't."

She raised shocked eyes to meet his gaze.

"If Sir George had been a different sort of man, then I would be shocked that you felt no sadness at his loss, but frankly, Lady Morgan, he was not a man anyone could mourn. It would be hypocrisy to mourn him."

She sighed and seemed to collapse into herself. "I have been so afraid to admit it. I have disliked myself and have been thinking I am unnatural. He was my *husband.* I *should* mourn him."

"One must earn the right to be mourned, Lady Morgan. He did not."

"I will try to remember. It is so hard when I have spent most of my life thinking I must obey every stricture, every shibboleth, of society. Watching over my shoulder, as it were, to see that I do nothing that he would disapprove."

"No longer."

She drew in a deep breath and then smiled. This time she was really pretty. Not in the way her daughter was pretty, but in a far more mature sort of way. James found himself surprised and found it difficult to draw his gaze from her features.

The smile faded. "What is it? What have I done?"

He shook his head slightly. "You have bemused me with your beauty, Lady Morgan. Yes that is it," he added, nodding. "You smiled just like that and drew my breath away."

The smile flickered and then held. "You should not say such things to me," she said. "You should say them to . . . oh, to Miss Ruthven. She is truly pretty."

"Do you think so? I find I do not care for red hair. Or the freckles that decorate my cousin's pert little nose!"

Drawn by her ladyship's soft skin, he touched her cheek with one gentle finger. "You will never show a freckle. You never have, have you?"

It was her ladyship's turn to be bemused. She could not have spoken if her life depended on it. Instead, she merely shook her head—but moving her head from side to side only complicated the problem, since it rubbed her cheek against that finger's gentle touch.

Across the room Babs nudged Lady Dewsbury-Morgan, pointed discretely when she had her ladyship's attention.

"I wonder . . ." breathed her ladyship.

"If a match is possible between them?"

Her ladyship frowned slightly. "I fear Anna is a trifle older than Mr. Ruthven."

"Do you think so? Surely not by much. Is it a problem, do you think?"

"She will never bear another child. Will he not want an heir?"

"I hadn't thought of that," said Babs, thoughtfully. "Oh dear, and I was thinking it would be such a very good thing."

"I still think it. Assuming he is willing to adopt a son to follow after him."

"Can a man do that?"

"Not where a title is involved, but merely to inherit property? Oh yes. It is done infrequently, but it is done. The boy involved often times adopts his new father's name or combines it with his own."

"I thought hyphenated names came about when large fortunes were combined by an arranged marriage."

Her ladyship nodded. "Then too. Or in cases such as mine. When I married and insisted that I retain my title. My husband agreed but only if I add his name to mine and thus the hyphen. I think," she went on, "I must see what I can do to promote that match. It would be good for Anna, but it would be marvelous for Louisa Maria who admires him as she does no other. She would never fear him and she would have time to extend her knowledge, to learn that not all men are like her father."

"I think she could talk now, if she would. It has crossed my mind more than once that she *deliberately* does not, not that she *cannot*."

Lady Dewsbury-Morgan turned to stare at her. "You think so?"

"Occasionally I swear I have heard her singing softly to herself. When she thinks no one is near, you understand? And she has allowed various squeaks and squeals to escape her, which she did not when I first knew her— as today when a bee stung her. I looked at her immediately and I would swear she was biting her lips to stop herself from saying more."

"Hmm . . ."

"It is very strange," said Babs softly. "Do you think she thinks that no man will bother her if she cannot speak?"

"It has not stopped Quentin Riverton," said her ladyship in the driest of dry tones.

Babs nodded. "Another possible match—if Louisa ever makes any match at all. I fear he has fallen deeply in love with her."

"Or with her music."

Babs chuckled softly. "Oh yes. There is that. I think it will bind them together and once she is certain he is true, then she will relax and allow him to court her properly and will, when enough time has passed, agree to wed him."

Her ladyship nodded. "But enough time has not passed. At the moment she is, very likely, a trifle embarrassed by the thought that he is cousin to the man she jilted."

Babs cast her a startled look and laughed softly. "I had not thought of that." And then they were both silent as the last notes of Louisa Maria's music floated into the air.

* * *

Lord Amrington rode over to Merrywood, after ascertaining that his son meant to go fishing and was unlikely to be anywhere near Miss Ruthven's estate. On his way he satisfied his curiosity that her estate was not only well cared for but prosperous and arrived in time to see the elder Morgan ladies drive off toward the dower house but without either Miss Ruthven or Miss Morgan. He gritted his teeth, hoping neither young lady was anywhere near the front door. A groom took away his mount and the butler took his card.

"Yes, my lord? What can I do for you?"

"Is Mr. Ruthven at home?" asked Amrington.

"I must ask which Mr. Ruthven, my lord. Mr. William or Mr. James?"

"Yes, of course." Amrington felt a bit of a fool that he'd forgotten. "Mr. William, I believe. The elder Mr. Ruthven."

The butler nodded, disappeared at a stately pace, and Amrington, tugging at his cravat, looked around still again. So far he'd been in luck. He wondered if it would hold, that he would manage to meet with Mr. Ruthven without either his son or Miss Ruthven becoming aware of his objective.

Luck was with him and, soon, he was seated in Mr. William Ruthven's private parlor, a glass of truly excellent wine in his hand.

The men spoke of trivial things while they sipped, each surreptitiously taking the measure of the other. Both were well pleased with what they discovered. Although one was of noble birth and the other a commoner, they were surprisingly similar in their outlook and values.

"You did not ride all this way in the hot sun to discuss the Prince Regent's latest folly," said William, after determining that Amrington would decline on a second glassful.

"No. I have a definite proposal in mind for discussion."

When he didn't continue and looked as if he very much wished he dared mop his brow, William took pity on him. "Proposal. . . . We both have children for whom we have long had responsibility," he mused. "It is the only thing of which I can think that we have in common. Why are you in such a pelter, my lord?"

"Pelter?" Amrington relaxed, chuckling. "What a word." His smile faded. "But you have taken my meaning. I want my son wed," he admitted. "I watched him the other night. He is not averse to your Miss Ruthven."

"I too have observed the growing attraction they feel for each other. It would be a good union, I think," said William, staring into his empty glass.

"Yes. A good match on both sides. Your niece will eventually gain a coronet when she becomes a countess. I believe she will grace the title with dignity and intelligence. My son will gain a woman of whom he may remain proud throughout his life, one who will have an understanding of the complications and responsibilities his peerage demands of him. She is such a one who is competent to oversee his houses and servants without the duty being a great burden, a burden she regrets and resents—as his first choice would have done!"

"Ah yes," said William thoughtfully. It crossed his mind that Lord Calder would gain far more from the union than merely his niece's ability to manage things and he wondered that Amrington did not mention it. Babs was an heiress, after all. "Lord Calder was on the verge of wedding the young Morgan lady, was he not?"

Amrington sighed. "I told him to find a wife. Or else. So he did—but not the sort of woman I wanted for him. I was actually pleased when the chit left him standing there at the altar! It was only much later I thought to check to see that she was all right. And, of course, by then Lady Dewbury-Morgan had taken them all away somewhere, no one knew where. That her ladyship had done so, however, did mean they were together and—I checked—she had the means of supporting them."

"But not very well, if what Babs has told me is true."

"Yes, but not starving or forced to live in a slum or a nasty damp village cottage with bad drains."

Ruthven nodded, but wondered if Lord Amrington might not think the rooms in which the women had lived very much a slum if he himself had been forced to occupy them. "To return to your reason for coming. I refuse to interfere to any great degree. Frankly, I think a union will result—but I am also afraid that my very stubborn niece will turn up her nose and have nothing to do with Lord Calder if anyone attempts to force her to the altar before she is ready to walk down the aisle."

"Blast all stubborn women!"

"I thought it was her independence which intrigued you?"

Amrington laughed. "Don't expect me to be rational about this. I want my son married and filling his nursery." He sobered, the comment calling to mind the reason why it was important. "The heir presumptive must be supplanted," he admitted, his mouth a hard grim line.

Ruthven's brows arched. "Ah. I begin to understand your insistence and why you push for an early ceremony. Still, if you will take my advice, you will leave well alone—although we could have all ready for when *they* are ready. They are adults. Neither is particularly stupid. They are attracted to each other. Have a bit of faith that they know their own business best and will come about—assuming we do not get in the way."

Amrington turned his empty glass between his hands while staring at nothing at all. "I do not like it. It is too important to leave to the young!" He sighed and nodded. "But I will attempt to contain myself for another . . . ten days?"

"A month."

"Two weeks, then. Surely two weeks is long enough for the business?"

Ruthven smiled tightly. "For some it would be more than enough. For others not a moment in time."

Amrington sighed. "Two weeks. I will say nothing more for two weeks."

Ruthven reluctantly nodded. "We will hope all is well at the end of two weeks."

For a moment the two were silent and then Amrington sighed again. "The boy has no notion how very lucky he was that that little widgeon ran out on the wedding. But that is past." He roused himself and straightened in his chair. "I would have all ready for a *real* wedding."

William nodded. "As I suggested." He continued, "Miss Morgan is a nice child, but very much a child. Not a proper woman for a great position." Willam tented his fingers, the tips tapping against each other and began speaking in a rather portentous manner. "I have admitted a reluctance to interfere and won't to the degree I think you would wish, but I have always done my duty by her and will in this case as well. She came of age a year ago and is her own woman and I can sign nothing for her. Nevertheless, as your son proved when he became affianced to Miss Morgan, the contracting of a marriage is, as you have said, too important to leave to the young. You and I should make our arrangements, as is proper, but we will wait for them to come to an agreement before informing them of our work and asking them to sign the settlements."

Amrington frowned. "I want my son wed."

"I," retorted William in an exceedingly dry tone, "do not wish to find my niece running off to Heaven only knows where, doing Heaven only knows what, and *not*, perhaps, meeting up with another Lady Dewsbury-Morgan if she finds herself in difficulties."

"What?" Amrington could not suppress a feeling a alarm. "She ran away? Why?"

"Because James returned to England and she refused to honor the marriage arranged when she was in her cradle. As it turned out, James, too, was unhappy with the notion, but we were unaware of that at the time I refused to listen to her demands that the engagement be broken."

"Ran away . . . but had she no notion of the dangers she faced? I had thought her a sensible woman, more highly educated than I like, but with obvious advantages. I have been told she manages her estate herself?"

"Yes."

Amrington's brows arched. "Oh, come now, you can be frank with me. Surely there is a caveat? You *do* advise her, do you not?"

"I do not." Ruthven shrugged. "Oh, very occasionally she will come to me for answers to some problem which has not previously come her way, but all too often, it is something for which I have no answer either and we must go to an expert. I saw she was well trained."

Amrington sighed. "Well educated. Yes. I feared it."

"You cannot have it both ways, my lord. Either you allow a woman to explore the limits of her intelligence, or you keep her in utter ignorance. Once you have set her feet on the path of learning she will move along that path, will ye, nill ye. At least I have found that to be the case with Babs."

Amrington grimaced. "I wish it were otherwise, but, since I still believe that, in most ways, she is the woman for my son, we will change the subject. Do you wish for our solicitors to draw up the contracts or should we do it ourselves?"

"I believe we should see to the general outlines, before

sending our decisions to the gentlemen trained to write up the results in proper form. For instance, I fear my niece would be unwilling to give up her right to Merrywood and will refuse to do what a woman does when she marries. I mean the transfer of the property into her husband's management. On the other hand, I understand that her responsibilities will increase drastically when she must manage several houses, their servants, provide entertainment for guests and . . . well, frankly I don't know what else is demanded of a peeress. Perhaps," he said thoughtfully, "we should put in a clause that she choose and train a factor who will, when the time comes—"

Amrington winced at the none-too-subtle reference to his eventual demise.

"—be prepared to take the reins from her hands so that she may concentrate on other responsibilities. The man she has now is very good, but is not young and we cannot expect him to carry on forever."

Frowning, Amrington pursed his lips. "Are you saying her fortune will *not* come under my son's care as is proper?"

"Merely that portion which is the Merrywood estate. What is in the funds and invested in other ways will fall to his management as is usual. Babs has a special fondness for her home, a tie to it and the land, that is as real as that of any man I have ever met."

Amrington stopped frowning, but continued to purse his lips. "She is," he finally said, "an exceptional woman if she truly understands the emotional attachment one has for one's land. Because of that, she will understand Matthew's involvement with his—" He grimaced and repeated William's words. "—when the time comes."

"She will be of aid to him, my lord, in ways most women would not. Have you studied England's history, my lord?" asked William, a seeming non sequitur.

"History?" Amrington suffered some confusion at the change of subject. "Of course I know England's history."

Mr. Ruthven nodded. "Then you know that, when our ancestors rode off to do battle with the Saracens, they left behind great estates. But are you aware that many of those estates were left in the hands of, and managed by, their wives?"

Amrington felt his mouth dropping open and instantly closed it. "I don't believe I ever thought about it."

"I have done much reading of documents from that time. It is a passion of mine, you see. I have been amazed at what was accomplished by the women of that age and I have wondered what it is about our own era that made us decide women have no use except to be decorative and, er, entertaining. Some men go so far as to believe that is all of which they are *capable.*"

Amrington looked thoughtful. "I understand what you would say. My own wife was an exceptional woman with a mind of her own, but I had not thought there was another like her, that she was a . . . a . . . well, an eccentric? All others, in my mind, were the mindless doll-women of whom you speak and I doubt, at my age, that I will change my ways, but I *do* understand what you would ask—and I cannot answer. I cannot tell you what my son feels about such things," he said, having finally, realized there was more to Mr. Ruthven's seemingly out-of-the-way comment about history than had been at all obvious. "I have never questioned him on the subject."

"It is something," said William gently, "about which *I* must think."

"Hmm. Yes, I see." Amrington rose to his feet. "Well, I assume we are still in agreement that a match between the two is to be desired. I've brought along the contract for the marriage that, thank the powers that be, did not come about. I wonder if perhaps you might peruse it and annotate it, and we can add and subtract from it?"

"Very well." William also stood. "Shall we agree to meet again—say, three days from now?"

It was not as soon as Amrington would have preferred, but he shook hands on it.

Then, while pouring each of them one more glass of wine, William frowned. "I wonder what I will say if my niece discovers you have visited me and becomes suspicious as to your reason."

Amrington's lips twitched. "Hmm. A problem. Perhaps I looked over her lands and wished to compliment her—but she is not at home. Then too, perhaps I offered to sell her a ram I am convinced would improve the grade of wool produced by her sheep."

William pressed his lips together and nodded. "That would be excellent—if you mean it. I have heard her mention that she must look out a new ram, that she is not happy with the one she has. If you are serious, I will tell her of your offer."

"I am serious. I have raised three for sale. They've proved out and now I wish to be rid of them. I will offer her the best of the lot." Amrington tossed back the last of his wine and rose to his feet. "It grows late," he said. "I had better take myself off and return to Hermione's— Lady Blackstock's, I should say—before she thinks me lost."

William rang a hand-bell that brought a footman who took a message to the stables that his lordship's horse was to be saddled and brought around. In less than a quarter of an hour, his lordship was on the road to Blackstock Manor reasonably well pleased with what he had accomplished.

Logan informed Babs that Lord Amrington had visited William Ruthven earlier that day and she immediately wanted to know why. Being Babs, she asked.

"Just a friendly visit. Oh, he did mention he wished to compliment you on the condition of your estate, although he thought your sheep could do with improving. He thinks he has a ram that would improve what you have. Are you still looking for one? He'd be willing to sell . . ."

And having turned Babs' mind to practical matters, William went off to write Lord Amrington a warning that Babs might soon accost him about buying the creature.

The next day Lady Dewsbury-Morgan rode with her when Babs drove herself over to Blackstock Manor. She watched Babs' light touch on the reins for a mile or two before saying, "I really must remember to ask Anna about acquiring a gig or perhaps a phaeton. We will need transport once we've moved into the dower house—other than that ostentatious monstrosity my son bought—I have rediscovered I enjoy driving. It was so many years since last I did so that I feared I'd lost the knack, but it came back almost immediately and I have asked your head groom to harness up a less docile creature the next time I go out."

"I have seen you tooling down the drive on several occasions and will admit I rather wondered where you went."

"These days it is to Woodbine House. Anna and I drive over to check on progress and make certain the paint the men mix actually comes near to the colors we've chosen. Would you believe that one man mixed an ugly plum color for the back bedroom and insisted it was mauve?"

"I have found that men rarely understand color. If you wish to buy a carriage, so be it, but if you would not mind the fact it is not quite up to the knocker—as they say— there is my mother's landau in the carriage house, just sitting there. Horses, however, are another matter. Perhaps my cousin James . . ."

"I think I will ask Mr. Riverton. I would ask Lord Calder but I don't quite like to. It is a trifle embarrassing even meeting him in company since Louisa Maria's very public rejection! But Mr. Riverton appears smitten with our Sissie and may actually like having something to do which, in part, will be for her benefit."

"Yes. Ah—here we are," added Babs, turning in to Lady Blackstock's entrance. The high gates stood wide, the grass growing up around the base of them in such a way as to indicate they were never shut. Ruts suggested the lane could do with some effort on someone's part as well. "I cannot understand how her ladyship can allow this estate to fall into disrepair as she's done. It is not as if she had gotten a trifle strange, as did Cousin James' father in his old age."

"You do not consider her . . . strange?"

"No, merely hunting-mad." Babs grimaced, her opinion of such sport not at all high. "That is no excuse for—" She bounced on her seat at a particularly nasty rut and set her foot against the front of the gig, steadying herself. "—for the state of this lane or of that hedge—" She pointed her whip to where a dead section of hedge was breaking down, the sheep beyond in danger of straying through it. "—or of any of the other things she's allowed."

"Perhaps if you wed Lord Calder and you live in the neighborhood he will see that things are improved at Blackstock."

Babs cast Lady Dewsbury-Morgan a quick sideways look, but her ladyship was facing straight forward, sober as a priest. "Don't press me."

"No, I won't," her ladyship said, smiling slightly. "But you can't stop me thinking it would be a very good thing for the both of you."

They had arrived and a well-trained groom ran forward to hold Babs' horses while a rather slovenly footman stood in the doorway, staring at them.

"Dratted idler!" muttered Lady Dewsbury-Morgan. "You," she called. "Yes, you," she repeated when the man put a thumb to his chest, his eyes widening. "Come put the steps down and help me to the ground."

The fellow pouted, but he did come and he did manage to help Lady Dewsbury-Morgan down without letting her fall, but he did it so awkwardly that Babs declined his help and got down herself.

"Is Lord Amrington at home?" she asked, once she'd done so.

He was, they met, and twenty minutes later Babs had bought her ram.

"Well, shall we drink on it?" asked his lordship, somewhat taken aback by Miss Ruthven's ability to drive a hard bargain.

"A glass of wine would be very welcome," she said. "I am glad to have that settled."

"I, too—Miss Ruthven," his lordship added, as he handed her her wine. "Will you think me too bold if I tell you I find you an amazing woman?"

She raised fine eyebrows, one slightly higher than the other and a bit of a frown adding a quizzical look to her features. "Thank you. I think . . . ?"

That made him chuckle. "May I also add," he said slyly, "that I would be very happy to welcome you into our family?"

Babs pokered up immediately. Was Calder pursuing her simply because his father approved of her?

"That," he said gently, "was supposed to be taken as a compliment. Or perhaps you think my family is not one that you'd find it to your advantage to join?"

"I will wed only if I am certain I will find something far more important in my marriage than prestige or financial benefit," she said, her voice cold, although she managed to keep it from dripping ice.

"And that is?" he asked, frowning.

"Affection and mutual respect, my lord," she said and rose to her feet, setting her partially filled glass aside. "I will send over a draft on my banker, my lord, and await the arrival of this paragon of a ram." She curtsied and swept from the room.

Amrington, holding his glass balanced between the fingers of both hands, stared at the empty doorway. Then he kicked himself, mentally, and scowled down into his wine.

Ruthven warned me, he thought. *Why can I not keep a still tongue in my head?*

Fifteen

James looked at Lady Morgan in surprise. "Did I hear you correctly?" he asked, startled from his usual savoir faire.

"Do not make me repeat myself. It was far too difficult saying it the first time."

"But, Lady Morgan, I do not *wish* to wed your daughter. If I had thought of it, which I will admit I did, I dismissed the idea immediately."

"But why? She adores you. She idolizes you!" Lady Morgan added what she felt the clinching argument. "She would never ever do anything to upset you or cause you distress."

James rubbed his chin, staring at the hopeful looking woman standing before him. "My lady, I do not wish to be idolized. Have you any notion how difficult it would be to deserve such devotion for the rest of one's life? And—" He hesitated, but it occurred to him he would never succeed if he never tried. "—there is a more important stumbling block. I am," he said with a twinkle in his eye, "thinking quite seriously of wedding someone else."

Lady Morgan sighed. "I knew it. You have decided to wed her after all."

His mind on Lady Morgan, James blinked. "Her . . . ?"

"Miss Ruthven, of course," said Lady Morgan and one

would not have been out of line to accuse her of sounding just a trifle cross.

"Ah! I have no more desire to wed my cousin now than I did before we met," said James firmly.

Lady Morgan's eyelashes fluttered. "You do not?"

"I do not. She is far too young for me. As is your daughter, Lady Morgan."

"But then . . . ?" She drew in a deep breath and let it out. "No," she said, "it is none of my business."

"But it is," he said softly.

She seemed to freeze in place, and then her eyes slanted up to his. "Is?"

He nodded. "Is." Her eyes widened and he grinned, nodded, and offered his arm. "Shall we walk, my lady?"

After only half an instant's hesitation, Lady Morgan rather shyly accepted his arm and paced beside him out the door and into the sunshine.

"It is quite beautiful here," he said when they had strolled down one path and turned onto another.

"Your own gardens will need a great deal of work" she said, glancing up at him to see if this was an acceptable statement.

"They certainly will. Do you know as much about gardens as you do about decorating, my lady?"

"Gardens? I only know what I like. I've no idea how one achieves the results I'd want."

"But you could direct a good gardener in the way to go on," he suggested.

Shyly, she smiled up at him. "I would enjoy it. It is too bad it takes years to produce a proper garden. I would offer to help you with yours as I've done inside the house, but—" She glanced at him and quickly away. "—one cannot accomplish a garden in the little time we will live here."

"Have you not thought it might be nice to live here forever?"

She stiffened. "Never return to London?"

"Oh yes. For the season. And it is not so far one cannot go for a week or two when there is reason."

Still unsure she had understood his hints that he meant to offer for her, she said, "We have taken the dower house for a year. Our year of mourning, you know."

"Do you mean to follow a strict code of mourning?" he asked.

"I . . ."

When she didn't continue, he squeezed the hand laying on his arm. "Never mind. It was not a proper question, but I do have a reason for my rudeness. If you were to agree to wed me—"

She let out a long breath she had been unaware she was holding.

"—I would hope to say our vows long before the year is over." He glanced down at her and found her staring at nothing, her mouth a little round "oh" and restrained a chuckle. "You must not try to answer me immediately, my lady," he said gently. "I have surprised you, of course, but I cannot have you thinking I might wed your daughter when it is you on whom I've my eye!"

"But . . . but . . ."

"Come now, you cannot be so surprised as all that, surely."

"I am too old. I think—" She cast him a quick look. "—I may be a trifle older than you."

"Yes, and will have grown sensible with it," he said, patting her arm encouragingly. "I have already seen how very good you are with decorating and I will enjoy watching you plan and execute my gardens and, although it should not play a large role in your decision, there is the fact that I like Louisa Maria and will try to be a good father to her."

"But of course that is an important factor." She

stopped and, perforce, he did too, turning to look down at her. "You know," she said earnestly, "that she may never again speak? She may *always* be a burden. I fear she will never wed, which *should* be the goal of all properly brought up young ladies. It is a terrible thought, that."

"Are you so certain?" James hid a smile at her belief that the only role for a woman was that of wife and mother. "I think she will."

"No man would wed a woman who will not speak! No one would consider it for an instant."

James thought of Quentin's growing affection for Louisa Maria and decided that, if Lady Morgan had not noticed, it might be wisest to refrain from mentioning it to her. She might interfere—in a well-meaning way—but the situation would not bear interference.

"You have not said whether I may hope," he said to turn her mind from her daughter.

Lady Morgan drew in a deep breath. "Sir, I am a new widow. I should not even think of a second marriage."

"You mouth the words of convention, Lady Morgan, but do you believe them?"

Her hands twitched and quivered, clung together, and then fluttered apart. "Oh dear. You should not encourage me to think bad thoughts, Mr. Ruthven."

"You think it wrong to consider a second marriage so soon." It was not a question. "Very well. But you will not forget that I've asked and that the question is still open?"

"How could I forget?" was her simple but obviously heartfelt response.

"Then I will be satisfied with that," he said. "There are young sheep in the meadow just beyond the grounds. If we walk up that rise ahead of us we will see them. Would you care for the exercise, or shall we return to the house?"

Lady Morgan indicated she would like the walk and it

was nearly an hour before they made their way home. James was not surprised to discover he liked her notions for the garden nearly as well as he'd liked her notions for the house. In fact, he had concluded that Lady Morgan was a surprising lady altogether.

But he thought it would be her ladyship herself who would be *most* surprised—once she regained confidence in herself and her own judgment.

While James Ruthven was finding his chosen lady still more suitable than he already thought her—something that would have surprised many people a great deal—Lord Calder arrived and asked if Miss Morgan was available.

He had decided he must put the chit's mind to rest. He had put it off for two reasons. The first was that it seemed particularly embarrassing to have the conversation at all. The chit should *know* he could no longer wed her. The second was the difficulty of holding any sort of conversation with her when she could not or would not speak.

"Perhaps," he added before the butler could do more than open the salon doors and indicate he was to wait there, "you will ask that Miss Ruthven join us? As chaperon?"

Logan nodded. Aware of Miss Morgan's disability, he went to find Miss Ruthven first, suggesting that *she* tell Miss Morgan the young lady was wanted in the salon.

"I see," she said after he explained that it was Lord Calder who wished speech with Miss Morgan. "I will go at once." She rose to her feet and then hesitated. "Just where, my good Logan, shall I find her?"

"She is, I believe, in the music room."

"Ah." Babs considered. "Perhaps I should collect Lord Calder and take him there . . ."

Louisa was most comfortable when near her music and this conversation might be a trifle difficult even in the best of conditions. Assuming, of course, that his lordship meant to tell Louisa he would not hold her to the engagement and she need have no fear he or anyone else would attempt to force her to the altar.

And surely he would not have requested my presence if it were anything less . . . proper? Babs nodded. "That is what I'll do."

She and Calder entered the music room to discover Quentin and Miss Morgan with their heads bent over a sheet of music, Quentin pointing to a particular phrase and Miss Morgan nodding her head in agreement with whatever it was he said to her.

Calder cleared his throat and the two turned just their heads to look at him. Quentin instantly straightened and stepped from Miss Morgan's side, but she turned on him an anguished look that drew him back.

"Hello, cousin," said Quentin. "Have you and Miss Ruthven come to join us in our practice?"

"No. I was unaware you meant to visit," said Calder, strolling forward and drawing Babs with him.

"I rode over an hour ago or so."

"Definitely 'or so,'" Babs laughed. "I believe when you and Louisa are involved with music neither of you has the least notion of the passing time."

Quentin pulled his watch from his fob pocket and looked at it. An expression of surprise widened his eyes. "So late as that? Miss Morgan," he said, turning to her, "I apologize for occupying so much of your morning!"

She shook her head, turned a very brief glower on her hostess and Lord Calder, and then dropped her eyes to the music in her hand.

"I believe Miss Morgan thinks it is I who should apologize," said Calder smoothly. "She is angry that I have interrupted the two of you."

He received a quick look at that, but not so quickly he didn't see the fear in her eyes.

"And she is right. I should have asked that someone see that she was free to hear me out. Miss Morgan, I've only a few words to say to you, and, having steeled myself to do it, I hope you will allow me to say them?"

This time Louisa Maria looked at Miss Ruthven. It was a pleading look and Babs freed herself to go to the girl. "My dear," she said softly, "I don't believe Lord Calder will say anything to upset you and, perhaps, will say what will set your mind at ease. Will you listen?"

After a moment Louisa nodded and, slowly, turned a wide-eyed gaze on his lordship.

Calder cleared his throat. "Miss Morgan, I believe we are both already aware of it, but I was told to put it into words. My dear, I release you, formally, from any and all obligation you had, or feel you still have, to wed me. I think you agree we will not suit."

Louisa's eyes grew still rounder and she looked first at Quentin and then, quickly, turned her gaze toward Babs who nodded. "Do you agree you will not suit?" asked Babs gently.

Louisa nodded once, firmly, and then she nodded several times in a row.

"You wish to be released from your engagement to Lord Calder?" asked Babs, wishing to make certain the chit knew what it was she was doing.

Again Louisa nodded.

"Then I think that completes our business," said Calder quietly. "Perhaps you would like to return to your music?"

Again Louisa nodded, but then looked questioningly at Quentin—who smiled and nodded.

After half a moment, Babs patted Louisa's arm, and, joining Lord Calder, she urged him from the room. "I am remiss," she said softly once the door was closed, "in allowing them to stay there, alone together, but I believe your cousin is to be trusted to hold the line?"

He grinned at her use of the cant phrase. "Quentin will do nothing to harm Miss Morgan."

"Excellent." But then she hadn't a notion what to say or do. Before she could offer him refreshment, which was the only thing she could think of to keep him near, he asked if she had time for a ride. "What an excellent idea," she said, brightening. "If you will accept a glass of wine while you wait, I will take only a moment to change. Our horses and my groom can be ordered up while I do so."

They found Logan who sent a message to the stables and brought Calder the mug of homebrew he requested instead of wine. Babs' maid was putting away newly ironed chemises and petticoats and ready to help her change. It was, of course, a bit more than a moment, but she did return far more quickly than Calder had expected.

He said so.

"You are overly familiar with the habits of London misses. I never understood why it took everyone so long to change. There was one young lady who spent more hours before her mirror than she did with companions!"

"She must have been a female Brummell," said Calder, grinning.

"You mean . . . ?"

"Brummell has said that one should never leave one's dressing room until one is certain everything about one's dress is perfection and then one should not think of one's attire again until time to change it."

"No, that wasn't Miss Grainer at all. Not only did she spend hours in her room, but then with every breeze, whenever someone crowded her the least bit or she stepped off the paving or along a gravel path, she bemoaned what must have happened to all that perfection.

I don't believe I ever heard her speak of anything but gowns, her coiffure, finding just the hat to go with some pelisse—you know the thing."

"If you had not said it was Miss Grainer I would have known exactly. It is likely she is still Miss Grainer because no one can entice her into speaking of anything else long enough to ask if she might wed them!"

They chuckled and continued to ride along the lane, talking of this and that, the groom, trailing far enough behind, he was, more or less, beyond hearing. When they reached the humpbacked bridge, Calder indicated the river path and asked if she'd like to walk.

He helped her dismount, ordered the groom to watch the horses, adding they would not be long and would not go far. The river just there was fairly straight, so the groom, as was proper, could keep them in sight, but they could, finally, feel assured he'd not listen to their conversation.

As soon as she felt it safe, Babs said, "Thank you for speaking to Louisa."

"I wonder if I would ever have done so if you had not insisted it was the thing to do."

"Why?"

"It was embarrassing. I very nearly turned tail when I saw Quentin."

"No one listening to you would have known you were the least out of frame. You handled the situation very well."

"Thank you, but I doubt it."

"Why?"

"If I did well, why did she not respond?"

Babs shook her head and they walked in silence for a space.

"Have *you* an answer for me?" he asked when they stopped to stare at a barge rounding the curve in the river.

"No."

"When?"

"I don't know."

"What else do you need to know?"

Babs searched her mind. "Tell me about your life in London."

He talked easily of the way he spent his days.

"And the nights?" she asked, casting him a teasing glance.

He grimaced. "Are you certain you want to know? I assure you I would not behave so once I am married."

She didn't press it. Instead she asked, "Are you satisfied with such a life?"

For a moment he remained silent and she wondered if he would answer. Then he sighed. "I was. That first year or two after coming down from my college it was new and exciting. And then it became habit. And then . . . it was necessary."

"Necessary?"

"My brother is dead. I have not wished to admit he is gone."

"So you kept to the life you knew, superstitiously thinking that if you did not change your life, then his had not changed?"

"Something of the sort."

"And now?" she asked after another long silence.

"Now it is time to go on. To learn to do the things an heir must do—and take some of the burden from my father's shoulders."

"Assuming," she said, "he wishes it taken from them!"

He laughed. "Yes, there is that. But I think he *has* reached that point. Napoleon will soon be finished and the Continent open to English travelers. I have long suspected he wishes to see again some of the people and places he visited when on his grand tour."

"Or is it that you wish a grand tour of your own and

therefore assume *he* wishes to return to the places and people he knew?"

Lord Calder was silent for an even longer time but Babs waited patiently, realizing his silence was because he actually considered his answers to her questions. "There was a time," he said, "when I listened to his stories and wished I too could have such adventures. Now . . ." He shrugged. "I may travel. Eventually. At the moment . . . no. Miss Ruthven—"

"Babs," she said.

"—what?"

"Do call me Babs. It is much more friendly and we are friends, are we not?"

He nodded. "I hope so. Will you call me Matt?"

"Your father calls you Matthew."

"He is not fond of pet names. I am."

"Then . . . Matt."

"Good. Now what was I saying . . . Ah! Babs—" He tipped a glance her way and smiled when she did "—will you be so good as to help me learn what a landowner must know?"

Babs instantly sobered. "Will I . . . what?"

"Will you teach me to fulfill the role I must eventually take to myself?" he asked, using different words.

"Do you think I can?" she asked, somewhat awed that he'd deign to ask her, a female, something so important.

"Yes. And with more patience than my father! He will expect me to simply *know* when it was never my place to *know.*"

She chuckled.

"You don't answer."

"Well, it is difficult, is it not? Learning what you must learn will not happen overnight. I believe I could help you, but . . ." She looked up and their gazes tangled.

He stared down at her—and then understood. He laughed. "You mean you might have time for the task if we were wed but that you are not yet ready to agree to that?"

"Lord Calder—"

"Matt," he said sternly.

"—Matt," she repeated obediently. And then drew in a breath. Equally sternly she said, "One thing I *will* give you is that you are *not* a slowtop!"

"No, there is nothing wrong with my cockloft when I decide to put it to use," he agreed with a straight face.

She cast him a glance and then laughed, glad to have an excuse to change the subject. "Should I not have said slowtop?"

"It is cant and not usually on a lady's lips."

"Does it bother you that I use cant occasionally?"

"Much to my surprise it does not. Which is strange." His heavy brows drew down over his deep-set eyes. "A year or so ago a young lady came up to London for her season who affected cant language. I despised her for it."

"Ah, but she *affected* the language!"

He nodded. "Yes, there is a difference, is there not? You do not watch for times when you may use the words you know. She did and then looked to see how she had impressed those around her."

"I can almost feel sorry for her," said Babs, slowly.

"Why?" he asked.

"Because there are so many young ladies brought to town each season, all looking for a match, and all filled with rigid propriety until there is no way to make themselves individuals in the eyes of the young men who gather round. She thought, I suspect, she had found a way to make herself recognized and remembered."

"I had not thought of it in that way. Yes, perhaps she is more to be pitied than despised."

Babs nodded. "Still, to return to the point, I am glad you are an intelligent man. I have been surrounded by intelligent men all my life and I could not bear to spend the rest of it in the company of one who was not."

"Does that mean you will wed me?" he asked, all innocence.

She flushed. "No, it does not. Do not put words in my mouth!"

He chuckled. "I think you will."

She glanced at him. "Why?"

"Because you have found a man who will allow you to be yourself, and will also make you stretch to keep up with him."

"Why you arrogant . . ." She looked over the fingers he laid over her lips.

"Don't say it."

"Why not?"

"Because it might start an argument and you know I cannot bear arguments."

She smiled and shook her head. "You do like . . . what is it called? Cross and jostle work? But pretend you do not like arguments?"

"I like *innocent banter* which is not the same, but cross and jostle work?" he asked, and shook his head. "More cant! And this time, boxing cant! Where, my dear Babs, did you learn that?"

She frowned. "I don't think I can tell you . . . oh yes, I can. From your aunt!"

He stared and then laughed. "Yes, my aunt would find the term perfectly understandable and would be likely to use it too. Do you dislike Aunt Hermie?"

Babs frowned. "I do not know her well, of course, and she is addicted to the hunt in all its various forms . . . but it is, really, impossible to dislike her. She is so very much herself . . . if that makes sense."

He nodded. "Oh, yes. There are few people in our world who have the strength or the courage to be exactly who and what they are and . . . and devil take the hind-most if others do not approve."

"Or she is completely oblivious of what others might think of her?"

He smiled but it soon faded. "I don't believe she is oblivious. Occasionally, I think, she wishes they would not disapprove, but I suspect she sees their disapproval as a failing on *their* part."

Babs nodded. "Up to a point, I can understand. I have never wished to change myself in order to make my character or personality agreeable to another—as Lady Morgan did when her husband insisted she change out of all recognition."

"She is an extreme case, of course. I have—" He glanced down at her. "—already said I will not attempt to change you. I like you. Much to my surprise."

"You are surprised?"

"Well, you did steal my gun, did you not? And you hid it away where it could not be found. By me, at least."

"You held a grudge all those years?"

"No. I had forgotten all about it."

"But you had *not* forgotten," she said, frowning.

"In one sense, perhaps, but not in the sense that I brooded on it and kept myself poised to discover a means of revenge. Babs," he said quietly, "I am not one to hold a grudge. I become angry occasionally, but once I have vented my temper, it is over. Done. Finished. Do you understand?"

She nodded. "I suppose I am much the same. I cannot tolerate injustice, for instance, and will rake the culprit up one side and down another—but then I go on about my business. Of course, I will not put that sort of person into a position of authority and I will never again trust them in quite the same way. Does that make sense?"

He nodded and they strolled on in silence until they

realized they had rounded the bend and gone beyond the groom's sight. Babs stopped. "We should go back," she said just as Matthew touched her arm, turning her toward him. He lifted his other hand and, lightly, held her before him. He stared down into her eyes.

A touch of color rose into Babs' cheeks but she did not turn her gaze from his. Matthew's hold tightened ever so slightly but still he said nothing. After another long moment he sighed, loosed her, and turned.

"I apologize," he said.

"Why?"

"Because I was tempted to kiss you and I've no right to do so . . . yet," he added, rather spoiling the innocence of his explanation.

Babs bit her lip. "You need not apologize. I . . . was rather hoping you would."

He turned back. "Why?"

She was silent for a long moment and then, determined to lighten what had become far too serious, smiled a rather mischievous smile. "Curiosity?" she asked, her head tipped to one side.

He chuckled and gestured up the path. "Shall we return before I succumb to temptation and satisfy your curiosity?" he asked.

She sighed an overdone and obviously put-on sigh. "If you insist."

His smile broadened. "You are, as I have suspected, something of a minx."

"Yes," she said, glancing at him from the corners of her eyes. "But you are a bit of a rake, so that is all right."

He stiffened. "I have never ever done anything to embarrass a young lady!"

"No, but you have thought about it," she said, "and if you were a proper monk you would not."

His shoulders heaved in silent laughter. "My dear innocent, I suspect even monks experience the occasional urge to . . . to embarrass the occasional woman. It is merely that they are not supposed to do so and very likely feel guilty. I do not."

She nodded. "As I said. A bit of a rake. All men are, are they not?"

"I suppose they are. In the sense you appear to mean."

"There is a different meaning?"

"A far more common and far less innocent one, I fear. The man we generally call a rake tends to have no concern for the object of his interest but only his own desires. Most men do care."

"I see." She thought about it. "Or do I?"

He pokered up. "It is not a subject I will discuss further—at least, I might with my *wife*, but not, Babs Ruthven, even with my fiancée! And you are not so much as that. Will you not say me yes and put me—" *And my father.* "—out of my misery?"

She didn't respond and he looked down at her, saw she frowned—but in a thoughtful rather than angry way—and decided the better part of valor at this point was to hold his tongue.

He was right. After half a dozen steps she stopped. A step later he did too and turned to look at her. Their gazes mingled, tied the one to the other as had occurred before, and finally, when he thought he could bear it no more, she drew in a deep breath and swallowed. Then she nodded.

One quick nod.

"Was that," he asked softly, "a yes? You have agreed to wed me?" he asked, putting it into words that could not be misunderstood.

Again Babs nodded.

His smile was brighter then the sun. "I am glad," he said.

It was a simple response but obviously sincere and was

perfect from her point of view. "I think I am too," she said.

"You only think it?" he asked, his heavy brows suddenly drawing down.

"It is, you must admit, a serious decision. One that affects the whole of the rest of our lives. I am uncertain I've done the right thing."

"We will, together, see that it is the right thing," he said and again his sincerity was obvious.

She nodded, but the corner of her lip disappeared between two pearly white teeth.

"You really are uncertain, are you not?" he asked a trifle tentatively.

"Yes."

His features hardened. "Do you wish to retract?"

She paused just long enough so that he feared she would, but then she shook her head. "No." And then she sighed. "I suppose we must inform Uncle William and announce it to everyone else."

It was his turn to pause. "If," he finally said, "you would prefer to wait . . ."

Again a silence fell. Babs was tempted, but shook her head. Matthew softly released the breath he'd held until she did so. And then he wondered why her response meant so much to him . . . but looking into his emotions was something he did rarely and had little practice at doing, so he set aside the feeling and smiled down at her.

"I wish," he said, "that we were still around the bend and out of your groom's sight."

She smiled. "Unfortunately we are not."

"Shall we return around the curve?"

Regretfully, she shook her head. "Better not," she said.

"No. I don't suppose we'd better."

They both sighed. Then, hearing each other, they

both laughed. And then, arm in arm, they returned to their horses and mounted up.

"Uncle William will very likely be found in his study at this time of day," she said.

"Then onward," said Matthew, "to Mr. Ruthven's study."

Sixteen

Babs entered her uncle's study only to stop short. Matthew's hands rose to her shoulders to steady her. He too looked across the room to where his father sat across the empty hearth from Mr. Ruthven.

"I suppose this isn't altogether a bad thing," mused Matthew, breathing the words into his brand-new fiancée's ear.

She sighed. "No, but it might be easier one at a time."

The men, when they perceived her entry, rose to their feet. "My dear child," said Mr. Ruthven, the faintest frown marring his brow, "you are looking more than a trifle windblown. Lord Amrington will excuse you while you change from your habit and remove the odor of your recent ride!"

"I have never minded a bit of the stables around me," said Amrington, looking from his son to Miss Ruthven and back again. His eyes narrowed. "It is my opinion they've something to say to us and, speaking for myself, I'd not care to delay hearing it."

Matthew gently squeezed Babs' shoulders and moved her on into the room. "We do have news. Miss Ruthven has done me the great honor of agreeing to wed me."

Amrington turned to Mr. Ruthven, grasped the other man's hand, and shook it vigorously. "They have done it," he said with satisfaction. "Their timing is impeccable, do you not agree?"

Ruthven made a motion as if to silence Amrington, but was either unobserved or ignored because his lordship turned to the newly engaged couple and, beaming, told them the papers dealing with settlements and so on had arrived from the solicitors only that morning and they could sign them now since they were both available for that duty.

Matthew felt Babs stiffen and, suddenly concerned, looked down at her. "No!" he said sharply but she pulled away from him, glaring at the men across the room. "Babs, please! Don't . . ."

"I'll not have it!" she growled. Her voice was pitched lower than normal and it was, actually, more frightening than if she had raised it. "Interfering old men! Cannot you keep your noses to yourself! Well, you can just go marry each other. I'm through. I'll never wed. I'm going to live and die a spinster!" She turned on her heel and, exiting, slammed the door behind her.

Ruthven sighed. "I tried to warn you, my lord. In fact, I did warn you," he said to Amrington who was staring, openmouthed, at the blank door.

"But . . . ?"

"She will not be driven," said Ruthven. "Led, but not driven."

"But . . . !"

"Yes, of course she had already agreed to marry your son. It was the idea we were just waiting for her to do so that set up her hackles. At least you did not suggest going directly from signing the contracts to informing the vicar he was to read the banns at tomorrow's service for the first time!"

Amrington grimaced. "How did you know it was on the tip of my tongue?"

"I have," said Ruthven dryly, "come to know you reasonably well, given how briefly we've been acquainted.

Lord Calder, there is wine on the sideboard. I think we could all do with a glass."

Matthew glanced toward the wine, glared at his father, and then, grimacing, turned on his heel and left the room without a word.

"What did I do to upset Matthew?" asked Amrington, bewildered all over again.

"He blames you for upsetting my Babs, of course, as do I. I hope he has the address to bring her around his thumb!"

"Surely she did not mean those things she said?"

Ruthven was silent for a long moment. "I would not care to venture a guess," he said and went, himself, to the sideboard where he poured them each a large glass of a heavy Madeira, a wine he did not favor in the usual way but, on this occasion, felt to be appropriate.

Matthew found Logan in the front hall. The man was staring, thoughtfully, up the stairs. He jumped slightly when Matthew addressed him.

"I've a message for Miss Ruthven. I wanted it delivered in these exact words." Matthew stared at the butler, his brows lifted, the dark bar across his forehead quite impressive.

Logan nodded.

"Tell her this. I didn't know a thing about it."

"I am to say only that? Lord Calder didn't know a thing about it?"

"Nothing else. I suppose you could clear your throat to engage her attention but do not try to say you've a message from me, or anything of that nature. Only those words."

"His lordship didn't know a thing about it," repeated Logan. "Very well, my lord."

"Now."

"Oh, no. She gave orders she is not to be disturbed for anything less than fire or flood."

"*Now,*" said Matthew more firmly.

"It would mean my position!" said Logan, backing away.

Matthew's lips firmed but a noise on the stairs drew his attention and he glanced up. Lady Dewsbury-Morgan was coming down and he ran lightly up the steps to meet her at the landing.

"I have need of your aid," he said, taking her hands gently but firmly into his own. "Logan will not do it. He says it is worth his job to interfere. Will you chance her temper and help me in his place?"

Her ladyship smiled up at him. "In a temper, is she?"

He nodded. "With some reason."

"Angry with you?"

"Only by association," he said with a smile that quickly faded. He told her what he wanted said and, after repeating the phrase, Lady Dewsbury-Morgan turned and climbed the stairs. She disappeared from sight down the hallway that led to Miss Ruthven's private apartments. Behind her Matthew didn't move. He stared after her for as long as he could see her and then listened until the tapping of her cane also faded to nothing and then, relaxing slightly, leaned against the railing.

And waited.

"Oh no, my girl. I once told you never to show me that temper!" said Lady Dewsbury-Morgan sharply. "You will listen and you will *hear* me."

"You have come from that . . . that . . ." Babs clenched her fists and turned her back on the woman who, without invitation, had invaded her room.

"He knew nothing about it."

"Ha!"

"He knew nothing about it."

"You would believe the devil if he smiled at you!"

"He knew nothing about it."

"How could he not?" she asked.

Lady Dewsbury-Morgan quickly suppressed a smile. "I haven't a notion. I don't even know what the thing *is* about which he knows nothing. I merely know that Logan would not deliver the message because he feared for his position. I believe that, if I had not agreed to come in his place, Lord Calder, knowing full well he has no business in your rooms, would be here telling you himself that he *knew nothing about it.*"

Babs frowned. Was it possible? Suddenly, sharp and clear in her mind, was a picture of her uncle, an alarmed look on his face and his hand rising toward Lord Amrington. *"Uncle William!"*

"I should bring him to you?" asked Lady Dewsbury-Morgan, confused.

"What? Oh. No." Babs's lips closed, firmed, and her eyes flashed. "How dare he?"

"Lord Calder?"

"No, of course not. My uncle. He knew how I felt. He *knew.*"

Lady Dewsbury-Morgan considered the angry young woman for a long moment and then, limping ever so slightly—she had perhaps hurried a bit more than she should have done coming down the hall—she moved closer and lifted her hand to slap the chit across the cheek.

Babs, without thinking, caught the elder woman's wrist but was startled by the attempt and allowed some of her anger to drain away. "What is it? I am not hysterical, you know. Merely angry."

"Yes, and irrational. I would have a round tale from you, miss, and then we will decide what to do. Ranting and raving and waving your arms about will accomplish nothing. Besides, Lord Calder is waiting to discover if you believe him and, assuming you do, what you mean to do about it. Whatever it may be."

"Matt! Where?"

"I left him on the stairs."

Babs swung around her visitor and left the room, running down the hall. At the top of the stairs she looked down. "I believe you," she said. "But I am still very *very* angry."

For a moment Calder almost seemed to collapse into himself, and then he straightened.

"My faith in you meant so much that you nearly faint?" she asked, slowly descending the stairs toward him.

"I hadn't a notion how much it would mean," he said quietly, "until it was necessary that I hear you say it." A surprised look had him blinking his eyes in wonderment. "How strange."

"What is strange?" she asked.

"The discovery that I have fallen in love with you, my dear." He caught and held her gaze. "Deeply and truly in love."

Her eyes widened and she mouthed the words, *You love me.*

"And you, my dear?"

She smiled, her eyes glowing. "I think I have loved you almost since I first met you," she said. "Well, since we met again, that is."

"So long?"

She nodded. "You must not ask why I took so long agreeing to wed you, knowing I loved you."

"I need not. I understand perfectly." Suddenly his voice deepened, softened. "I love you. I love you so very much. I never expected to ever love anyone as I love you."

She stood before him on the landing, looking up into his face. He stared down. Their hands rose and clasped. Each leaned a trifle toward the other . . .

. . . and Logan cleared his throat.

They straightened, looking ever so faintly embarrassed. Matthew looked very slightly irritated as well.

"Now," said Lady Dewsbury-Morgan from the head of the stairs, "will one of you please inform me of what tempest roiled the leaves in this particular teapot?"

They returned to the upper floor where Babs led the way to a lady's parlor which would not, in the normal way, be open to guests. But this, she felt, was an emergency.

"You tell her," said Babs once they were seated.

"I can tell her what happened. I cannot explain why you reacted in quite the way you did," said Matthew, staring at her.

Babs sighed. "I will not be dictated to. Those . . . those . . ."

"Our elders," suggested Matthew with a glance toward Lady Dewsbury-Morgan who attempted—not very successfully—to hide a smile.

Babs' lips compressed and then she sighed. "My temper. They meant us to wed whether we would or no. They planned it. They have already drawn up the settlement papers. They have them all ready for us to sign. At what point, if we had not come to them today, would they have sat us down, handed us a pen, and pointed out where our signatures were required?"

"Never."

"How can you say that?"

"They would not have done it. What they *would* have done—my father, at least—was to nag-nag-nag us to get on with it."

"And why not?" asked Lady Dewsbury-Morgan. They turned to her, having half forgotten she was there. She smiled at their expressions. "It has been obvious," she explained, "that the two of you were meant for each other. What is surprising is that it took you so long to discover it for yourselves."

Babs, still irritated, turned back to Matthew. "Does it not bother you that they would organize our lives? That they would decide what was best for us and not consult our wishes?"

"They *did* wait for us to announce that we had become engaged. I imagine we have your uncle to thank for that. My father would be far more likely to hand us the contracts, suggest it was time we stopped our shilly-shallying, sign them, wed, and get on with our life together."

Babs' eyes narrowed and her lips pulled into a tight little bud.

"My dear," asked her ladyship, "why do you feel it wrong of them to wish to see that everything is done for the best?"

"What *they* perceive to be the best."

"Yes. Of course. But think, dear. Have you *objections* to wedding Lord Calder?"

Babs, her lips tightly compressed, shook her head.

"You have, in fact, agreed to do that very thing?"

Babs nodded.

"Then you realize that contracts must be drawn up and the banns called?"

Slowly she nodded.

"You wish to do it all yourself?" asked her ladyship politely.

"I would wish to be consulted!"

Matthew touched her hand. "No one should sign important papers without reading them," he said softly, suggestively. "If," he added, "there is anything to which you object, then it must be changed, must it not? Even—" He smiled a quick smile and his eyes twinkled. "—if-it-means-postponing-the-wedding."

He drawled that last in such a way he gave it extra meaning and Babs met his steady gaze, frowning ever so slightly.

"I, for myself, would prefer we wed as quickly as may

be," he continued, "but if you wish to punish your uncle and my father, then I am certain you can find first one thing and then another to which you object or can think up additions or alterations for-as-long-as-you-wish."

Again that drawl. Babs's eyes widened. Her lips spread slowly into a tight smile. Then she chuckled. And then she sobered. "Will you mind very much?"

"If you keep them jumping for overly long, I will—but if you mean to change things only three or four times? I will manage to contain myself and await your pleasure, madam."

Babs nodded. "You are generous, my lord."

"No. But I begin to understand you and I will not begin our marriage with resentment coloring your vows!"

She grinned. "Yes, I think perhaps you do understand me. Shall we go down?" she asked, rising to her feet.

He did likewise, offered her his arm, and led the way to the door where he turned them. "Thank you, my lady, for taking my message to my love." He bowed.

Babs cast him a quick look. His love? He had said so on the landing and she had believed him. But should she? Could she?

Ah! If only he meant it. Was it at all possible he *truly* meant it? Babs suspected she would have another long, one-sided, conversation with her bedpost when she finally sought her bed that evening!

The contracts went back and forth to London three times before William Ruthven realized the game in which his niece was engaged. When they returned again he himself read them carefully, made a tick against two points, added a clause in another place, and then gave the whole a final reading before taking them to Babs.

This time when Babs skimmed through the closely written pages, looking for the next change she meant to make, she discovered what he had done. She looked up at him and discovered him sitting across her desk from her, his arms crossed and a scowl on his face.

"Well, miss?" he asked, a stern look about him she'd not seen in years. "Will you finish making a Maygame of Lord Amrington and myself?"

"You have guessed? Oh dear, that is too bad," she said with pretended innocence.

"How long did you mean to carry on with this nonsense?"

"Oh, for another time or two. Actually, you discovered one change I had not considered." She laid one slender finger against a tick mark. "But, since you have guessed my game, we will make the final changes all at once—" She made a moue. "—although it is too bad of you, that you spoil it. You and his lordship deserve to be punished!"

"And Lord Calder?" asked William.

"He understands. It was, in fact, his suggestion."

William's brows arched. "Now that puts another complexion on things, does it not?" he said in musing tones.

"In what way?"

"It had not occurred to me that his lordship had that particular sort of a sense of humor. You had best watch your p's and q's, Babs, or he'll learn to manage you and you will never know it."

A frisson ran up her spine but then she considered. She grinned. "If I never know it, then it will not worry me, will it? Now here," she said, pointing to the page before her—and went on to discuss the change she wanted made in that particular clause.

When they finished, the documents were bundled up and tied up and Logan told to order up a groom who could find his way about London, a man prepared for a long hard ride there and back again.

That done, William turned to his niece. "This has gone on long enough, Babs," he said sternly. "You will tell Lord Calder that it is time to ask the vicar for the first reading of the banns."

She stood, her arms crossed, her toe tapping. "Uncle, would you care to rephrase that?"

"No." He smiled a rather wolfish smile she had never seen. One that had her understanding how he had, for many years, managed the family's business—not just her inheritance—with panache and great success. "For once you will listen to common sense and not make objections merely because you do not like the tone or the phrasing!" He turned on his heel and left the room.

Babs smiled fondly after him. She had, she knew, pushed him just as far as he would go and she, on the whole, was not displeased. She turned to Logan. "I would like John to bring around my horse and another groom who is to take a message to Lord Calder." She pulled a notebook and tiny pencil from her pocket, something she was rarely without, wrote a few quick words, tore out the sheet, and formed it into a twist that she gave Logan. Then, picking up her skirts, she ran lightly up the stairs to her room to change into her habit.

"So, Mr. Ruthven is on to us, is he?" asked Matthew, smiling fondly at his fiancée.

Babs tipped her head. "I like that 'us.' It has a nice sound to it," she said.

"Lady Dewsbury-Morgan was right, was she not?"

"In what way?"

"She said we were a match. When we first met again I had no notion of it."

"Nor I. In fact—" She cast him a quick glance from under her lashes. "—there are still issues between us, are there not?"

"If you refer to my hunting," he said, brows rising, "I remember telling you I do not hunt for sport."

She nodded. "I understand that, but what is your thinking about closing your land to the fox hunt?"

The brows snapped together into a single bar. "Forbidding them to cross my land?"

"Hmm . . . ?" She watched him carefully.

"I . . . cannot make a decision which affects so many without more thought."

"So many."

"For instance, I have one estate, inherited from a godfather, which lies in excellent hunting territory. Quorn country. You ask that I make of myself a pariah among my friends, many of whom are members."

She nodded. "I would respect you less if you had given me an easy answer. Merrywood is forbidden territory. Everyone knows it and no one does more than grumble when a particularly good run must be aborted at my borders. I am thought to be more than a trifle eccentric, of course," she finished with a grin.

He smiled. "So what else would you ask me? Because I doubt you've only the one thing in mind."

Babs turned away. "Matt . . . that day I discovered your father and my uncle had been so presumptive as to have ready those contracts . . . you . . . well . . . Oh dear, I feared I would find this an exceedingly embarrassing conversation."

After a glance back to where the groom had settled himself against a tree and closed his eyes, Matthew carefully placed his hands on her shoulders. "Nothing should be an embarrassment between us, Babs. I hope I can say anything to you and, likewise, you to me. Ask your question and I will try to answer honestly."

"Well . . . you—" Her voice became very nearly inaudible "—called me your love. Did you mean it?"

For a moment he was silent and Babs felt her heart racing. On the other hand, she had come to understand that he did not instantly respond to questions that were important, that he actually thought about them, and that was something she liked in him.

But this . . . it was so important . . . what if . . . oh dear. . . .

Babs' mental dithering was cut short.

"Love. It is something I never expected to feel. I didn't, I think, understand what it is," he said slowly.

Babs held her breath.

"I thought I disliked you, your independent ways, your argumentative nature, your insistence you will not be ordered about, but will be an equal partner with the man you wed . . . you were so different from what I planned for my life."

He stood there behind her, silent, his fingers firm about her shoulders and she found she was frightened. *Have I come to love him so much that his answer is this important to me? Did I not decide the love of our children would be enough?*

His hands slid from her shoulders down her arms. "I have changed a great deal, Babs. For the better, I hope. And you have done that, made me see so much to which I had previously closed my eyes. Thank you." His hands tightened momentarily.

The longer this goes on the more I am sure he will tell me he cannot love me, she thought, despair growing.

"Love. It is very important, is it not?"

"Very," she managed, her voice muffled.

"It is very hard to say," he murmured.

A sudden hope had her turning between his hands until she looked up at him.

"I do love you, Babs," he said quietly, his gaze locked with hers. "To my amazement, my joy, to the bottom of my very frightened soul . . ."

His words were cut off when she drew her arms up between them and threw them around his neck, drawing his head down to hers.

As kisses went, it was the usual awkward first kiss . . .

but the second, of which Matthew took command, was exceedingly satisfactory to both.

Back near the horses, the groom opened one eye, smiled, and closed it again. *Lord Calder,* he thought, *has everything well in hand.*

When, finally, Matthew lifted his head, he smiled down into her bemused face. "Does this," he asked politely, "mean that you spoke truly when you said you love me too?"

Babs laughed. "Yes. Oh yes, forever so long, it seems. I feared you did not return my feelings, feared I must hide it from you, must be satisfied with the innocent love of our children. I am so glad you love me too."

"And I, my independent lady, am glad you had the courage to make us discuss it. We might have gone on for a long time not quite trusting that our love was mutual," he said, holding her close. "You are very special, you know."

Just under a month later, friends and relatives crowded the village church to watch Miss Barbara Ruthven and Matthew Adam Woodward Milton Riverton, by courtesy, Lord Calder, repeat the vows that made them man and wife.

Miss Morgan, her eyes wide, watched the whole in silence—but once the service and wedding breakfast were in progress, she came to Babs, put her arms around her, and, softly, asked, "But does he not frighten you half out of your wits?"

"No. Never. The secret is to forget those ridiculous eyebrows. Without them, he has a rather pleasing countenance." And then she stared. "You spoke!"

"No one can make me wed him *now,*" said Louisa, a certain complaisance about her.

"No, no one can, that is true," said Babs. "The thing is,

my dear, that no one would have done so at any time if only you had said no and held firm to saying it. From the very beginning."

Miss Morgan shook her head, sober featured, even a trifle pale. "You did not know my father. I hope you never know such a man." She frowned. "But how can one *know?*"

"Know?"

"If a man will behave in such a way. They are so much bigger than we are. They rule our world." She frowned. "I cannot understand how you *know.*" She turned on her heel and moved away to where a potted orange tree gave her a corner in which she could hide and still observe the guests.

"What did our silent friend want?" asked Matthew, joining Babs just then.

"I think to let me know she would no longer be quite so silent!" said Babs. "She spoke."

He nodded. "I thought perhaps she would. She has been more relaxed since we announced that we would wed—but still watchful. Now there is no way anyone can force her to wed me and she may relax utterly."

"That is what she said. She also asked if I were not afraid of you."

"Are you?"

"You know I am not."

"Then—" He eyed her speculatively "—will you trust me now and come away with me? May we begin our journey through life with a more prosaic sort of journey?" He gestured to where a traveling carriage piled with luggage waited outside the door.

Words, she thought. *I wonder if I will ever learn his easy use of words.* "You never did tell me where you meant to take me," she said.

"North. I'll say no more. I think you will like it, however. If we are at all lucky with the weather!"

"The Lake District?"

"You have guessed," he said, disappointed.

"And you have pleased me exceedingly. I have wished to visit the lakes ever since a neighbor went and came back full of tales and a most delightful sketchbook full of the most interesting scenes."

He smiled again. "Then, if you are ready for our adventure, we shall be off."

She looked around at her neighbors and friends. She saw her uncle talking to Lord Amrington, the two of them deep in discussion. Briefly, she wondered what it was about. The three Morgan ladies, even Louisa Maria, were talking to James Ruthven and Quentin Riverton. Quentin had just said something to draw a laugh from the others. She glanced around, checking that the servants, under Logan's watchful eye, were serving the guests as she would wish and, finally, turned back to Matthew.

"I am ready for our adventure. Do let us go."

She was ready later that night for another sort of adventure as well, perhaps a trifle nervous, but both curious and in a state of anticipation. Matthew's kisses had given her a clue to the joy she'd know . . . and, as it turned out, neither she nor he was disappointed.

Epilogue

When Babs and Matthew returned nearly three months later to Merrywood Hall where they meant to spend the greater part of each year, they discovered many changes had occurred.

Lady Dewsbury-Morgan had taken up residence in Woodbine house along with an old friend, an invalid who, although very nearly helpless, remained cheerful and excellent company.

Lady Morgan was no longer Lady Morgan. She had married James Ruthven in a private ceremony with only a few witnesses a few months after becoming a widow and now lived, with her daughter, at The Oaks where James Ruthven was slowly convincing Louisa Maria that not all men were monsters and some were actually quite nice.

Invitations to musical evenings held at The Oaks were sought after. One of the primary guests, always, was Quentin Riverton who was in permanent residence with his Aunt Hermie where he had taken on some of the duties of a land agent, bringing the Blackstock estate back to what it once was.

The work, however, was an excuse. Quentin admitted to Matt that he hoped to earn Miss Morgan's trust and, eventually, her love. But he was a patient man.

And there was always their music . . .

Lord Amrington and William Ruthven had become close friends and his lordship was often a guest at

Merrywood, the two men never finding it difficult to discover something to keep their discussions interesting. They had also discovered in each other the perfect opponent across a chess board so that when their talking palled, they could be found staring at the finely carved set of men and, occasionally, reaching to move a piece, holding it with one finger while they studied the board and then releasing it—or occasionally returning it to its place and the mind to contemplating, again, the next move.

Babs' only disappointment was that she was not yet enceinte. Lord Amrington was not the only one who wished to begin filling the nursery on the floor above the master suite. Babs longed to hold her first child—but it was something over a year later before she was able to do so.

And then it was twins. A boy and a girl, who were, little more than a year later, joined by another set of twins, also a boy and a girl. More children followed and, never again, was the Merrywood estate a lonely place for a child.

Matthew discovered that wedding an independent lady had a great many advantages. In fact, as time went on, he was quite pleased with Babs' ability to hold her own in any argument in which they indulged. Besides, there was—as his father had once hinted—the fun of making up to which one looked forward! On the other hand, unlike his mother and some other wives among their *tonnish* friends, Babs never ever wished to forbid him her bed.

To their great joy, their deep and abiding love allowed them to enjoy a long and extraordinarily happy marriage.

Dear Friends,

I had fun with AN INDEPENDENT LADY. Babs was just the sort of independent lady I like to write about.

Georgie, the heroine of my next book, is another such heroine. She gets up to all sorts of mischief in THE FAMILY MATCHMAKER, appearing in July 2003. I'm not certain whether it is fortunate or unfortunate that Georgie is a very small woman, tiny in all directions, who isn't always so careful as she should be about her attire. When the hero first sees her, she is, thanks to her ladder disappearing, stuck high up on the base of a statue that she has scrubbed free of grime and less delicate matter—birds are not as careful about such things as they might be! She is dressed appropriately for the work, but *not* for meeting the man of her dreams who thinks her a servant set to the work and a mere child as well. He is disabused of that notion when Georgie's grandfather introduces the two—but makes no reference to her age. Our hero is appalled at the emotions he develops for his neighbor's grandchild. Unmixing all the mix-ups requires a matchmaker's greatest efforts!

Wishing you all the wonderful happy reading you desire.

Cheerfully,
Jeanne Savery

P.S. I enjoy hearing from my readers and may be reached by e-mail at JeanneSavery@earthlink.net or by snail-mail at P.O. Box 833, Greenacres, Washington, 99016 (please enclose a self-addressed, stamped envelope for snail-mail reply). I try to answer promptly but travel frequently and sometimes I'm a snail myself at getting letters answered. Please be patient.

Embrace the Romances of
Shannon Drake

Discover the Romances of

Hannah Howell

Put a Little Romance in Your Life With
Georgina Gentry

__Cheyenne Song
   0-8217-5844-6   **$5.99**US/**$7.99**CAN

__Comanche Cowboy
   0-8217-6211-7   **$5.99**US/**$7.99**CAN

__Eternal Outlaw
   0-8217-6212-5   **$5.99**US/**$7.99**CAN

__Apache Tears
   0-8217-6435-7   **$5.99**US/**$7.99**CAN

__Warrior's Honor
   0-8217-6726-7   **$5.99**US/**$7.99**CAN

__Warrior's Heart
   0-8217-7076-4   **$5.99**US/**$7.99**CAN

Call toll free **1-888-345-BOOK** to order by phone, use this coupon to order by mail, or order online at **www.kensingtonbooks.com**.

Name _____

Address _____

City _____ State _____ Zip _____

Please send me the books I have checked above.

I am enclosing $_____

Plus postage and handling* $_____

Sales tax (in New York and Tennessee only) $_____

Total amount enclosed $_____

*Add $2.50 for the first book and $.50 for each additional book.

Send check or money order (no cash or CODs) to:

Kensington Publishing Corp., Dept. C.O., 850 Third Avenue, New York, NY 10022

Prices and numbers subject to change without notice. All orders subject to availability.

Visit our website at **www.kensingtonbooks.com**.

BOOK YOUR PLACE ON OUR WEBSITE AND MAKE THE READING CONNECTION!

We've created a customized website just for our very special readers, where you can get the inside scoop on everything that's going on with Zebra, Pinnacle and Kensington books.

When you come online, you'll have the exciting opportunity to:

- View covers of upcoming books
- Read sample chapters
- Learn about our future publishing schedule (listed by publication month *and author*)
- Find out when your favorite authors will be visiting a city near you
- Search for and order backlist books from our online catalog
- Check out author bios and background information
- Send e-mail to your favorite authors
- Meet the Kensington staff online
- Join us in weekly chats with authors, readers and other guests
- Get writing guidelines
- AND MUCH MORE!

Visit our website at
http://www.kensingtonbooks.com